Chase The Legend

HANNAH KAYE

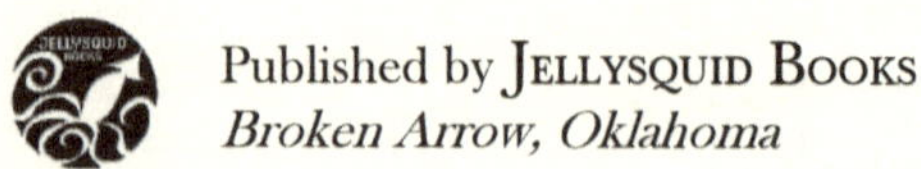

Published by Jellysquid Books
Broken Arrow, Oklahoma

For Katy

For sharing all the joys, heartaches, victories, and struggles
that come with this crazy adventure we're both on—
The days when we snuggle tiny humans,
And the nights when we slay dragons.

(Don't read the last chapter first.)

ALSO BY HANNAH KAYE

Middle Grade Fiction

The Sadie & Clyde Adventures
GOLDWATER RIDGE
SILVERSTONE VALLEY

Adult Fiction

THE FISHERMAN WHO STOLE THE STORM
(Published as H.K. Tindle)

A CLASSIC RETOLD SERIES

Break the Beast – Allison Tebo
Crack the Stone – Emily Golus
Steal the Morrow – Jenelle Leanne Schmidt
Unearth the Tides – Alissa J. Zavalianos
Raise the Dead – Nina Clare
Summon the Light – Tor Thibeaux
Chase the Legend – Hannah Kaye
Kill the Dawn – Emily Hayse
Riddle of Hearts – Rosie Grymm

Learn more at AClassicRetold.com

Contents

Where lies the final harbor,
whence we unmoor no more?
In what rapt ether sails the
world of which the weariest
will never weary?

HERMAN MELVILLE, *MOBY DICK*

PART ONE

The End of the Map

My Dear Professor Bay,

If, by some act of mercy, you choose not to throw this letter into the hearth unopened, I hope that it finds you well.

Enclosed you will find my formal resignation, if I may trouble you to pass it on to the administration. There is also a note that can be read to my students, for I could not bear to say goodbye to them face-to-face. If I must be the cause of children's tears, I'd rather be half a world away when it happens. Call me a coward; it is no more than I deserve.

Which of course brings me to the inevitable: I'm sure you are miffed—perhaps even angry, though I hate to think it of you—that I denied you the opportunity to talk some sense into me. For four years, you advised and guided me. I was practically a daughter in your eyes—and so I would have been, had I stayed and honored my engagement to your son. But I cannot change my mind; my course is set, and to try to dissuade me now would be painful for us all.

So here I am, hiding behind pen and paper so that I don't have to meet your eyes as I break your heart.

Please assure Phillip it's better this way. I am not the wife he needs or deserves, and in his heart, I think he knows it. Tell him it is far better to admit defeat before vows are made. He would have grown to resent my shortcomings, no matter what he says now. Tell him to move on quickly, and to forget me if he can manage it. I sincerely wish him all the joy. Heaven knows he deserves it.

And as for me? I cannot yet guess where my journey will end. All I know to do is to go back to my beginning. I have much to think through, and I cannot do it in thick air. I need clear skies and fair winds, open water with nothing but rolling blue for leagues in any direction. The shining heavens, the fathomless deep, and honest work to busy my hands.

I sail from Map's End at my earliest opportunity. Please give my regrets to any who ask after me. Tell them I've gone to sea to find the happy sailor girl I used to be—the one I lost somewhere among the waves.

I remain, no longer your daughter, but ever your penitent student,

Ilsa Starling

CHAPTER ONE

Call Me Ilsa

THE FIRST TIME ILSA STARLING found herself face to face with a dragon, she knew she was no Hunter. The timing of that realization could not have been worse.

She'd always envisioned herself in this moment as something larger than life, standing tall in the bow of a mighty ship with a battle cry on her lips. The ice-sharp wind would whip through her hair as she defiantly brandished a harpoon at the beast, unflinching at its deafening roar.

But there was no weapon clutched in Ilsa's hand as she stood in the dark street, staring into the monster's leering jaws. Just the scuffed handle of a faded carpetbag, containing the few remnants of her old life she had deemed worth saving. They'd be no help now, of course.

As if on cue, the contents of the carpetbag shifted impatiently in her hands.

"Be still," Ilsa hissed, pressing the bag to her chest. The wiggling stopped, but Ilsa heard a mournful squeak from inside.

It's for your own good.

The dragon's enormous head loomed in the darkness above her, wide as a jollyboat and white as polished marble. Its skeletal grin hung suspended in the darkness, close enough that Ilsa could have reached out and touched it if she hadn't been numb to her core. Frigid damp clung to her with the weight of a blanket—but none of its warmth—pulling her shoulders into a defeated slump.

Somewhere beyond the reaches of her vision, hidden by the sea fog's thick veil, she could imagine the rest of the beast lurking—a lithe, serpentine body, powerful wings built to slice through both air and water with knifelike precision, a tail as strong as a cedar yet flexible as a whip.

Anyone raised at sea, as Ilsa had been, would be familiar enough with the old tales to know that running from such a monster was pointless.

Dimly, Ilsa realized that the thought should scare her. But it had been many weeks since any feeling as sharp as fear had pierced the veil of apathy that settled over her heart, thick as the freezing fog that filled the silent street. The past few days, she'd been strangely grateful for the familiar numbness; it dulled the sting of her departure.

But now, the apathy that had brought some comfort seemed to be Ilsa's undoing. A Dragon Hunter's instinct and quick action were critical to survival, yet there she stood, so detached from the moment that she could do nothing but stare.

A heartbeat passed in frozen silence. Then another.

No roar from the dragon. Just a faint dripping of condensation against cobblestones. Ilsa shifted from foot to foot, unsure whether to attempt an escape or to stand still and bet her life on the chance that the dragon might not look her way. Neither option seemed viable, and if she was honest with herself, she was too tired to express a preference between the possible outcomes.

Her stocking was wet. Of all the sensations she could be feeling, that was the one her mind latched onto.

Thanks to the coachman not bothering to call out a warning, Ilsa's first step into the seaside village of Edgewater earlier in the evening had been directly into a slushy puddle. Dirty street water filled her boot, and the damp chill had clung to her steps ever since, following her through the streets like a beggar child pleading for shelter.

It was absurd. She was about to get eaten by a dragon and her last thoughts in this life would be about her sock.

Some Hunter she'd turned out to be.

The beast grinned down at Ilsa through rows of yellow teeth, but it didn't appear to be in much of a hurry to sink them into her. She exhaled slowly. Her breath formed a small cloud in the icy air, then dissipated a moment later.

And still, the dragon didn't move. Didn't even breathe.

"Beautiful, ain't she?"

The unexpected question split the eerie silence in two. Ilsa clutched her carpetbag with white knuckles and whirled to face the voice. She was seized with the wild impulse to crack its owner over the head with the tattered piece of luggage, though she suspected it would do more harm to the bag than to him.

Two shapes emerged from the fog. The figures—a pair of local fishermen, if their well-worn oilskins and long gray beards were any indication—eyed Ilsa from beneath bristly brows. Scrambling to recover her sensibilities, she tucked the carpetbag under her arm in hopes that it would look less like an intended bludgeoning weapon. A muffled squeak from the bag's occupant expressed its displeasure, and Ilsa loosened her grip.

"Sorry?" she managed, shrinking a bit beneath the bigger man's disapproving gaze. Or perhaps she only imagined the scornful tilt to his lips and the slight arch of his wiry eyebrow; she'd been seeing disapproval everywhere she looked of late, even in the mirror.

Especially in the mirror.

"The dragon," the fisherman replied with a sideways glance. "I said she's a beauty."

He reached up a calloused hand to pat the monster on the jawbone as if it was some sort of humongous pet.

Understanding washed over Ilsa, a cold mix of relief and shame.

Dead. It was dead. Of course. Nothing but an empty skull, propped up on display.

Ilsa tugged at the ribbon that secured her limp braid. She could almost hear Phillip's mother chiding her over the action: *"A young woman of your standing oughtn't to fiddle with her hair like a schoolgirl."* At her urging, Ilsa had started wearing it up to be more fashionable—and to curb the nervous habit. Strange that now, after years of piling her hair atop her head, Ilsa's fingers remembered their old ways without her even giving it a second thought.

The familiar ribbed texture of the ribbon under her fingertips felt reassuring as Ilsa studied the dragon above her for signs of life. Its frozen grin stared back, completely still.

"Is it normal in this part of the world to display hunting trophies in the middle of the street?" She asked, trying to speak steadily. She didn't take her eyes off the leering skull, not even for an instant. She had the unsettling suspicion that if she looked away, it might move.

"Normal?" The man guffawed. "Nothing about a skull like this is *normal*. No one's ever seen anything like it! She's the pride of Edgewater! That's why she's out here in the square for us all to admire. Crew of the *Talisk* brought her here just last week." The fisherman went on bragging. "Only dragon of its size any Hunter's ever encountered and lived to tell about!"

"Eh, that's what you'll hear in Edgewater, sure enough." His companion chimed in with a coarse laugh. "But I heard tell Adam

Chase's crew fought one twice as big out on the Edge."

"Says who, Adam Chase?" the big man scoffed, shoving his friend's shoulder good-naturedly. "When *he* brings in a head this big, I'll believe him, and not a minute before. Tides, I'd even take a tooth for proof. But all Chase has got to show for his tale is a wrecked career and a chip on his shoulder."

"Well, that and a dragon bite that nearly did him in," his friend countered with a half-shrug. "Hard to deny that; everyone's seen him limping about on that peg of his."

"Ah, anything coulda taken that leg off and you know it. Chase coulda got himself shot in a barfight. Or maybe that first mate of his finally lost his patience and shot the hothead himself."

"Wouldn't blame him a bit if he had."

Ilsa suppressed a shiver, but whether it was caused by the cold or by the loud carelessness of the fishermen's conversation in the otherwise quiet street, she couldn't tell.

"Excuse me," Ilsa said as she pushed past the fishermen. The dragon skull melted into the fog behind her, but the memory of its haunting grin lingered in the corners of her mind, like a ghost drifting just beyond the edges of sight.

A determined chirrup from the carpetbag demanded attention.

"Fine." Ilsa sighed. "If you insist."

Stepping to the side of the street, Ilsa unbuckled the latch. Immediately, a long-eared, whiskered face poked up from the recesses of the bag. The creature fixed Ilsa with a hurt stare and sniffed as if to inform her that a well-bred homing tammer with a pedigree that stretched back to the time of the kings oughtn't to be subjected to the indignity of being stuffed in a bag. Some of the effect was lost, however; the tammer's fine, pure-white fur was mashed comically upward, giving him the appearance of a child who'd just woken from a long, deep nap.

"I know, I know, I promised you wouldn't be in there long."

Ilsa stroked the tammer's rabbit-like face in an attempt to smooth his fur and soothe his wounded pride. "I am sorry. Things got...strange out here."

The tammer scampered up Ilsa's arm and onto her shoulder, his favorite perch ever since he was a kit. He pressed his velvet-soft nose against her neck with a grateful nuzzle. Apology accepted. Then, yawning, he stretched out his folded wings, nearly a yard across from tip to tip, and shook himself all over. His long, tufted tail swished behind him, brushing against Ilsa's back.

"Only for a moment, now, understood?" Ilsa warned, though she could already feel her sternness weakening. "It isn't safe yet. There was a dragon around the last corner. Who's to say what will be around the next one?"

The tammer cocked his head, nose and ears twitching at the unfamiliar surroundings. Ilsa knew the intelligent creature was probably already constructing a mental map from what he could see, plotting the best route back to the aviary on the grounds of Baywood Estate. His hundreds of generations of breeding and training would lead him with uncanny precision, straight back to the only home he'd ever known.

"It's too far, Mobius." Ilsa shook her head. "We're not going back there now."

Or ever, in fact.

"All right, you've had your stretch." Ilsa beckoned the tammer. "Back in the bag, now; be a good boy."

Mobius turned imploring eyes on her, and his ears lost a touch of their perk. Ilsa could swear she saw his chin quiver.

"Fine, you manipulative little scoundrel," she said, giving the creature's head a soft pat. "But you know what to do if someone's coming."

Mobius burrowed his head in the hood of Ilsa's cloak, showing his understanding.

"Good enough, I suppose," Ilsa said. "Now let's keep walking. This damp is miserable."

Beyond the town square and its skeletal resident, the cobbled road grew rough. Ilsa stumbled as she picked her way along the uneven stone. She couldn't see the buildings on either side of her in the darkness, but she could feel them growing closer together as her path narrowed. The smell of salt and fish-rot hung in the still air. Although she'd never walked these streets before, a long-slumbering instinct awakened inside of her, and she knew without a doubt that she was nearing the sea. The famous cliffside docks of Edgewater must be very close.

A glimmer of something suspiciously akin to hope flickered through Ilsa's heart. So many years far from the sea, and now, at long last, she'd come back.

"Moby," she said, reaching up to stroke the tammer's fur. "We've made it."

When she'd arrived in Edgewater just after dusk, Ilsa had planned to find lodging for the night and then make her way to the docks in the morning. But now that she'd tasted salt on the air, she couldn't wait any longer.

Her heart filled with the memory of how once, in her girlhood, her journey home from a school term was delayed, resulting in a midnight arrival at Grandfather's stately manor. Disregarding the advice of his housekeeper to wait and surprise him at breakfast, Ilsa had rushed to his room and climbed, high-buttoned boots and all, into his enormous bed—the one that looked like a sailing ship, complete with a dragon-shaped figurehead carved into the footboard, and great wooden posts draped with voluminous curtains that reminded her of billowing sails.

Grandfather woke up laughing.

"Come on, little fluff," Ilsa whispered to Mobius. "It's time to go home."

CHAPTER TWO

Riptide

ILSA'S PACE QUICKENED. The cold stung her cheeks, but she didn't care. The prospect of seeing the coast again after so long spurred her steps along; she was almost running. Mobius, though perhaps not understanding the cause, caught his mistress's infectious excitement. He leapt off her shoulder, spread his wings, and turned a somersault in the air.

"Been cooped up too long, have you?" Ilsa smiled at him. "Well, that makes two of—"

Pain knifed through her chest, cutting off her words. With a sharp gasp, Ilsa stumbled to a halt. It took all the strength she could muster to keep from collapsing onto the glistening cobblestones. She doubled over, huddled against the dizzying pain.

Mobius fluttered next to her in a tight circle. He nipped at the folds of her cloak in a futile attempt to pull her up.

"All right, Moby, I'm all right." Ilsa gasped, trying to soothe the agitated animal even as she struggled to catch her breath. She reached for him, and he came gratefully to her arms. He nuzzled his face against her heart. "It's nothing out of the ordinary."

A few more shallow, stinging breaths, and the tightness began to ease. Thank goodness.

The moment passed, but it took Ilsa's burst of excitement with it, leaving her weak and tired.

Mobius nudged his face against her cheek and chirruped for attention. Spreading his white-feathered wings, he glided down to the cobblestones and took a few short hops away. He turned his head back to make sure Ilsa was following before continuing to the west side of the street.

Ilsa let Mobius lead the way. A few steps further, a slumpy, shadowy building with a sign announcing itself as the Riptide Inn appeared out of the mist. Built of dark, salt-stained planks, the inn smelled of woodsmoke even from the outside. Muffled voices drifted out from behind the crooked plank door: the familiar homey murmur of a seaside pub after dark.

"Message received." Ilsa sighed, looking down at her companion. Mobius's ears twitched at the familiar words he'd been trained to equate with a job well done. Guilt tugged at Ilsa's conscience. Usually, those words were accompanied by a fat, glistening wolfberry, but in Ilsa's rush to leave Baywood, she'd neglected to pack any of Mobius's favorite treats. Praise would have to be its own reward this time.

Although Mobius had obviously made up his mind about their next course of action, Ilsa hesitated, tugging indecisively at her ribbon. Part of her wanted nothing more than to move on, to travel through the night and not stop until she'd put as much distance between herself and her old life as possible. But the warm glow and comforting smells from the inn beckoned her to come in from the cold, to drink something hot, to stay a while. Ilsa shivered. It had been such a long day.

Maybe for a minute or two. Warm up. Ask for directions. Then keep moving.

"Very well," Ilsa said. She bent to scoop Mobius off the cobbles. He didn't like being cradled; he was far too fond of his freedom of movement to stay in her arms for long. But for whatever reason, this time he held still as Ilsa hugged him to her chest. Perhaps he sensed she needed his closeness.

"Riptide, is it?" Ilsa read the name on the establishment's sign. An irresistible force dragging one out to sea. If that didn't strike her as ironic in her present situation, then she had failed the sisterhood of schoolteachers everywhere. She could already hear her sixth-year students' groans as she explained the nuances of literary analysis, trying to drill into their distracted minds why each word choice mattered, and—

With a flinch, Ilsa dropped her gaze from the sign.

She wasn't a schoolteacher. Not anymore. She would never see those bull-headed sixth-years again.

Ilsa swallowed back a bitter taste in her mouth. As much as she knew it was for the best, it was easier not to dwell on it.

She was caught in the riptide, being pulled out to sea. Struggling would only drown her.

Ilsa shuddered. Her eyes stung, but she knew better than to expect tears now. She had none left to cry.

Ducking to avoid the low beams, Ilsa pushed open the Riptide's crooked, slatted door. The weak protest it gave was a welcome sound after the silence of the street. Warm yellow light spilled through the mist like a lighthouse beacon, and she stepped into it gladly.

Mobius sensed the change in atmosphere, too. He wriggled free of Ilsa's grasp, and, satisfied with the warmth and light he found, climbed to his perch on her shoulder. He settled in and began to preen his wings, entirely at ease.

Ilsa wove her way through the murmured conversations and amicable laughter of the late-night patrons. Some had drinks and food, others smoked pipes or tossed dice across the rough-hewn tables. A few sat in silence, the firelight flickering across their care-worn faces. No one looked her way as she passed through. Just another invisible stranger.

The boy at the counter slouched across the bar as Ilsa approached, with his shaggy head resting on his arms. A book lay open in front of him, and Ilsa couldn't resist a glance over the tiny, upside-down print. She didn't recognize it, but she could tell it was a science text of some kind—cetology, from the looks of the diagrams. That would put anyone to sleep.

"Can I help you, madam?"

The formal term of address from the boy's sleep-heavy voice shook Ilsa from her snooping. She was not technically a madam, she was a miss, but the assumption stung. She ought to be married and settled by now, and even a half-asleep serving boy could see it.

"Are you the proprietor?" she asked, clearing the discomfort from her throat. She didn't bother to correct him.

"No, my father is. Peter Coffin. I just watch the front at night."

Coffin. Now there was a name ripe for literary analysis. It was almost too obvious. Not particularly comforting, either.

"You're wanting a room for the night, I suppose. Or rather, what's left of the night." Without waiting for a response, the boy opened a ledger on the counter in front of him. "We've had a busy evening, what with that Hunting ship in from the Edge, and most of our rooms are full. But you're in luck—there's one bed left in the bunkroom, and it's yours for half price."

"A generous offer, but I'm afraid I can't stay." Ilsa shook her head. "I do need to post a letter, though. And would you be so kind as to point me in the direction of the docks? I've got to catch a ferry."

"Can't go near the docks," Young Coffin replied, pursing his lips. "Fog's too thick. No ferries will be running tonight. Or tomorrow either, if this doesn't clear up. Could be days before anyone leaves the cliffs. I'll get that letter sorted for you, though."

His words hit Ilsa like cold sea spray. No ferries till the fog cleared? And how long might that be? The last thing she wanted was to be stuck in Edgewater, pinned at the shoreline.

Her hand slipped into her pocket. The letter to the professor, the one penned with guilt and sealed with tears, lay cold against her palm. Dear old Professor Bay, with his bushy gray mustache and merry eyes. He'd always looked out for Ilsa; he'd always been so kind. How long would it be, really, until he got it in his head to come after her? Or worse yet, Phillip? Surely the fog would clear long before then.

Wouldn't it?

"Madam?" Young Master Coffin cleared his throat with a twinge of annoyance he didn't bother to hide. His outstretched hand hovered expectantly. "I'll take that letter for you."

"I'm sorry," Ilsa said. She withdrew her hand from her pocket, leaving the letter where it lay. "It appears I've misplaced it."

The boy rolled his eyes, an ungracious gesture Ilsa chose to overlook. She wasn't *his* teacher, after all.

"Does the offer still stand on that bunk?"

"Your, uh, rabbit is trained, yes?"

"Better than most children." Ilsa assured him, stroking Mobius's chin. "And he's a tammer, actually. He doesn't like to be called a rabbit."

Mobius gave a prim little sniff.

"Um... sure. Whatever." Young Coffin shrugged. "It'll be five shillings."

"We'll take it," Ilsa said, handing over the fee. She wasn't above sleeping in a bunkroom. The community sleeping space was not unlike a dormitory—where she'd slept most of her growing up years—or even a ship's foc's'le strung with a hundred swinging hammocks. A room full of quiet strangers, all wishing to be left alone, was somewhere she could comfortably disappear.

Of course, Phillip's mother and her bridge club would be scandalized by the very idea.

Good.

Clutching her carpetbag with all her worldly goods inside, Ilsa headed toward the stairs and left Young Coffin to his reading—or dozing, as the case might be. The imminent prospect of a bed reminded her body of its weariness, and her feet grew heavy as she trudged toward the bunkroom. Mobius concurred with a wide yawn that bared his prominent incisors.

At the top of the stairs, a narrow hall stretched the length of the inn. On the right side stood doorways to private rooms: Mr. and Mrs. Coffin's, perhaps, and those snatched up by the wealthier—or simply earlier—patrons. On the left was a single door, which, according to Young Coffin's directions, opened into the bunkroom.

Ilsa pushed the door open as quietly as she could manage, but the old hinges creaked despite her best efforts. The man in the bunk nearest the door tossed fitfully as the light from the hall spilled onto him. Ilsa stepped inside and closed the door quickly behind her. The man snorted as he settled back down.

The air in the narrow, slope-ceilinged room hung thick and hot with the exhalations of sleeping travelers. Somewhere in the darkness, a sailor muttered in her sleep, something about Rigsby and getting the knots all wrong.

Iron lanterns containing moonstones hung at intervals along the near wall. In their dim silver light, Ilsa could make out the tightly packed bunks lining both walls of the long room, with a narrow aisle in the center. She picked her way through the passage in near darkness, silently judging the travelers who didn't have the decency to keep their personal effects out of the walkway. Her foot caught on one sailor's trunk and landed in a pile of another's boots as she stumbled toward her assigned bunk.

"Of course it *would* be the farthest one from the door," she whispered to Mobius.

Eventually, Ilsa reached her bed—with a bruised shin for her trouble—but a glance revealed her frustrations weren't over.

In the thin glimmer of moonstone light, Ilsa saw a lumpy pile of bulky shapes, haphazardly stacked on her mattress. Trunks and cases, she guessed as she squinted at the shadows, piled up with careless disregard for...well...her.

After everything today had put her through, this was the final straw. Ilsa blew out an exasperated sigh and glared at the sleeping forms in the darkness around her, wondering which among them was guilty.

Mobius didn't seem to mind the new inconvenience. The agile creature jumped down from her shoulder and alighted at the foot of the bed, curling into a ball against one of the smaller traveling cases.

"Make yourself comfortable," Ilsa muttered. Mobius, immune to her sarcasm, was already asleep. A bit of pity tempered Ilsa's annoyance. Mobius wasn't built for the kind of travel she'd put him through, poor thing. He needed rest. They both needed rest.

There was nothing else for it; she'd have to clear off the bed. Briefly, she considered going back downstairs and asking Young Coffin for help, but she quickly rejected that idea. Better to deal with the problem on her own than to make herself a burden to anyone else.

Ilsa set to work, reaching for the topmost boxy shape. It didn't come away easily.

Must be stuck on something a little further down, she decided. *What I wouldn't give for a little more light.*

She changed her approach and attempted to push at the largest shape she could find, probably a sea chest. If she could dislodge it, maybe the rest would follow.

The mound didn't budge. It was like pushing against a brick wall.

What's in these boxes? Rocks?

A few attempts later, Ilsa was struggling to keep quiet as she shoved and yanked at the pile. She was panting hard when she stepped back, at a loss for ideas.

Should she start shaking people awake and asking them to move their things? Give up and sleep on the floor? Frustration clouded her good sense, and she settled on the least logical but arguably most satisfying option: Ilsa picked up her carpetbag and smacked it against one of the offending cases with all her might.

The mound shifted and, at long last, began to move. But the movement wasn't the predictable tumbling of good, sensible boxes falling to the floor. Rather, the whole bulky pile moved as one form, and then...

Sat up?

Ilsa's heart jumped to her throat as the whatever-it-was got out of the bed and rose up before her. She was no longer staring at a pile of trunks, but rather a hulking form: a boxy head, massive shoulders, and an expansive, thick torso—easily confused with a sea chest. Then, from the darkness, two perfectly round dots of yellow light flickered into focus and glowed down at her.

Eyes, she realized with a start. Those things were eyes.

And they were far too high above her head for them to belong to a human.

A scream rose in her throat, but a hand clamped over her mouth before any sound could escape. Or at least, Ilsa thought it was a hand. It was rough and stony, cool to the touch, and large enough to cover the entirety of her lower face.

"The others sleep." The voice that dropped out of the darkness above her was deep and coarse, like the grinding of millstones against each other. Judging from the tone, Ilsa wondered if the creature thought he was whispering. A thick accent laced his words, but it was one she couldn't place.

Ilsa said nothing in response; She couldn't.

"Do not yell," the giant said. "Agreed?"

Ilsa nodded rapidly as best she could—anything to get that great stony hand off of her face. The giant drew it back, and she gasped for air. Her heart thundered in her ears.

For a moment, all was quiet as Ilsa stared at the shadowy thing she'd roused, and it looked back at her. Though, with those glowing golden eyes—similar to a cat's, but seeming to produce a light of their own rather than reflecting it—Ilsa got the uncomfortable sensation that their owner could see her much better in this darkness than she could see him.

The glimmer of a moonstone lantern sitting on the floor a few bunks down caught Ilsa's eye, and she backed up, reaching for the light. Once she had it in her hand, she raised it slowly. The light trembled a bit as she tried to get a better look at the thing she'd awoken in the darkness.

The creature towered over her at nearly eight feet tall; his head brushed the planks of the ceiling. He probably weighed hundreds of pounds—most of it pure, chiseled muscle. His head was shaved, aside from a tight cluster of short, thick braids left on top. Rings and jewels in bright colors hung from both of his oversized, pointed ears, and a narrow rod of shining crystal pierced through his nose. His skin—or perhaps it would be more accurate to call it a hide—was grayish purple, and had an oddly polished quality to it, like well-worn leather.

But of all the giant's oddities, one feature in particular arrested Ilsa's gaze. Every inch of his body—his arms, chest, neck, and even his face—was covered in tattoos. Ilsa had seen her fair share of tattoos on sailors, and a comparison of this creature's markings to those inky scribbles would fall woefully short. The intricate, angular patterns were not drawn on, but rather carved directly into his rocklike skin, leaving deep canyons on its surface. Some kind of pigment must've been rubbed into the carvings, for they all glistened a deep, metallic blue.

Ilsa knew in an instant what he was: a Stoneman.

She'd never seen one of his kind before—only heard stories. But she knew enough of these mysterious, primitive natives of the Underneath to start trembling. Stonemen had haunted the stories children told each other in the dark for centuries. Few explorers dared to delve into the sprawling world of tunnels and caverns that endlessly spiderwebbed beneath the surface of the earth, but the ones who did swore that the legends were true. Tribes of these formidable hunters ruled the dark world of the Underneath but were rarely seen under open sky.

And yet, here was one standing before her in the bunkroom of an Edgewater inn, looking exactly like he'd be described in the stories, complete with a wicked mouth full of sharpened, charcoal-colored teeth.

And Ilsa Starling had just hit him in the head with a carpetbag.

CHAPTER THREE

Chowder and Stone

CRUMPLED FRAGMENTS OF INK-SMEARED PAPER chased each other through Ilsa's dreams, carried on a bitterly cold wind. Somewhere, Phillip called her name, but he could not find her; the fog was too thick. Ilsa tried to run, but everywhere she turned she stumbled over piles of stone.

Slowly, Ilsa realized she was coming out of a disturbed, stiff sleep. She forced her eyes open. As her vision slowly swam back into focus, she could make out the wooden beams of a slanted ceiling above her.

Somewhere in the room was a high-pitched hum, like a nervous tide bee buzzing about in search of flotsam to nest in. Or perhaps the buzzing was in her own head. Why did it ache so much?

Ilsa blinked around her unfamiliar surroundings, disoriented.

What on earth happened?

Ilsa rubbed her temples and attempted to get her bearings. She could see now that she was in a bed in a long, crowded bunkroom. There were no windows, but some pale moonlight wormed its way through chinks in the slatted wall. She blinked hard a few times, trying to piece together clues from jumbled memories that blurred together with a dull headache.

The Riptide Inn, in Edgewater. She could remember that much, at least. But wasn't there something wrong with her accommodations...?

Ilsa sat up, then regretted it as her head throbbed in protest.

The Stoneman. She remembered him. And then...

Ilsa moaned, burying her face in her hands. She'd fainted dead away at the sight of him, hadn't she? She could only remember bits and pieces after that: Young Coffin babbling out apologies, a deep, angry voice that must've been his father berating the poor boy for accidentally double-booking a berth, and then that grinding, stony voice interrupting them both, insisting he'd give up the bunk for the rest of the night.

The bunk that he'd bought and paid for, just as much as Ilsa had.

And then, while she'd still been senseless, somebody had carried Ilsa back to bed. And she'd bet a month's wages it hadn't been Young Coffin.

Ilsa groaned again, wishing she could melt straight into the floor. Had she really made such a fool of herself?

Someone a few bunks down grunted in sleep, but no one else was stirring. It must not be morning yet. Ilsa fished Grandfather's gold watch from her pocket and squinted at its face in the dim glow of the moonstone lanterns. Barely half past two. Good. She would be able to slip out unnoticed. Ilsa didn't give much thought to where she would go, so long as it wasn't here. There was no sense trying to go back to sleep. Embarrassment alone would keep her tossing all night, not to mention the guilt of stealing a stranger's bunk.

"Mobius," Ilsa whispered to the ball of white fur at the foot of her bed. The tammer's back rose and fell with deep, rhythmic breathing. "I'm sorry, little fluff, but we've got to go."

Mobius raised his head slowly in response to her persistent nudging. He opened one eye, but he didn't seem committed to the idea of being awake.

"I hate to do this to you again," Ilsa said. "But we're not staying."

Mobius yawned, baring his front teeth, but he obligingly stretched one back leg. Then the other. Then both wings, giving them a few test flaps. He set to preening the fur around his face, fluffing it up with his front paws. That was a surefire sign that he was planning to wake up. Mobius never left his roost without making sure he looked his best.

Ilsa, on the other hand, didn't give her appearance any more thought than to pat her rumpled blouse and skirt as smooth as she could in the few seconds she devoted to them, and then comb the wispy flyaways back toward her braid with her fingers. While Mobius was still grooming his pristinely pointed ears, Ilsa reached for her carpetbag. But instead of finding its worn wooden handle, her hand brushed cold metal. She looked down, surprised to see a small pile of belongings that weren't hers: a scuffed leather haversack, an oversized cloak the color of coal, and a long, heavy iron spear.

Though Ilsa wouldn't have been able to guess what sort of equipment a Stoneman would travel with, these were certainly his things. If he had left them behind when he gave up his bed, then he probably hadn't strayed far.

All the more reason for Ilsa to be gone before the sun.

"That's enough now; you look fine," Ilsa whispered to Mobius. She stooped to grab her bag, about to make her escape, when something caught her eye.

Red light, bright and glowing like a live coal. It was coming from inside the Stoneman's half-open pack. A stray ember from someone's pipe perhaps, that had landed amongst the clothes inside? But no, that wasn't possible; anyone who could've been smoking was asleep, and if it had landed there sometime in the night, the ember would've fizzled out or ignited a blaze long before she saw it.

Glancing over both shoulders, Ilsa poked a cautious finger into the stranger's bag. The heat coming from inside was unsettling.

It took a second of fumbling among the other contents of the haversack before she located the source of the light. Ilsa gasped as she drew it out.

Resting in her palm lay a solid gem, as big as a lime, crimson as blood, and shot through with white-hot streaks of light that shone and danced along its facets. Even among the wealthy socialites with whom Phillip's family mingled, Ilsa had never seen the stone's equal. But she doubted a gem like this, despite its obvious worth, would ever sit atop a crown or hang from a lady's neck. It was too wild, too primal. Too much like its glowing-eyed owner.

Ilsa stared at the jewel a moment longer. Warmth seeped from it into her hand, not hot enough to burn, but sending tingles up her arm nonetheless. Something about the jewel seemed almost alive, like the pulsing sense of expectancy one felt when holding a nearly hatched egg.

That thought was unnerving enough to break the spell. Ilsa stuffed the gemstone back into the pouch, burying it deep in the folds of cloth for good measure. She held her breath, glancing around to make sure nobody saw her—or the Stoneman's treasure.

"Now we've *really* got to get out of here, Moby," Ilsa said. Mobius's grooming ritual would have to wait. She picked up the disgruntled tammer mid-fluff. With something of that obvious value in his sack, the Stoneman would come back for it, probably as soon as he could.

And Ilsa would rather not have to face him when he did.

After picking her way back through the crowded bunkroom, Ilsa headed for the stairs. Despite the hour, the gentle murmur of sound drifting up from the common room told her that the inn wasn't deserted yet.

As she reached the bottom of the stairs, Ilsa took in the room with a sweeping glance, hoping to see exactly the same group of sailors and fishermen who'd been there before.

No such luck.

It would've been hard to miss him: he was as obvious as a lonely mountain rising from an open plain. The Stoneman sat hunched over a table—which was far too small for his bulk—next to the inn's only window. He had no food in front of him but instead held a book. He thumbed methodically through the pages, eyeing them with interest. But he wasn't reading; Ilsa could tell that at a glance. The book was upside-down.

It wouldn't be easy to escape without being seen, since she would have to pass right by him to get to the door, but Ilsa thought it might be possible. As long as she moved quickly and the Stoneman didn't look up, she could probably manage it.

Coward.

The thought hit Ilsa out of nowhere, and she stopped short.

What are you going to do? the voice in her head prodded. *Disappear without a word of acknowledgment or apology? Again?*

That was hardly fair. What was she supposed to do about it now? What, as if somehow, facing up to the Stoneman would rectify the way she had left things with Phillip? What sort of nonsense logic was that?

But the sting of guilt was hard to ignore. Ilsa glanced again at the Stoneman. He was still as hideous as he had been at first sight—grayish skin, carved tattoos and all—but it was hard for Ilsa to see him as a monster when she remembered how gently he'd treated her when she'd been vulnerable.

"Stay put." Ilsa placed Mobius on her shoulder. Then she straightened her spine and headed for the counter. Young Coffin, no longer dozing, wrinkled his nose at her approach.

"Oh. It's you."

Apparently, he hadn't forgiven her for her part in the evening's mishap. Ilsa chose to ignore the flat tone and accusatory glance he gave her.

"Yes. Can I get something to eat? One for me and one for... a friend." Ilsa stumbled a little over the word.

The boy pointed toward the hearth without looking her in the eyes. He shoved two wooden bowls across the counter.

"Chowder's in the pots," he mumbled begrudgingly. "We've got clam or cod, leftovers from dinner. We keep 'em warm all night. Meals are included with the room fee, so help yourself."

The pots in question were large iron cauldrons hanging on a spit near the fire. Both were about half full of thick, bubbling soups, indistinguishable from each other. Ilsa supposed one might be clam and the other cod, but it was difficult to say. No matter. Either one would be hot and salty, which is all she required of a bowl of soup on a cold night. Ilsa ladled out two portions from the cauldron on the left, taking care to avoid the crisp bits burned to the cast iron, and hoped for the best.

Balancing the bowls, Ilsa wove her way through the tables, back to where the Stoneman sat alone. At the sight of his stony bulk, her courage quailed.

Was she really about to share a meal with this terrifying stranger? She could walk away. There were plenty of people about; Ilsa was wonderful at melting into crowds. He probably didn't even want company. Ilsa certainly wouldn't want to be approached by a stranger at a restaurant. Besides, the Stoneman might not even like chowder. Now that she thought about it, Ilsa didn't even know what his kind ate.

Wayward children, of course. Or at least, that's how the stories told by exasperated governesses usually went.

In that wavering moment of indecision, the Stoneman looked up from his book, and those yellow eyes locked onto Ilsa. His gaze was no less arresting than it had been in the bunkroom's darkness, though here his eyes didn't glow as much. His carved, fierce face broke into a smile, displaying a mouthful of pointed black teeth.

And despite herself, Ilsa smiled back.

She'd only ever half-believed those old tales, anyway.

Ilsa approached the table. Her heart pounded wildly, but she tried not to focus on it. The Stoneman offered no greeting except to watch her expectantly. Mobius, for his part, was supremely unbothered; he sat on Ilsa's shoulder inspecting the claws on his front paw, occasionally giving them a small nibble to correct their shape. That, at least, was a comfort. Ilsa trusted the tammer's instincts. If his acute sense of danger wasn't triggered by the Stoneman, maybe there was no cause to worry.

Ilsa glanced about for something to keep from having to stare into those intense yellow eyes of his, and her gaze caught on the book he held in his enormous hands. She recognized it as the same volume the boy at the counter had been reading earlier. A cetology text, if she remembered correctly.

"So, you like whales?" she blurted.

As soon as she said it, Ilsa knew how foolish she sounded. But she couldn't snatch the question back, at least not before the Stoneman's expression twisted in confusion. He stared at her, and Ilsa's face flushed.

"What—" he rumbled, after a moment of quizzical silence. "What is a whales?"

"Oh, whales?" Ilsa stammered. "Um, they're big animals, you know, they live in herds in the sea. Like cows, sort of, but they swim? I think some of the tribes in the far north hunt them for food, but..." she trailed off, realizing she was babbling. "Your book, it's about them." She finished. Her cheeks were nearly on fire.

The Stoneman looked down at the book in his hand with a confused smile. "Ah, yes, the inn boy gives this to me. A thank you for not eating him, I think."

"Right." Ilsa shifted her feet, wondering if he was joking or not. Anxious to stop feeling utterly ridiculous, she held a bowl of chowder out to him.

"Are you hungry?"

"It is not custom of my people to eat with strangers."

"Oh!" Ilsa faltered, taking a step back, fearing she'd violated some sacred custom. "I'm sorry, I—" but she stopped midsentence when she noticed his golden eyes were shining with barely-contained laughter.

"But I think after what happened upstairs—" the Stoneman winked at her, an expression that looked entirely out of place on his fierce features. "We are no strangers, yes?"

"Certainly not." Ilsa smiled with relief. "And I'd rather be friends than enemies, though I daresay I didn't make that very clear with my carpetbag. Hence the chowder." She offered it again, and this time he took it. His mighty hands made the bowl seem to shrink, but he nodded his thanks and gestured for Ilsa to sit across from him.

She sat, rather stiffly, picking up a threadbare napkin from the tabletop and folding it over her lap. Mobius, on the other hand, regarded no such formalities. The tammer scurried down Ilsa's arm and bounded across the table. Before Ilsa could snatch him back, Mobius stuck his nose into the Stoneman's chowder and helped himself to a chunk of celery.

"Mobius!" Ilsa scolded, but the tammer, his whiskers dripping with creamy soup, ignored her. He was too busy with his impertinent munching.

"I'm terribly sorry." Ilsa shook her head, exasperated. "That's Mobius. He's... not great with personal boundaries."

"Greetings, Mobius." The Stoneman lowered his head in a solemn bow. "I am Yuri T'berris of Agna'varkis, the Realm in Heart of Earth, guardian of the Firestone and heir to crown of my father." Yuri looked up expectantly. "You are?"

"Ilsa." It sounded so weak and plain after Yuri's string of titles. But there wasn't much else to add. Any further introduction of who she was or where she was from seemed outdated and irrelevant, left behind with Phillip and the rest.

There's nothing left but me.

"Call me Ilsa."

Yuri repeated her name, but it sounded foreign on his lips. He gave its inflection a slightly different flavor. A soft consonant at the beginning. A slight lift between the syllables. And a lingering at the end, gentle as a sigh.

Yil'saa.

"Very close," Ilsa said, unconsciously slipping into the encouraging tone she used with struggling students. "It's Ilsa. It starts with the soft sound, like 'inn' or 'illness' or—"

"I know what I said." Yuri interrupted with a chuckle. "Though I was not born to it, I know your language many years. Your name. Ilsa—" Ilsa noted that he pronounced it perfectly— "it is very close to word in my people's tongue. *Yil'saa.* Hearing you say it made me think..." He trailed off.

"What does it mean?" Ilsa asked. Why did she feel like there was much more riding on his answer than a mere linguistic coincidence?

Yuri smiled softly.

"Little sister."

Whatever Ilsa had thought to say next was lost. She swallowed hard as the dull ache of loneliness in her chest swelled to a painful surge.

She looked away, past Yuri to the window behind him, but all she could see in the darkness outside was the persistent swirl of fog, thick as the confused feelings that had come over her.

In the silence that followed, Yuri turned his attention to his chowder. Ilsa did the same, but she hardly noticed how it tasted. After a few minutes, Yuri spoke again.

"Your legends are wrong about my people," he said in a low, careful tone that revealed he knew his words had had an effect. He extended his hand, offering his open palm to Mobius. The tammer gave Yuri's finger a cautious sniff. "We do not harm the small and lost. We protect our own."

"And what about those who are not your own?"

"We *choose* our own," Yuri said, looking directly into her eyes. Ilsa couldn't hold his intense golden gaze for long. She glanced away, clearing her throat.

Mobius, satisfied with his preliminary examination, climbed into the Stoneman's massive hand. The mere size of Yuri's palm made Mobius look more like a mouse than a tammer, but he didn't seem to mind. He folded his ears atop each other—a sure sign of relaxation—and started preening his tufted tail, as comfortable as if he'd sat there every day of his life.

"He likes you." Ilsa remarked with a note of surprise in her voice. "Usually, he takes a little while to warm up to people."

As if determined to make a liar out of her, Mobius scampered up the Stoneman's arm and settled in on his shoulder—a perch he'd only taken with one person other than Ilsa.

Phillip.

Mobius nuzzled Yuri's fierce, tattooed face with his velvety nose, then looked straight at Ilsa. His message was as clear as if he had spoken the words himself.

I get it, Mobius. You think he's a good one. And you're probably right, as usual.

"I hope you don't mind my asking," Ilsa said, trying to shift to a more casual vein of conversation as she stirred her spoon in her nearly untouched soup. "What brings you out here, so far from your people?"

"Many things." The Stoneman replied between shoveled spoonfuls. "But most recently, I am setting out on a voyage, to pursue the great beasts at the edge of the world."

"Really? You're going to be a Hunter?" Ilsa said. "So am I."

Yuri nodded as if that didn't surprise him in the slightest.

"Rotten luck to be stuck here, isn't it?" Ilsa asked, grateful to have found common ground. "When do you think we'll be able to make it out to Map's End?"

Yuri cocked his head at her and gestured toward his chowder with his spoon.

"When this bowl is empty, I think."

"Oh, well, not tonight, of course." Ilsa corrected him.

He slurped the dregs of his dinner and shrugged as if to ask why not.

"It's the middle of the night," Ilsa said. "And the fog is too thick. None of the ferries are running; that's what they're saying."

"No ferries, true. So, I have hired small boat for myself," Yuri said, wiping his mouth with the back of his hand. "Good soup."

"But the fog—" Ilsa protested, growing increasingly concerned. "You wouldn't dare try to navigate the cliffs without being able to see where you're going, would you?"

"Ah," Yuri grinned. "Yes, if I had small pale eyes like yours, a little fog would stop me." He blinked his glowing yellow eyes to emphasize his point. "I was not born in place called Agna'varkis—in your language, Vale of Steam—for nothing. I see fine in dark, dim, and mist."

"How very fortunate for you and your superior eyes," Ilsa said dryly, but her attempt to hide a smile was unsuccessful.

"Hm," he said. "Very." Yuri pulled himself up to his full towering height and smacked his empty bowl back down on the table. Then he smiled again—a sharp, black grin Ilsa was growing to like more and more each time she saw it.

"So." Yuri extended an inviting hand down to her. "You are coming with me or not, Little Sister?"

Almost without thinking, Ilsa started to reach up, to take his hand.

You're going to do this to him, too?

The accusing thought was sharp and sudden. Ilsa jerked backward, shaking herself. Everything in her wanted nothing more than to accept Yuri's offer. His caring smile. His gentle words. His hand, reaching out for her, so willing to look after her.

Abruptly, she stood, pushing her chair back with a harsh screech against the floor.

"I'm afraid I can't," she said, her words rushing out over each other. "I wish you all the best. And thank you again for your kindness."

Yuri cocked his head, frowning in confusion at her sudden change in tone, but Ilsa didn't give him the chance to argue.

"I really do need to be going. Come, Mobius."

The tammer shot her a hurt look, but he reluctantly obeyed. With a lithe motion that required no use of his wings, Mobius sprang from Yuri's shoulder and landed on Ilsa's.

The cold night air knifed into Ilsa's chest as she hurried from the inn, but she didn't dare look back. She knew she couldn't afford to stay. She couldn't allow herself to get close to Yuri—the sting she felt leaving him after just a few minutes was a testament to that. No doubt it would grow with time.

"It wouldn't be fair to him, Mobius," she whispered into the frigid darkness, more to herself than the tammer. "You know it better than I do."

Ilsa shoved her hands in her pockets to ward off the cold and felt the crumple of paper against her fist. The reminder of the unsent letter only served to reinforce her decision.

She was far too hard on her friends.

CHAPTER FOUR

The Ghost of True Power

ILSA'S FEET ACHED AS she trudged along the cobbled street with uncertain steps. The night hours crawled on, and freezing rain began to drizzle around her. The lights of Edgewater floated in the fog like lost ghosts, wandering the night with no hope of shelter. Their bright spots against the mist gave off an eerie, disorienting glow. Ilsa stumbled as a wave of dizziness made her vision swim. Her breath came in short, painful gasps.

Mobius nipped at a wisp of Ilsa's hair. She brushed him off, but he persisted, catching the strand between his teeth and tugging harder.

"I'm fine." Ilsa told him with a weary shake of her head. "It'll be all right. I just need to rest a few minutes, that's all."

Another burst of pain tore through Ilsa's chest, proving her assurances false. She lurched forward, gasping. Instinctively, she put out a hand to steady herself and was met with a smooth, wet surface, cold and clammy against her palm. She looked up.

Her heart skipped a painful beat at the sight of the dragon skull looming above her.

With a chirp of alarm, Mobius scurried into her cloak's hood. Ilsa could feel his little body quivering against her back, but she lacked the strength to comfort him.

It's all right, she thought, though the words didn't make it to her lips. *We must've gotten turned around and wandered back into the square, that's all.*

That was the logical explanation, of course. But it was hard to escape the sensation that perhaps the dragon was following her.

Ilsa leaned against the skeletal beast, sheltering from the sleet beneath its leering grin. A strange thing, taking refuge in the maw of a monster.

"Lost, traveler?"

The question from the shadows sent a jolt through Ilsa's thoughts. Startled, she turned to see where the low voice had come from.

Ilsa could barely make out the shadow of a slope-shouldered form, huddled under the dragon skull a few yards away. A dark hood obscured the figure's features, leaving Ilsa with the unsettling feeling that perhaps he had none. A warning crawled along the back of her neck, but she didn't have the strength to retreat.

"Your pardon, sir. I thought I was alone." Mobius poked his head out from the folds of her cloak and ventured a cautious sniff in the stranger's direction. Ilsa put a hand on his head and shoved him back into hiding. "I'll only take a moment, then be on my way."

The glow of a pipe flared in the darkness, illuminating a fraction of a face beneath the hood. Ilsa caught a glimpse of a thin, pale jaw, which bore the sharp marks of prolonged hunger.

"A moment." The stranger's thin voice rasped like a knife scraping across iron. "Such an insignificant thing. And yet, in the presence of true power—even the ghost of true power—a moment is a rare treasure indeed. Most never come so close as to take one."

The stranger raised a clawlike hand and scratched at the jawbone of the beast. A faint glimmer of something flecked off of the bone at his touch, like sparks springing from a whetstone.

"Ah," the stranger's gaunt features twisted into a facsimile of a smile. "Still good."

He shook the embers from his pipe stowed it away, then drew a long, serrated knife from somewhere within his cloak. He scraped the blade across the bone, carving a deep groove into the side of the skull. A shining streak of liquid seeped from the crack, dribbling down the monster's face like a tear.

"Is that oil?" Ilsa couldn't restrain her surprise. It was her first glimpse of the powerful substance that gave this corner of the world its place on the map. But to the best of her knowledge, dragon oil had to be extracted from the beasts by an arduous process. She'd never heard of it being scraped from their bones.

The stranger cupped a hand beneath the flow and let the oil pool in his palm.

"Remarkable, is it not?" He chuckled, holding his prize out for her to see. "Even in death the dragon holds more raw power than you or I could ever dream of achieving in life."

The oil rippled across the stranger's hand, seeming to move with a life of its own as it wove through his fingers.

"So short-sighted, these coastal people are." The stranger scoffed. "Melvians. The *advanced* civilization. The ones with all the answers. They fuel their machines and warm their hovels with power they cannot understand. They look at a dragon and see its parts. Boiling down a god to light their hearth."

"Dragons aren't gods." Ilsa shook her head. "That much I do know."

"No?" The stranger's unflinching smile was beginning to make Ilsa's skin crawl. "Tell me, what about this power is less than godlike?"

"I'm not denying they have unique biological properties, but that doesn't—"

"You do not even begin to grasp what power you could possess." The stranger snapped, cutting her off. "Strength from weakness. Life from death. Health from frailty. I have seen it. I have lived it."

He raised his cupped hand to his mouth and took a long, slow sip of the liquid. Ilsa cringed.

"You *definitely* shouldn't be drinking that."

The stranger slurped the dregs of the oil. When he pulled his hand away from his mouth, a bright smear lingered on his sharp face.

"Long ago," he said. "I was not very unlike you."

Did she only imagine that his voice sounded stronger than it had a moment ago?

"I don't know what you're talking about." Ilsa looked away, hugging her arms tightly across her chest, unconsciously shielding her heart.

"You doubt," he said. "Because you have not seen. You do not know. But you will, Ilsa Starling. You will."

A chill shot through Ilsa that had nothing to do with the rain. She stepped backward. "How do you know my name?"

The stranger ignored the question. "Let me show you what is possible. One taste and your doubts will die. I know you're tempted. Give in. Give me your hand."

Ilsa hesitated, tugging at her hair ribbon. The urge to turn and run, to get as far from this unnerving stranger as she could, was strong. And yet...what if...? Her gaze flicked to the slick of oil still shimmering on the dragon's skull.

Strength from weakness. Life from death.

The stranger's dripping hand hovered, outstretched, waiting.

A burst of bright light flooded the plaza. In an instant, shadows scattered, and Ilsa saw the stranger's face beneath his cowl for the first time.

If he'd been human once, he certainly wasn't anymore. His features were skeletally sharp, eyes sunken deep in their hollows. His skin had long since moved beyond pallor; it was a nearly translucent gray. His nose was nothing more than two reptilian slits along a narrow ridge of bone. Uneven patches of flaky scales scattered sporadically across his neck and face.

Ilsa reeled backward with a horrified cry.

The stranger hissed, drawing his threadbare cloak tightly around himself, but he could not erase what she'd seen.

"Be gone, foul creature!" A booming voice rang out from behind Ilsa. She whirled to face it and had to shield her eyes from the intensity of the light. With an enraged shriek, the stranger fled, vanishing into the mist.

As soon as he disappeared, the light retreated, shrinking from a blinding blaze back down into a concentrated glow—a glow that emanated from a large red gemstone.

"That creature did not hurt you, *Yil'saa?*"

"Yuri!" Ilsa sagged with relief at the sight of the Stoneman. "I'm so glad to see you! Whatever made you follow me?"

"Your pack," Yuri said as he slipped the gemstone's braided cord back around his neck. The shining stone lay against his chest, its light dancing across his carved tattoos.

"My what? Oh." Ilsa blinked as Yuri indicated the faded carpetbag he'd set on the cobbles beside him. "I hadn't even noticed I'd left it."

Yuri handed it to her, but his attention was on the darkness beyond. Ilsa followed his frowning gaze.

"Yuri, what *was* that thing?"

"I am not sure." He replied, his brow furrowed. He knelt, dragging a finger through the ash that the stranger had shaken from his pipe. "What did it say to you?"

Ilsa hesitated. The stranger's alluring promises and veiled predictions echoed in her mind, tantalizing and repulsive all at once. Her gaze lingered on the groove he'd carved in the dragon skull, still wet with a lingering ooze of oil.

"He didn't say much," she lied. Another shudder ran down her spine.

"Hm." Yuri grunted as he got to his feet, still frowning into the darkness. With an almost unconscious adjustment, he pulled his cloak tighter around his chest, obscuring the glowing gemstone.

Ilsa studied him.

We protect our own, he'd said, back in the inn. She wasn't quite sure what he'd protected her from, but deep down she was grateful he'd been there. She couldn't make it alone. And if it was a choice between risking a friendship with Yuri, or taking the advice of a suspicious stranger, she knew who she'd rather trust.

"Thank you," she said quietly. "And I'm sorry about leaving earlier."

Yuri broke his pensive gaze and turned to her with his black-toothed smile.

"So," Ilsa said, stooping to pick up her bag. "Does that offer of a boat still stand?"

Chapter Five

Map's End

THERE WAS NO WATER at the Edgewater Docks. Just beached boats strung out along the cliffside drop-off, ready to launch into thin air.

Ilsa sat in the bow of a small, single-masted craft. If she closed her eyes, she could almost imagine she was sailing. The gentle rocking motion of the boat was familiar. Familiar, but in the way a friend's face appeared in a dream—distant, and somehow, in a way she couldn't quite name, deeply wrong.

Ilsa risked a glance astern and saw the towering Cliffs of Edgewater falling away behind the little boat. The frowning crags seen from this angle would have been breathtaking—beautiful, even—if she could have somehow made herself forget that she'd sailed straight off of them and was now gliding along with nothing beneath her hull but a thousand feet of mist, and below that, the restless northern sea.

In a moment, the fog swallowed the cliffs, leaving nothing but whiteness to the boat's stern. Wispy tendrils slipped over the gunwales like sea spray in slow motion. The voyage was eerily silent without the splashing of surf against the hull. The only sounds were the flapping of the sails and the creaking of the mast.

Ilsa turned her attention to the key that made sailing through the sky not only possible, but commonplace in this part of the world: the iridescent liquid ribboning its way through the auxiliary sails that stretched from the boat's flanks like great wings. It played tricks on her eyes—sometimes purple, the next moment aquamarine, and then again nearly invisible but for a faint shimmer on the canvas.

Seeing the oil in action was like witnessing something out of the bedtime stories Grandfather used to tell her when she was little:

"They fly, like the dragons themselves," he would say, his dark eyes sparkling. "Can you imagine? A boat in the air? And all that to harvest oil to fuel our engines, to power our industry, to give us a better life. See this?" Here he would usually hold up his watch or point out some other nearby convenience. "The only reason we have it is because a brave Hunter risked his life to slay a dragon and harvest its power. So, any time you ride a train, my girl, or buy a dress you didn't have to sew yourself, you be sure to thank a Hunter."

"But Grandfather." Ilsa would giggle. "There aren't any Hunters here. They're all off the map."

"True, true. Well, that proves my point. Only the very bravest sailors dare to sail to the edge of the world."

Somewhere in the mist far below came the piercing cry of a seagull, drawing Ilsa back to the present. She shuddered. The very bravest sailors? She didn't feel brave at all.

"I see the lights of Map's End." Yuri called from behind her, breaking into the flurry of her thoughts. Yuri sat in the stern, a small mountain hunched against the fog. The tiller looked no bigger than a twig in his hands. Ilsa strained her eyes, but it was a futile effort to try to compete with Yuri's keen vision.

"We sail the rest of the way," Yuri said.

"You do know how to get this thing down, don't you?" Ilsa glanced over the side of the boat, but even the sea was shrouded.

Yuri's only answer was a rumbling chuckle. Not terribly reassuring.

The blind descent tested Ilsa's courage more than she cared to admit. The sensation of dropping through clouds, all the while hearing crashing breakers ring out ever louder below, was not one she was anxious to repeat anytime soon. When the boat finally met the waters with a mighty splash, Ilsa blew out a tight breath of relief. She didn't even mind the chill of the spray; she was just glad to be out of the sky.

"Well done, *Yil'saa.*" Yuri rumbled, leaning forward to drop a heavy hand on her shoulder. The solid pressure of his touch was comforting, but his intentional mispronunciation of her name was even more so. *Little Sister.* "You survive your first dragonsail ride without being sick."

Ilsa gave a weak smile.

"I'm happy it's over." She confessed. "Though I suppose we'll all have to get used to it."

"Your companion was not troubled," Yuri remarked. He was right. Mobius, not having slept much last night, was nothing but a round ball of white fur tucked amongst the bags. He hadn't even twitched an ear the whole time they'd been skyborne.

"He's done far more flying in his life than I have." Ilsa smiled at the sleeping tammer. "But once we're aboard a Hunter, maybe I'll give him a run for his money."

They sailed through the pre-dawn in companionable silence. The movements of piloting the small craft came naturally to Ilsa, her instincts forgetting the years she'd spent away from the sea. As the sun rose over the breakers, the fog thinned, and with it, the heaviness of her heart started to lift. She felt, for the first time in a long time, that perhaps everything would be all right. She could never go back to what she'd left behind, but an ocean stretched before her. At least here, on a boat, Ilsa knew what was expected of her. At least here she wouldn't feel inadequate, unworthy, or broken. At least here...

Her thought trailed off, lost in an ache of loneliness, of yearning for what once was but could not be again. No "at least" could give it back. She blinked back a well of sudden, unwanted tears.

Not now, Ilsa. It'll do no good.

She set her gaze toward the horizon, determined not to look back. A gust of wind pulled aside the last wispy curtain of fog. All at once, the little boat broke out into clear air and wide-open seas. A gray shadow appeared, no more than a smudge on the horizon, but Ilsa knew land when she saw it.

"Yuri!" she exclaimed, leaning forward to grasp the bow of the boat in excitement. "There it is! I can see the island!"

ILSA AND YURI RETURNED their rented boat at a small public pier on the southern shore of Map's End. A local informed them they needed to get to the north harbor if they were looking for Hunters, so they set off through town.

Map's End had always existed in Ilsa's mind as nothing more than a small mark in the far northeast corner of Grandfather's sea charts. Nothing lay beyond the island but open ocean, so most cartographers didn't even bother extending their maps past it—a practice that earned the island its fitting, if somewhat prosaic, name.

The gray, weathered little village was built into the dips and rises of the rocky island. Despite the cold, the islanders went about their business with determined faces and squared shoulders, as if daring the foul weather to keep them from their way of life. Fishermen rigged their nets to set back out into the foamy waters while their wives hawked the morning's catch. Dockworkers loaded and unloaded the supply ships moored at the pier. Merchants and tradesmen haggled over goods and prices. Somewhere nearby, Ilsa could smell fish cooking on an open flame, though she couldn't tell where it was coming from, and in the distance she could sense the underlying hum of a busy market.

There was something inspiring about it all. The tiny island stood at the remotest edge of the map, the last outpost of civilization before it gave way to the expanse of the sea. The buildings were battered and storm-lashed, but still stood strong and grim against the gray sky. It struck Ilsa as a resilient, defiant place, impervious to the hardship that raged around it.

It was everything she wished she could say about herself.

The farther they pressed into town, the busier the streets became. Ilsa had never seen such a diverse crowd, even in some of the busiest port cities she'd anchored in. Native Melvians like her were present, but they were barely the majority, even though Map's End technically fell within Melvian borders.

Ilsa sidestepped a pair of long-lived Sylacians from the Svygard Mountains, clothed in thick furs and carrying bone weapons. A minute later, they passed a tight cluster of dark-complected Eelni from the Central Plains, known for their wisdom and fortitude. They came only to Ilsa's waist when full-grown—though to equate their size with weakness was a mistake many had been made to regret. Stalls and Crans shouted loudly in the common trade language as they hauled their cargo toward the docks, exchanging the latest news from their neighboring regions in the far south, and complaining loudly about the cold here at the edge of the sea. Representatives from more races and nations than Ilsa could recognize chattered and thronged in this tiny cross-section of humanity.

And yet, even in such a diverse mix, one creature stuck out. Ilsa felt the burn of dozens of eyes following her and Yuri through the streets. Conversations hushed as they passed by. She glanced up at Yuri, but the tattooed Stoneman walked by her side with languid strides and a pleasant expression, seemingly oblivious to the stares he drew.

"Don't you ever get tired of them gawking at you?" Ilsa asked as a gray-haired woman pointed indiscreetly at Yuri before whispering something to another villager.

Yuri chuckled. "It is port town," he said. "You see how many different sorts are here. I'm sure I am not the first of my kind seen in Map's End."

"Then why do they keep looking at us?"

"Hmm. Not unusual to see many races here. But yes, unusual to see Melvian girl and Stoneman traveling together. My guess? They stare at *you.*"

Ilsa stopped walking and gave him an open-mouthed stare of her own. But the glimmer of mischief in Yuri's eyes betrayed that he meant to poke fun at her. And by the grin that split his face, it was clear he got exactly the reaction he wanted.

Ilsa laughed out loud, surprising even herself. Mobius's sleepy head popped out from inside Yuri's haversack—a hideout he'd immediately preferred over Ilsa's carpetbag—and twitched his ears at the unfamiliar sound. Ilsa hadn't laughed in...well, who was counting, anyway? But she couldn't deny that it felt good. Perhaps Yuri's joke carried some truth. And perhaps she didn't care at all.

The road turned sharply upward, and they began to climb, all the while still surrounded by the houses and establishments of Map's End. At the town's highest point, Ilsa let out a little gasp. For the first time all day, the fog had thinned enough for her to see the north end of the island spread out below. The great sailing ships that lay at anchor in the north harbor transformed the crescent bay into a vast forest of masts and canvas.

"Somewhere down there, Yuri," she said. "Somewhere down there is our ship. Our way out. We need only to find it."

Yuri sent her a questioning glance, but Ilsa didn't look up to meet his eyes. Instead she swept the harbor with her gaze, as if somehow the ship she was to sail on could give her a sign.

"Let's go now," Ilsa urged.

She took Yuri's broad hand and started down the hill toward the ships. But he pulled her to a stop in the middle of the cobbled street.

"Little Sister," Yuri said. Concern radiated from those persistent yellow eyes of his. "You ask me last night what I am doing so far from where I belong. An odd question, I think, when of us two—" he raised a knowing eyebrow at her. "—*you* are the one who is running away."

"I'm not running away," Ilsa said quickly. A little too quickly. Mobius peered at her over Yuri's shoulder; his whiskered gaze was accusing, as if demanding to know why, if they weren't running away, had Ilsa pulled him from his cozy hutch in the middle of the night and coaxed him into a carpetbag—and in such a rush that she'd neglected to pack wolfberries, at that!

Ilsa's face grew hot, and her nervous fingers reached for her hair ribbon. "I mean, I *am* leaving a rather significant chapter of my life, but it was over before I left."

"So why hurry?" Yuri prodded. "You race to sea like your life depends on it."

His words hung in the air between them. Ilsa chewed her lip, trying to decide how to reply. But she knew without trying that no clever excuse or attempt to brush off Yuri's concern would be successful.

"Maybe it does." Ilsa admitted quietly, looking down the hill, past the town, and to the gray ocean beyond.

Yuri waited, his patient silence giving Ilsa the space to form her thoughts.

"It's...complicated," she finally said. "For as long as I can remember, I've had times when it's harder to see the joy in life. My grandfather used to call it a damp, drizzly November of the soul. Doctors call it a 'delicate melancholy constitution.'"

"I like your grandfather's name better."

"He was rather poetic, wasn't he?" Ilsa agreed. "Well, whatever you want to call it, I find that the best way to drive it off is to go to sea. Grandfather—he raised me after my mother died—he was a sea captain; he worked for the merchants' guild in our province. So, when I was young and I had a bad spell, he would withdraw me from school, even if it was in the middle of a term, and take me on his voyages. I'd sail with him until I was well enough to return to my studies."

"A good man," Yuri said.

"He was." Ilsa nodded, feeling a brush of sadness. Five years gone, and she still missed him every day. "So, I suppose that's why I see the sea as a sort of medicine for when life becomes too heavy to bear. And it's been quite heavy, of late." She added quietly, more to herself than to Yuri.

Tell Phillip it's better this way...

"At any rate." Ilsa forced a lighthearted shrug. She pushed away thoughts of Grandfather, and Phillip, and everything else she'd left behind. "Going to sea for a bit to clear my head is a decent sight better than stepping out into the street and knocking people's hats off for no reason."

Yuri tilted his head to one side and frowned in confusion.

"Would...would that make you feel better?" He asked slowly, as if trying to decide if she was serious or not.

"It might make me feel *something*." Ilsa smiled sheepishly, a little ashamed that she wasn't entirely joking. "Which, if the alternative is numb detachment, I think it's worth the risk."

"I am not sure," Yuri said with a quizzical frown, but he didn't press the matter further.

When they reached the harbor, Ilsa hardly noticed the cold fingers of fog that grasped at the hem of her cloak. Everything about this place—the creaking hulls of ships lying at anchor, the gentle swaying of the dock beneath her feet, the thick smell of salt and rotting wood—felt like whispered greetings from old friends. For once, Ilsa didn't have to hurry to keep pace with Yuri's long strides; she stepped lightly through this damp maritime world.

Oh, how I've missed it all.

She didn't regret leaving the seafaring life, of course; Grandfather's gift of a secure living for her when he died was a great kindness. And despite the abrupt and painful way the years she'd spent inland had ended, Ilsa could never dream of calling them wasted. But here—among the lines and masts and salt-weathered figureheads—here was where she belonged.

Ilsa turned to Yuri to see if he shared her excitement. Her companion stood paused on the pier, his arms folded easily over his broad, carved chest. Yuri squinted up into the forest of masts with a thoughtful gaze. Ilsa was struck once again by how inconsistent his fierce appearance was with his gentle manner. He seemed so out of place, and yet so confident that he was where he needed to be. What chain of events had led him to this moment, standing here on the edge of the known world, next to her?

"What about you, Yuri?" Ilsa asked abruptly.

He raised a questioning eyebrow at her. "About me?"

"Well, I told you what I'm doing here, but all I know about you is that you want to sail on a Hunter. Why?"

"Hm." Yuri smiled, gazing out again at the ships. "That is a question with many answers."

"What's your favorite one, then?"

Yuri's brow furrowed. After a moment of thought, he turned his full attention to her.

"When the Creator formed the world," he began, in a tone like someone about to recount a legend. "He gives dominions to peoples he put there. Your race stewards the seas. Mine, the depths. Sylacians are masters of the mountains and skies."

"And the Eelni tend the green earth." Ilsa finished for him. "Yes, everyone knows that. What does that have to do with you?"

"To each race was given means and wisdom to care for its homeland. Each has spent the ages honing its crafts, forming its culture. And yet, very often they do not mix. My people are among the most isolated of any on earth. You had never seen one of my kind before last night, true?"

"Yes."

"It should not be so." Yuri shook his head. "I am firstborn of my clan. One day, I will be chief of my people. So, ten years ago, I make a vow to travel the world, gathering wisdom from all its children, to bring back to my homeland. Since that time, I cross many seas, travel many lands. See." Yuri spread his hands, indicating the carved tattoos on his forearms. "These tell story of my journey."

They were beautiful, symmetrical marks. If Yuri hadn't pointed out the difference, Ilsa would have thought they were merely extensions of the tribal pattern that covered the rest of his body. But when she looked closely, she could discern a jagged snowcapped peak on his left forearm, and a pattern like a leafy vine on his right.

"I climb the highest peaks with the Sylacians." Yuri nodded toward the mountain outline. "And glean wisdom from the skies. Then I live among Eelni, learn to work the ground with my hands, bring forth life from dirt."

Yuri turned his face toward the sea again, taking a deep breath of salt air.

"Now, for my final journey, I must sail to the edge of the world with your people, test the limits of what is possible, and witness the power and majesty of the ocean," he said. "When at last I listen to the secrets of farthest sea and gaze upon that great mystery, the space beyond the Edge, I will finally be ready to return home, carrying the blessings and knowledge of the whole world with me. And—" a twinkle of mischief glinted in Yuri's golden eyes "—I will have to get dragon tattoo, no?"

"Ten years a wanderer," Ilsa murmured, glancing at Yuri with a new measure of respect, and a little sadness. "All that time alone, out of place, belonging nowhere."

"The prize is worth the sacrifice," he said, and his emphatic tone testified that he believed it. "My people suffer and die from ailments that Sylacians found cures for long ago. The Melvian way of life is full of useful tools my people have never dreamed of. And your food!" Yuri clapped a hand over his stomach and moaned. "*Yil'saa,* I am not sure how I survived so long without tasting surface-dwellers' food. The first thing I will present to my father when I return is a jar of Eelni spices." He chuckled. "But I am ready to go home. One last journey."

A wave of grief washed over Ilsa at his words.

One last journey.

"Then we'd better get started," she said, straightening her shoulders and forcing a smile. "Come on then, let's get ourselves a ship."

"...AND WE ENTREAT THE BLESSINGS and protection of our Creator upon Captain Chase, his crew, and this voyage. May the lights of this harbor welcome them home upon their journey's end."

The reverend's voice boomed out in the little stone chapel. It was a simple, humble place, unadorned but for a tall white pillar to the left of the lectern.

Ilsa didn't want to be here, listening to the traditional commissioning service for an outbound ship, but she had to admit that after a disappointing morning, it did feel good to sit down for a spell.

She rubbed her temples, fighting the ache that never quite faded. None of her plans had accounted for the possibility of not even being able to get on a ship. She'd thought that would be the easy part, but truth be told, she didn't really know what she was doing when it came to trying to sign onto a ship's company. Despite her long history at sea, she'd never had to navigate that part of it before. Being the captain's granddaughter did come with some advantages.

The first ship they'd inquired at was a disaster. The officer on deck had merely looked her up and down. Ilsa squirmed under the scrutiny, painfully aware of her thin frame and washed-out complexion. If she landed a berth, it wouldn't be because of her looks.

"We don't let socialites walk onto Hunting ships, you know."

"I'm not a socialite; I'm a schoolteacher," Ilsa replied. "And before that, a sailor. I did nine voyages in the South Ardan Isles."

The officer waved away Ilsa's credentials.

"You wouldn't last a month on a Hunting ship. These are the toughest seas in the world, and Map's End only sends her strongest sailors to brave them." He eyed Yuri. "Interested in you, though."

"We go together, or not at all," Yuri replied.

"Fair enough," the officer shrugged. "Sorry lass, but I can't help you. You want to sail? Head back to the Ardans."

"Or check with *Relentless.*" A passing sailor called with a coarse laugh. "They'll take anyone with a pulse."

"Don't be cruel, Tom." The officer cut a glare at the sailor, then gave Ilsa an apologetic shake of his head. "Off you go, then."

A similar reception met them at the second ship they tried. After the third rejection, Yuri pulled Ilsa aside.

"Come, we will rest now," he'd said, leaving little room for protest. "I heard bells; a chapel is nearby. We will go in. Our ship will not leave without us."

"How do you know that?"

"Because if it did, it would not be our ship." Yuri smiled. "Come. It will be warm inside, and we will sit."

So here she sat, slumped in a stiff-backed pew, weary and discouraged. Ilsa's gaze wandered the ceiling above the congregants, a stone dome that served to amplify the reverend's voice. But despite the magnitude of both his volume and his passion, Ilsa found it hard to focus. She caught herself studying the pillar instead. A carving near the top of the marble monolith read:

> *Sacred to the Memory of Those Taken by the Sea.*
> *Map's End Remembers You.*

The list of names memorialized on the white stone was lengthy. Some of the engravings were weathered and worn nearly smooth, but others bore no such signs of age.

Ilsa and Yuri sat amongst a small gathering of islanders—sailors, fishermen, wives, and widows. They sat apart from each other, like scattered islands in a silent sea, each isolated in their private prayers. Ilsa wondered how many of the somber, black-draped women in the chapel could point out their loved one's name engraved on that bleak pillar.

Looking over the small gathering, Ilsa was grateful that she and Yuri had arrived late to the service when the congregants' attention was focused on the reverend. Slipping quietly into the back pew during the benediction had saved them the stares Yuri's savage appearance surely would have drawn.

"Captain," the reverend continued, raising a withered old hand in blessing toward a man sitting in the front pew. His back was to Ilsa, so she couldn't discern much about him aside from his dark hair, which fell past his shoulders and was tied back with a slate-gray ribbon. "As you sail, know that the hearts and prayers of all on this island accompany you."

"Thank you, Father," the captain answered. His words may have been well-mannered, but the anger in his tone caught Ilsa off guard. He stood abruptly, pushing the whole pew backwards with the suddenness of the movement. "But I doubt many of these good souls will waste their prayers on me. Now, I must see to some final matters on my ship. You'll excuse me."

Captain Chase strode down the aisle with a jerking, unsteady gait, and Ilsa got her first good look at him. Two things stood out to her immediately: his youth—he looked barely thirty—and the rather striking fact that he had only one leg. In place of his left, he wore an ivory peg, and leaned on a wooden crutch tucked under his arm. The captain's face was drawn and hardship-worn, but the firm set of his jaw and determined crease of his brow gave him the look of one who sees trouble and dares it to try and shake him.

He was everything a dragon-hunter ought to be.

"Godspeed, Captain," the reverend called after the captain as he stormed out. When the slam of the chapel door had faded to echoes, sadness stole across the old man's face. "And may he have mercy on your soul," he added softly.

"Yuri!" Ilsa hissed, tugging at his arm as she stood. "Come on; we've got to follow him."

But Yuri shook his head. "The preacher said he sails with the evening tide. There is time. Sit down. We find him after prayers."

Ilsa wanted to protest, but Yuri didn't seem to be asking her opinion. Reluctantly, she sat back in the pew and tried to listen as the service continued, but her mind had already followed the one-legged captain all the way to the harbor, onto his ship, and out to sea.

Ilsa didn't hear much of the message. At the end of the service, though, she bowed her head, and recited the Sailor's Prayer along with the rest of the congregation. The blessing given by the Creator and passed down through hundreds of generations of sailors was as familiar to Ilsa as her own name; she'd spoken it numberless times on behalf of herself and others. Grandfather had taught her to say it as soon as she could lisp out the words.

"They that go down to the sea in ships, that do business in great waters; These see the works of the Lord, and his wonders in the deep."

Ilsa spoke the words, but her heart was not in the prayers. Her faith, like her joy, had been thirsting for too long.

"For he commandeth, and raiseth the stormy wind, which lifteth up the waves thereof." The congregation around her continued in unison. "They mount up to the heavens, they go down again to the depths: their soul is melted because of trouble. They reel to and fro, and stagger like a drunken man, and are at their wit's end."

Ilsa hung her head.

"Then they cry unto the Lord in their trouble." She whispered the next line. "And he bringeth them out of their distresses. He maketh the storm a calm, so that the waves thereof are still."

The words felt heavy on her lips. Ilsa's eyes flicked up to the list of names on the memorial. Doubtless this prayer was recited over those lost sailors when they left home for the last time.

Did they not cry out in their trouble? Why didn't he calm their storm?

Why won't he calm mine?

Ilsa shifted uncomfortably in her seat. It didn't seem right to be having such thoughts. But she couldn't help but wonder.

"Then are they glad because they be quiet," the reverend recited, drawing the prayer to a close. "So he bringeth them unto their desired haven."

"Amen," Ilsa murmured in unison with a dozen other voices. She hardly heard the reverend's final blessing and dismissal. She and Yuri slipped out the back of the chapel before the other petitioners could file out of their seats. As the cold sea air hit Ilsa's face, the final promise of the prayer turned itself over in her mind:

He bringeth them unto their desired haven.

CHAPTER SIX

Relentless

RELENTLESS RESTED LOW IN THE WATER, heavy-laden and rigged for sail.

"This ship has seen many seas." Yuri nodded solemnly at the weathered blackwood hull. "Good."

Ilsa agreed. *Relentless* was a smaller ship than any Grandfather had captained, but she could tell at a glance that it was sturdy and seaworthy. Mobius, refreshed after his long morning nap in Yuri's haversack, now sat on Ilsa's shoulder, eyeing the ship with suspicion.

"We go aboard now, yes?" Yuri asked, gesturing toward the gangplank.

"I'm not sure..." Ilsa trailed off. She fiddled with the worn edge of her hair ribbon. Despite the tip they'd gotten earlier that *Relentless* was taking on crew members, the ship looked strangely deserted to Ilsa.

"Do not worry," Yuri said, giving her a reassuring smile as he strode up the plank. "I will find us what we need."

Yuri's alert yellow eyes swept the deck, then turned upward. He tilted his head as he peered into the ship's rigging. Then he smiled.

"Habari za asubuhi," he called upward. It sounded like a greeting, but it was no language Ilsa recognized. But something shifted up in the ropes above, and Ilsa realized that there was a

small person up there, peering down at her.

Ilsa hadn't noticed her, tucked amongst the lines and spars, her dark skin nearly blending in with the blackwood mast she leaned against. She held a silver dagger, methodically scraping the blade against a small whetstone in her other hand.

"A Stoneman who speaks Eelni?" the woman grinned at Yuri, flashing a row of glittering white teeth. "That's a new one."

"I traveled long among your people," Yuri replied, dipping his head in a bow. "They always be kind to me."

"The Creator forbid I break that noble tradition, then," the woman said. Without sheathing her blade, she clasped a line in her fist and swung down to the deck. Her bare feet hardly made a sound as they hit the planks. When she stood upright, the Eelni woman's head came to Ilsa's chest, which would make her tall for her race. Hundreds of thin black braids hung to her ankles, and they sparkled with brightly painted beads woven throughout the strands.

"Tashtanna Ngozi, chief harpooner for five voyages aboard the good ship *Relentless*," the sailor said with a deep bow that swept her hair across the deck. Her accent was deep and rich, hinting at faraway places.

Five voyages? Ilsa's eyes widened. This tiny woman had probably felled dozens of dragons. Ilsa tried to imagine Tashtanna wielding a harpoon, but it was a difficult image to conjure; the weapon would be nearly twice her height.

"So, a Melvian, and Stoneman, and a rabbit walk onto a Hunting ship." Tashtanna chuckled. "Sounds like the start to a terrible joke, doesn't it?"

Mobius sniffed, then primly extended a wing in a not-so-subtle display of proof that he was not, in fact, a rabbit.

"Oh!" Tashtanna exclaimed, inclining her head toward Mobius. "My sincerest apologies, little friend. That fellow's a harbinger, isn't he? I've never seen one up close before. Where on earth did you get one?"

A knot tightened in Ilsa's chest. She tried to answer casually, but her mouth was suddenly dry. She swept Mobius off her shoulder and cradled him in her arms, as if that somehow would hide the obvious.

"He, um... he was a gift," Ilsa said quickly, hoping that would be the end of it.

"That word. Har..bin... It means bad news, yes?" Yuri gave an uncertain frown. "Why do they call Mobius that?"

"A leftover term from the old wars, I think." Tasha shrugged, oblivious to Ilsa's discomfort. "They used to use these things as messengers. So, if you saw one in the sky, it was a sign that news was coming. Like an omen."

"Keeping them is more of a gentlemen's hobby now." Ilsa agreed, holding back a sigh of relief as the nervous moment passed. Mobius squirmed in her grasp. "Though—" she amended, patting his head obligingly. "Mobius is very good at delivering messages."

"Fair enough," Tashtanna said. "So. What can I do for you?"

"We want to join voyage," Yuri said. "Man at the harbor said your ship need sailors."

"Not from around here, are you?" Tashtanna asked. The question struck Ilsa as an odd follow-up to Yuri's statement, but she answered it anyway.

"No, I've just traveled from Central Melvia, and Yuri comes from—"

"I can tell *he's* not local." The woman laughed. "Good. If you're looking to sail, and you're not islanders, then you're in the right place." Tashtanna thumbed the edge of her knife. "*Relentless* sails in a matter of hours and we've barely got a skeleton crew signed on." She gave a wry smile. "Captain's orders are to take on anyone who can stand on two feet and has a vague idea of which end of the boat goes in the water."

"We might be *overqualified* for this one," Ilsa muttered to Yuri.

"I'll go ahead and save you the trouble of asking." Tashtanna cut in. "Nothing at all is wrong with *Relentless*, or Captain Chase either. Besides that," she added with a wink. "With fewer crew, we each get a bigger cut of the voyage's profits, eh?"

Ilsa worried the end of her ribbon between her finger and thumb. Tashtanna's light explanation was hardly reassuring. "Why can't you get anyone to join your voyage?"

The harpooner's face grew fierce.

"People of this island are prejudiced, that's all it comes down to," she snapped, cutting a glare toward the town beyond the harbor. "The locals won't sail with Chase because of his accident."

Ilsa thought back to the captain in the Hunter's Chapel, with his limping gait and pain-lined features. She hadn't yet stopped to question how he'd lost the leg.

"But I'll have you know the truth." The little harpooner continued, a fiery note of passion in her voice. "He's one of the greatest Hunters out of Map's End, always has been. The very fact that he's setting sail again after his last voyage ended in disaster proves that more than a hundred barrels of oil would. If you can accept that, and not buy into the nonsense that Captain Chase is cursed, then you'll do fine on this ship."

"Curses don't scare me," Ilsa replied. "I believe in the providence of the Creator. Nothing happens outside of his care."

Even as she said it, Ilsa felt as though she was merely repeating something she'd been told she believed.

"I'm sure Captain Chase is more than capable." Ilsa hugged her cloak around herself against a gust of sharp wind. She tried a light smile. "He has an apt name for the job, at any rate."

"True enough." Tashtanna agreed, "but don't ever let him hear you say so. His leg wasn't the only thing that dragon took from him; Chase's sense of humor never recovered from the disaster."

"What happened to the crew?" Yuri asked. "In disaster you speak of. A leader's greatness must be judged by fate of his people."

"Not one was lost." Tashtanna replied firmly, tossing a stray braid over her shoulder. "Though," she continued, a little begrudgingly. "I do have to admit that was probably more to the credit of our first mate, Mr.—"

"Edwards!" the shout that came from belowdecks cut off Tashtanna's next words. The harpooner stiffened.

"Well." Ice crept into her tone as she glared toward the hatch leading below. "It looks like you'll get to meet him yourselves."

"Edwards! Get back here!"

A man burst from the hatch, mounting the stairs to the deck with long strides. He was tall, clean-cut, and handsome, with the gait of a sailor and the determined posture of an islander. If Ilsa had to take a guess, she'd say he was in his early forties, and he wore his years of experience on his face. Three steps behind him came the captain from the chapel, his face flushed and angry. He caught up to Edwards on the main deck and grabbed his arm, forcing him to stop and face him.

"You have my answer, Chase." Edwards shook off the captain's grip. "I can't help you."

"Of course you can!" Exclaimed Chase, throwing his arms up in exasperation. "You've been with me every time before. Just give me one more voyage, and I will prove everything worth it."

"I thought you were going to sell the boat," Edwards said with an accusing arch of his eyebrow. "That's why I let you bring me out here. I was going to help you assess the value, and then sell it. That was the deal."

"Well, I changed my mind."

"Of course you did." Edwards replied drily. "It couldn't possibly be that you never intended to sell, and only told me that to lure me aboard and try to pressure me into staying?"

"I'm not luring you to anything! What do you take me for, some kind of charlatan?" Chase grasped Edwards's elbow again. "I'm offering you the opportunity of a lifetime."

"And how will it be different than last time?" The first mate sighed.

"I have resources I didn't have back then." Chase insisted. "Trust me, it *will* be different."

"You also have a life-altering injury that you didn't have back then." Edwards pulled away, glancing pointedly at the captain's ivory leg. "Have you forgotten that this time last year you were little more than a dead man?"

The captain flushed with anger and opened his mouth to retort, but Edwards cut him off before he could begin.

"This voyage will end worse than the last. I won't sail, that's final, and you'd do wisely to decide the same."

"Since when did you become such a coward?" Chase snapped.

Edwards flinched. Ilsa could tell the words cut deep. But he took a deep breath, schooling his temper before replying.

"I have more to consider than ambition and profit now," he said calmly, glancing back over his shoulder at the captain. He started walking toward the gangplank. "I believe I did inform you that I'm recently wedded? I sent you an invitation, if you recall."

"You widowed that girl the day you married her!" Chase shouted after him. "It's what she signed up for when she married a Hunter, and you know it!"

"You won't sway me, Chase."

"It's a poor excuse," said the captain. "Family matters never kept you ashore before."

"You know that's not all." Edwards stopped, then turned back around. "You shouldn't be doing this, and I think deep down you know it. If I can help you realize that, then I'll have done my duty."

At that, Chase laughed, a harsh, abrasive sound.

"You think by refusing me, you'll keep me ashore? That I'll give up?" The captain shook his head firmly. "I'm sailing, Edwards. With or without you."

"You are not thinking, Adam. Please, as your friend, I must—"

"As my friend?" The captain's face twisted in anger, and he stepped threateningly toward Edwards. "Would a friend commit me to a life of misery and pity, with no hope of escape or reprieve? Would a friend dash every attempt I make at breaking out of this vile prison of an island? If you dare call yourself my friend, then where is the support and help I asked for, *friend*?"

The question hung between the two men in air that fairly crackled with tension. Finally, Edwards sighed. His strong shoulders slumped in defeat.

"I cannot do what you ask of me." His voice broke a little. "I will not take part in your downfall. Don't ask me to."

The captain's face hardened.

"Fine," he said. "Have it your way. I don't need you. I can do this without you."

"Adam, please, I am begging you to come to your senses." Edwards pleaded.

"No, I mean it. I could complete this voyage with a half dozen of the greenest hands in the Northern Continent!" Chase said. "And what's more, I'll be hanged if I have a first officer so dead set against me. I wouldn't have you aboard on this voyage, Edwards, not if you were the last sailor in Outer Melvia. I'd take anyone in the world over you. I'd take—" he cast about the deck, and his eyes locked onto Ilsa.

"You!" he shouted, pointing straight at her. "What's your name?"

"It's Starling, sir. Ilsa Starling." She heard herself answer without thinking.

"You're looking to sign onto this ship, aren't you?" the captain demanded.

"Well, yes, I mean," Ilsa stammered, glancing wide-eyed at Yuri for help. "I suppose we were hoping to inquire, but..."

"Wonderful." Chase cut her off. "You're hired. First officer. Can you handle it, Miss Starling?"

"Don't do that to her, Adam." Edwards interrupted, stepping between Ilsa and the captain. "You've made your point clear enough already. Don't drag anyone else into it."

The captain shoved him aside. "Get off my ship before I have you arrested for trespassing, landsman. I need to speak with my *first mate.*"

"I'm flattered, Captain," Ilsa said, shaking her head. "But I'm afraid you must have mistaken me for someone else. I'm not a Hunter. Well, not yet, at least."

"But you do have experience sailing? And can you take orders?" Chase looked pointedly at Edwards.

"I was unofficially brought up before the mast, sir." Ilsa replied, standing up a little straighter and lifting her chin. If there was one thing she knew well, it was the workings of a sailing ship. "And then I was officially on the articles for six years on a merchant ship in the South Ardan Seas. Nine voyages, sir."

"Impressive," Chase said. Warmth crept into Ilsa's cheeks at his acknowledgement. "Any leadership experience?"

"Well, no," she admitted. "Unless you count teaching school to children."

"If you can keep order in a classroom," Chase said. "You can keep order anywhere. No ship's crew will test your mettle more than children will. What did you teach?"

"Literature and geography, sir. And, um, celestial navigation."

The captain arched his eyebrows.

"It was an elective study." Ilsa shrugged with a modest smile. "But surprisingly popular."

"Never fully left the sea behind, did you?" The captain said. "That's good enough for me. It's settled, then."

Adam Chase extended his hand. An offer.

A chance.

Ilsa took it. His hand was cold in hers, but his grasp was firm. When he let go, Ilsa knew everything in her world had shifted.

She was the first mate aboard a Hunting ship.

"You'll do grand." Chase flashed a tight smile. "Tash, see her settled, will you? And the big fellow, too, we'll take him. You know how to use that spear on your back, I hope?" he asked Yuri.

Yuri gave the captain a solemn nod.

"Perfect. We could use another harpooner. We'll be glad to have you." Chase had to reach up to clap Yuri on the shoulder. "Now then, you must excuse me. It's a long, hard voyage to the edge of the world, with many dangers and trials between here and there. My advice? Go ashore and get yourselves one last good hot meal before we sail. You'll regret it if you don't."

Without waiting for a reply, Captain Chase turned and limped back to the stairs, concluding the interview. He disappeared belowdecks without a backward glance.

Mr. Edwards watched him go, a look of broken resignation on his face. "May the Creator protect you... my friend."

Tashtanna cleared her throat, and Edwards turned, looking surprised to see her standing there.

"I suppose you told him no, then?" she asked, her voice thick with sarcasm.

"Tasha..." Edwards spread his hands out toward her imploringly. "Can't *you* talk sense into him?"

"Forget it, Mr. Edwards." Tashtanna crossed her arms and shook her head. "You know where I stand."

"But why? This is madness!"

"I don't know anything about madness," Tashtanna retorted with a toss of her braids. "What I do know is that loyalty still means something to some of us. I'd sail straight off the Edge if he asked it of me. Now if you'll excuse me—" she gave him an icy glare. "I need to show the first mate to *her* cabin."

She linked her elbow through Ilsa's and turned her back on the former first mate. "Come along, Miss Starling, Yuri. I'll take you to your quarters."

Ilsa's mind whirled with the suddenness of what had just happened, but she let the Eelni harpooner lead her toward the stairs.

"Oh, and before I forget to make it official," Tashtanna added, flashing her glittering white smile. "Welcome aboard *Relentless*, Dragon Hunters."

"I DON'T LIKE IT."

"What?"

"The captain." Yuri answered, shoving a heaping forkful of fisherman's pie into his mouth and mumbling around it. "The argument. All of it. Too many bad feelings."

They sat in a small pub near the harbor, having taken Captain Chase's advice to avail themselves of shore food one last time. Yuri attacked his plate with vigor, but Ilsa couldn't bring herself to do much more than push flakes of pastry and chunks of lobster around with her fork. It might be her last decent meal for a while, but that knowledge only served to make her stomach churn more.

"I don't know about that," she said, not meeting Yuri's eyes. "Captain Chase seems to know what he wants on his ship. You want a captain to be decisive."

"Too rash. Too angry." Yuri shook his head.

"His harpooner spoke highly of him," Ilsa said. "That should count for something."

"True..." Yuri mused. "But she is Eelni."

"What's that got to do with anything?" Ilsa offered a bit of lobster to Mobius, but the tammer turned up his nose.

"Her people count loyalty as highest virtue, and treachery as basest sin. I would take her thoughts with... what is saying? Take with grain of sand?"

"Salt." Ilsa corrected.

"Hm." Yuri nodded. "I think we would be wise to listen to Edwards. You are not going to eat that?"

"We didn't have the full story," Ilsa argued, pushing her unfinished plate toward him. "There could be any number of reasons why the captain fell out with Mr. Edwards. Besides, a dragon killer ought to be fierce."

"I do not doubt his ability to kill dragons." Yuri shrugged, finishing off her pie in two huge mouthfuls.

"Good." Ilsa breathed a sigh of relief. "We could do a lot worse than *Relentless*."

Not to mention it's the only ship that would take me.

But she didn't voice that thought. Instead, she added, "I think Chase will prove an able captain."

"Perhaps you only say that because he make you first mate?" Yuri arched an eyebrow.

"Don't forget, he prefaced that offer with a statement that he'd take anyone in the world," Ilsa retorted, pointing her fork at him for emphasis. "That was hardly meant to flatter my vanity. But I won't try to deny it; the responsibility does excite me." Ilsa allowed herself a small smile and pushed a stray strand of hair out of her face. Yuri watched her closely.

"Be careful, *Yil'saa*," he said softly. Something about his tone sent a spike of panic through her.

"You're still planning to sail with me, aren't you?"

"Of course I am." Yuri gave her a reassuring smile. "I came to see edge of the world, and I can get there in one ship as good as next. But your reasons to be here are more complicated, so you must be cautious. Will this captain help you find what you seek?"

Ilsa looked away, busying herself with stroking Mobius between his folded wings. In truth, she couldn't quite name why she felt so strongly about sailing with Adam Chase. There was something compelling about his fiery determination, even when others urged caution. Perhaps the thing that drew her to him was the very thing that made Yuri wary of him.

"I don't know." Ilsa finally answered. "I think so. To be honest, Yuri, I'm not quite sure if I even know what I want."

He bringeth them unto their desired haven.

"The wind went out of my sails a long time ago," she admitted quietly. "I want to get back on course. And something tells me that Captain Chase wants that too."

"It is enough." Yuri nodded at her. "But I caution you: do not look to Captain Chase to give you worth. That cannot be found in any mortal, no matter how many dragons he has felled."

Ilsa looked away, not wanting to meet Yuri's eyes. Outside the pub's salt-grimed window, the sunlight was waning.

"Come on, Yuri. Let's get out of here." Ilsa urged, scooping Mobius off of her lap. "We need to get back to the harbor."

They left the pub and made their way back through the town's winding narrow streets. Dark came early in this far part of the world, and already the daylight felt thin.

"Fog closing back in." Yuri remarked, and he was right. A damp cloud was settling over the island, seeping the warmth from everything it touched.

"I'm tired of it." Ilsa sighed. "It'll be good to get out into the open sea where the air is clear, and I can..." she trailed off as the words died in her throat.

From an alley across the street, a dark figure stared at her, shrouded in a hooded cloak that covered everything except his ravenously thin jawline and unnerving smile. Ilsa's blood ran cold at the sight of him. She was sure she could hear his horrible, rasping whisper in her head: *Beware, Ilsa Starling.*

"Yuri!" she gasped, clutching at her friend's elbow.

But when she pointed toward the alley, there was no one there. Nothing but swirling mist. Yuri's heavy brows knitted with concern.

"What is it, *Yil'saa?*"

Ilsa bit her lip. She'd been so sure a moment ago, but fog could be deceiving. She took a shaky breath, forcing herself to think rationally.

"I... I think I'm just nervous. That's all," she said, not fully believing it. But she straightened her shoulders and lifted her chin. "Let's go. We've got a ship to catch."

"I could complete this voyage with a half dozen of the greenest hands in the northern continent!"

When Adam Chase had shouted those hot words at Edwards's retreating back, he'd intended them to be hyperbolic. But as he stood on the deck of his seabound ship, surveying the crew, he was keenly aware of how close his declaration was to the truth.

Chase grimaced as he stumped his way along the assembled sailors, an expression only partially caused by the pain that shot through his leg with every step. He looked up and down the line, putting faces to the names that would be engraved below his on the Hunter's Chapel memorial pillar if they didn't make it home.

This was as motley a crew as he'd ever seen. Aside from Chase himself, there was not a single veteran Map's End sailor among the lot of them.

That, at least, was a comfort.

First in the lineup stood Brigid Gardiner, a lifelong ship's cook from Edgewater with a quick temper and sharp tongue. She'd been advised to retire three voyages ago and had flatly refused, despite her steel-gray hair and many wrinkles. Chase had been the only captain willing to offer her a berth, but from the proud tilt of her chin, it was easy to see that Brigid felt she was doing him a favor, rather than the other way around.

Next to Brigid stood a black-skinned, silver-haired Sylacian with an unpronounceable name. For as long as Chase had known him, the man had answered to Bones, a moniker earned by his collection of immaculately polished cloudbear bone jewelry. He was one of the few crewmen that Chase had sailed with before. An expert in the field of processing and storing dragon oil, Bones had been recruited by Edwards years ago. While most sailors came and went, Bones had never left *Relentless*, though Chase suspected it was less out of loyalty, and more due to the Sylacian's natural bent to avoid change in any form.

Then there were the Steelkilt brothers, Radney and Pippin by name, a pair of teenaged landsmen who hadn't been too keen to answer many questions about where they'd come from. One or the other of them always seemed to be looking over their shoulders. They were textbook runaways, but Chase felt no guilt hiring fugitives. Whatever trouble the boys were in, life aboard a Hunting ship would serve as ample punishment. Should they survive the voyage, they'd reenter society as wiser men.

Beside them stood Nell, a redheaded eleven-year-old, thin as a rail but eager to work. Chase smirked. Would it even be a true Map's End ship without at least one scrappy orphaned islander aboard? Chase himself had once filled that role. It was like a rite of passage among island children, a coming-of-age ritual that transformed them from urchins to sailors.

Next to Nell, leaning on her harpoon, stood... Tash. Of course. Where else would she be? Adam met the harpooner's glittering black eyes briefly, nodded acknowledgement, then glanced away. He wouldn't have wanted to sail without her, and her loyalty was admirable, but having her aboard was a different sort of difficulty. Adam stepped past her without a second glance.

He had to crane his neck to meet the next sailor's eyes. Yuri T'berris, the tattooed Stoneman with the spear. He was untested, but if he was half as fierce as he looked, the dragons wouldn't stand a chance.

Chase came to the end of the line and stopped in front of his final crew member, Ilsa Starling.

First Mate Ilsa Starling, to be precise. Chase still hadn't quite come to terms with the fact that he was setting sail without Edwards at his right hand. In some sense, it was a relief to be free of Edwards, but his replacement was a complete mystery to Chase.

Physically, Miss Starling was nothing impressive. She was handsome enough, as women went, but her looks would be far better suited to a drawing room than a quarterdeck. Her thin face and hollow eyes made her look tired and wan, and desperately in need of sunlight. Neither Chase nor Starling had yet mentioned the stark-white tammer that perpetually perched on her shoulder. It would appear the creature assumed it was coming along for the voyage, and Chase didn't plan to argue against that. He wasn't about to risk losing another first mate, especially not over a rabbit.

After the rash and unconventional manner in which he'd hired her, Chase had half expected Starling to vanish into the mist, never to be seen again. But she'd reported for duty, ready to sail, which was more than could be said for plenty of others Chase had asked to join him on this voyage.

Perhaps Ilsa Starling would surprise him.

"Well, shipmates." The captain finally spoke, addressing his crew for the first time. His voice was as strong and defiant as a declaration of war as he repeated the age-old words that had begun every Map's End ship's voyage for centuries:

"The end of the map lies far behind you now. Here there be dragons."

Pinpricks of sea spray spattered across Ilsa's face as she stood at the stern of the ship, straining for a final glimpse of shore. It would be the last she'd see of land for...well, she didn't know how long, exactly.

The launch went off flawlessly—an encouraging start to her first voyage in several years—and now *Relentless* glided silently out of the harbor.

Only the endless, featureless ocean lay ahead.

Ilsa took a slow breath of cold, salty sea air. Only one small thread still tied her to the shore.

With trembling hands, she drew the crumpled letter from her pocket and looked at it one last time.

Please tell Phillip...

Ilsa shut her eyes tightly and pressed the unsent farewell to her lips.

"Goodbye, Phillip," she whispered.

A tug at the paper in her hand drew Ilsa's attention. Mobius, ever dutiful, had a corner of the letter in his mouth, ready to take it from her hand. Dear little thing. Even so impossibly far from home, he knew what was expected of him, and he was ready to attempt it.

"No," Ilsa said, stroking the tammer between his ears. She gently detached him from the letter and held it out over the rail of the ship. "Not this time, Mobius."

Ilsa let go. The letter fluttered from her fingers, dropping toward the water like a wounded dove. There was no splash when it landed. The ink bled, running like tears over the page. Then a wave washed over the letter, and Ilsa lost sight of it.

It was gone now, and so was she.

Taken by the sea.

PART TWO

The Expanse of the Sea

AS WITNESSED BY GEORGE EDWARDS,
FIRST OFFICER AND ACTING CAPTAIN

To the officers, owners, and shareholders of the MAP'S END HUNTER'S ASSOCIATION, to whom a vested interest in the success of our joint venture belongs.

Dear Sirs:

Due to a series of misfortunes that have befallen our ship's company, it is incumbent upon me to relate the reasons for the premature termination of our voyage.

After a remarkably successful outward journey, Relentless sailed through the storm band and came out upon the calm seas at the edge of the world. Captain Chase pressed his crew to the utmost, and our success was unparalleled. It is my personal belief that the good fortune of the voyage leading up to the disaster is what convinced Chase that he could set his sights on even bigger prizes.

Many are the tales of the ancient dragons that live beyond the Edge, and few are those who have dared to challenge them. Captain Chase correctly believed that felling one of those great beasts would launch his name into legend. That ambition led him to a fight that he could not win.

Relentless gave chase to a great white dragon, a monster of legendary renown. In some old tales and songs, the beast is called Avatheon, which in the Sylacian tongue translates loosely to "the white devil." Up until the moment we saw its wings on the horizon, many of the crew doubted such a beast could even exist, let alone that this monster could be killed with human hands. Despite my doubts, Chase believed he could do it. And his crew rallied to him, ready to follow him off the very Edge if he asked it of them.

His hubris cost him dearly.

Our battle was long and fierce. We were stretched to the limits. At times it seemed the beast was nearing its end, but it outlasted us. The White Devil shattered one of our chasers midair, sending its hapless crew spiraling to the sea. I believed them lost, especially when the beast began to dive. Had it reached the water, it would've made quick work of the survivors. But it did not get the chance.

Chase leapt from his own boat, flinging himself at the dragon's face with nothing but a dagger in his hand, which could not so much as scratch its scales. But the momentary distraction occupied the beast's fury long enough for Mr. Flask's boat to dive to the surface and rescue the fallen crew. Captain Chase's swift action saved those sailors' lives, but he nearly paid with his own.

I witnessed the horrible moment when Avatheon tossed its mighty head, flinging our captain into the air. When the dragon snapped him in its jaws, catching him by the leg, we lost all hope. The beast shook Chase violently, like a dog shakes a rat, and his leg was torn off. His body crashed to the waves below as the great dragon, satisfied that it had driven off our attack, retreated into the clouds beyond the Edge.

We pulled the captain's broken body from the sea. It was a miracle to find him alive, gracious Creator be praised, and another wonder still that our surgeon was able to staunch the wound enough to keep him from bleeding to death. But his condition remained critical, and as first officer, I took command of the ship in place of our incapacitated captain. It is therefore my duty to confess that it was I who made the costly decision to abort the voyage.

I authorized the use of what oil we had already processed to speed along our return journey, as every day we delayed could reduce our captain's chances of survival. I also allowed the experimental medicinal use of dragon oil to treat our captain's condition, and it is the belief of our surgeon that the measure might have made the difference between his life and death. Due to emergency circumstances, the majority of our cargo was depleted upon our return to Map's End.

I have spoken with the captain's physicians, and they are in agreement that it would be unwise for Captain Chase to return to sea and are advocating for his retirement from active service.

Thus, when he has regained enough of his faculties to see the wisdom of that, I mean to encourage Chase to sell Relentless. Perhaps the profits from such a sale would be enough to recoup the damages of your lost investments. For my part, I know no amount of money will ever sponge the stain of this voyage from my memory.

May you be more fortunate in your future endeavors.

CHAPTER SEVEN

Wings on the Horizon

"ILSA? ARE YOU DOWN HERE?"

Ilsa folded the loose papers of Mr. Edwards's account and quickly tucked them back between the pages of the logbook, out of sight. She snatched the pen that lay forgotten on the rough galley table and tried to resume a pose that looked somewhat unaffected. A half-second later, Tashtanna's face appeared in the low doorway.

"There you are!" Tasha exclaimed. She reached into a woven pouch that hung from her belt and drew out a handful of a dry muesli mix comprised of nuts, oats, and dried fruit. "What are you doing down here in the middle of such a fine day?"

"I, uh..." Ilsa trailed off with a guilty little shrug. She'd had a good reason, originally, but had forgotten it upon discovering Edwards's letter hidden in the logbook.

She didn't know why she felt the need to hide her discovery. It wasn't as if Captain Chase could hide his injury. But to see all the details laid bare felt so raw, so private.

"You ought to come up on deck." Tashtanna said around a mouthful of her snack, not seeming to notice anything out of the ordinary about Ilsa's manner. "Fresh air and sunshine would do you good. Come on; up you get."

Ilsa obliged, standing stiffly and suppressing a wince as she followed Tasha out of the galley and up the steps to the deck.

Tasha was right; it was a fine day, one of the best they'd had in the two months since leaving port. Bright sunshine bathed the ship with light—if not exactly warmth in this far northern reach of the world—and the deck was pleasantly active. Yuri and the Steelkilt boys were aloft while Bones manned the helm, but the captain was nowhere to be found. That wasn't too uncommon; Chase spent quite a bit of time locked away in his cabin. And knowing what she did now, Ilsa couldn't blame him.

Mobius sat upright on the starboard rail, facing out to sea. His tail swished contentedly as he watched the tossing waves. Ilsa smiled. Deep down, she'd always felt that he'd make a good seafarer, despite being born and raised on the central continent. Ilsa walked over to the rail and stroked the tammer's back, between his folded wings. Mobius looked up at her and twitched his nose.

"What are you watching out for, Moby?" Ilsa asked him, her gaze sweeping the horizon.

Mobius looked down at the water directly below the ship's hull, and Ilsa followed his lead. At first, she saw nothing; then, for a brief instant, a sleek gray fin cut above the surface, trailing a thin white wake behind it.

"Ah, ballast," Tashtanna muttered, leaning over the rail as the shark disappeared beneath the waves. "They've found us. They always do, eventually. I've lost more than one fat prize to scavenging sharks before I could even haul it aboard." Tasha rolled her eyes and shook her head, setting her gold earrings sparkling in the midafternoon sunlight.

Today her long braids were coiled atop her head and wrapped with a brightly patterned turban of teal and coral silk. It was a beautiful piece, standing out in stark contrast to the weather-beaten, faded look of everything else on the ship.

"A gift from an old beau." She'd explained with a grin when Ilsa had complimented it that morning. Ilsa couldn't tell if Tasha was joking or not; the harpooner had quickly changed the subject.

"The sharks don't know what's good for them," Tasha said, scooping another small handful of muesli into her mouth. "If they'd just wait their turn, we'd give back the carcass after we process it. All we need is the oil. Which I don't imagine they have much use for. Probably turns their stomachs sour. Want some?" She held her pouch out to Ilsa, who took a pinch of its contents. It was delicious; the sweetness of the dried apples blended beautifully with warm spices and bright tang of the nuts.

"That's very good," Ilsa said. She tossed a bit of dried fruit to Mobius, who caught it midair and set to nibbling contentedly.

"It's from home." Tasha smiled. "You'll only find flavor like that on the Plains of Adisa. It's the one thing I really miss about living inland. My mother sends me some every so often. You're welcome to as much as you like." Mobius's ears twitched at the invitation, and Tasha laughed. "*You* need to ask first, though," she told him.

In the weeks they'd spent at sea together, Ilsa had grown fond of Tashtanna. She'd halfway expected some trace of rivalry or jealousy to crop up between them, considering the harpooner's long history and experience aboard this ship and Ilsa's position as first mate. But Tasha had been nothing but kind. It was thanks to her constant help and instruction that Ilsa was able to learn the rhythms of life aboard a Hunting ship so quickly.

"I wanted to show you." Tasha pointed off the bow, toward the horizon. A cluster of thin white streaks shot up above the water, then faded to vapor a moment later. "See that?"

"Whale spouts." Ilsa nodded with mild interest. "Been seeing a lot of them the last few days."

"It's a good sign," Tasha said. "Dragons tend to follow the herds. They hunt the whales, we hunt them. General rule of the hunt: look for spouts. Where there's whales, there will be dragons. Mark my words, we'll hear that sweet call of 'wings on the horizon' before the week is out."

"I'm looking forward to it," Ilsa said. "I didn't think we'd be at sea two full months without so much as sighting a dragon."

"Not that uncommon." Tasha shrugged. "And aren't we grateful they keep this far out to sea? You wouldn't like them near the coast."

"Fair point."

"Still though..." Tasha pondered a little. "Inshore hunting would come with its perks. Imagine if we could do the hunting, and then take them back to shore and let someone else deal with the mess."

"Is it that bad?" Ilsa asked.

"Oil processing? That's where the *real* glory of our job starts!" Tasha laughed. "Most of the oil is stored in the dragon's scales. You have to melt them down in try-pots, then skim the oil off the top once the heat extracts it. But bigger brutes have an extra chamber in their skulls that's just full of the stuff, pure and uncontaminated. And much more powerful—meaning, more valuable—than the more common scale oil. To get that out, we have to drill a hole in the dragon's skull and dip out the oil with a bucket, like water from a well."

Ilsa wrinkled her nose.

"On our last voyage," Tasha continued, not noticing Ilsa's discomfort. She popped a bit of dried apple into her mouth. "I was standing on the horn of a downed dragon we'd tied alongside the ship, and I slipped." Ilsa shot her a horrified look, but Tasha just laughed. "Fell straight into the dragon's skull and ended up nearly drowning in the oil chamber before Bones pulled me out!"

"That's the most disgusting thing I've ever heard."

"Tell me about it. I smelled awful for weeks! I was tempted to cut all my hair off, just to get the stink away, but that would've upset—" Tasha stopped herself. "Well, anyway," she said quickly. "It took years to grow it this long, so I decided to tough it out until the smell faded."

"Well, whatever the case—" Ilsa glanced sideways at her friend. "It gave you the absolute most horrifying story to tell at parties."

"Dragon hunting will keep you humble, that's for sure." Tasha chuckled. "One minute you're sailing through the sky in valiant pursuit of the greatest beasts on land or sea, and the next, you're up to your earlobes in smelly, sticky brain juice."

Ilsa nearly choked on an almond. "You *had* to say that while I'm eating?"

Tasha clapped her on the shoulder. "Give it a few hunts, and that sort of thing won't even faze you."

"I'm not sure I could ever get used to *brain juice,*" Ilsa said. Mobius shuddered, flicking his tail in disgusted agreement.

"In all seriousness, though," Tasha said. "You do have to respect the messy parts of the job. Processing oil is complicated, and storing it is rather delicate. There's a lot of power in this stuff, and when it's not treated with care, things can get volatile. But don't worry, I'll walk you through it your first few times."

"You know," Ilsa said. "You ought to be first officer, Tashtanna, not me." It was a thought that had plagued Ilsa constantly since she accepted the job, and she often wondered if Tasha thought so, too.

"Mm, probably." Tasha shrugged, unbothered.

"So why aren't you?"

"Ha! I could do *your* job, Ilsa, no doubt about that." Tasha tossed her head proudly. "But there's not a chance in the world that you could do mine."

"Fair enough." While Ilsa doubted that was all there was to it, Tash did have a point. "Nobody wants to see me throw a harpoon."

"Leave it to the professionals." Tasha winked. "Yuri and I have the harpoons well in hand. So, let's review your job, shall we? Little Nell's up there in the lookout, watching for dragons. When she calls out, where do you go?"

Ilsa gave Tasha a longsuffering sigh and rolled her eyes. They'd been over this dozens of times in preparation for Ilsa's first hunt, but she played along. She half suspected Tasha was pestering her on purpose because she knew Ilsa had been a schoolteacher, and this was her way of getting revenge on behalf of students everywhere.

"I report to the starboard pursuit boat," Ilsa replied dutifully. "I'll pilot, and Yuri will be in the prow with his spear."

"Correct. And I?"

"You're the harpooner in the port boat. Your pilot is Bones."

"Unfortunately." Tasha grimaced. "He's a fine seaman and a good friend, but the man sails a chaser like he's trying to toss a barrel of fish. No finesse." She sighed. "What I wouldn't give to have Adam back on the tiller."

"The captain?" Ilsa's surprise was evident in her voice. "I didn't know he piloted a chaser."

Of course, on a small ship with an even smaller crew, it was to be expected that everyone would fill multiple roles aboard. Brigid, the ship's cook, was also the closest thing *Relentless* had to a surgeon aboard. Bones piloted Tasha's chaser, but he'd be the first to claim that his real job was to head up the processing and storing of the oil. Yuri, Ilsa, and Tasha each regularly took turns being helmsman. Even Nell was originally signed on as a cabin girl, but lately had found herself assigned to the lookout more often than not. But despite all the double-duty being pulled across the ship, Ilsa hadn't considered it applying to the captain.

Even more surprising, however, was Tashtanna's casual use of the captain's first name. In the two months she'd been aboard, Ilsa hadn't heard anyone call him that.

Tasha looked away and cleared her throat.

"Anyway." Tasha flicked a hand as if to swipe a braid away from her face, seeming to forget that her hair was tucked under her scarf. "Once we're skyborne, then what happens?"

"We go after the herd, get in close..."

"And?" Tasha prompted, arching an eyebrow with a mischievous smile.

Ilsa rolled her eyes. "And I pull back and let you get the first strike so you can win your petty rivalry with Yuri."

"Exactly!" Tasha grinned.

"You know, I really shouldn't have let you drag me into your silly games, even though you offered to take my overnight watch." A first mate ought to stay out of such foolishness and Ilsa knew it, but Tasha's offer of a little extra sleep was more tempting than she could bear to pass up.

"He stuck my harpoon to the deckhead, Ilsa. Practically the *ceiling*!" Tasha threw up her hands in exasperation. "Normally I wouldn't feel the need to retaliate—I consider myself to be above such things—"

"Naturally," Ilsa remarked drily.

"—but nobody touches my harpoon, or gloats about my size. Not even a giant like Yuri."

"Here's an idea," Ilsa said. "Why don't you switch boats? I'll be your pilot and Yuri can ride with Bones, and then we can win fair and square."

"Well... I *did* ask the captain about that." Tasha admitted.

"Oh really?" Ilsa raised her eyebrows. Mobius cocked his head to one side, as if just as invested in the conversation.

"Yes, but he doesn't want the two of us in a boat together." Tasha shrugged. "Probably concerned we'll realize how powerful we are when we join forces, and we'll take over the ship."

"You're not serious." Captain Chase had no need to worry about mutiny. Nobody doubted who was in charge on this ship.

"It's actually about spreading out our skills," Tasha said, her tone growing uncharacteristically serious. "We don't have any reserves on this voyage. The captain can't afford to have his best sailor and best harpooner in a single pursuit boat. If we go down, the success of the voyage dies with us. That's something he won't risk."

Ilsa knew she should feel a little sobered by Tasha's admission, but instead, what came out of her mouth was:

"He said I was his best sailor?"

Ilsa had spent most of the last two months at sea learning to pilot the little chaser boat she'd be responsible for in a hunt. Dragonsail proved fickle and difficult, and piloting a boat through the sky didn't come nearly as naturally to her as sailing on the water. It had taken plenty of trial and error, but in the last few days, Ilsa had felt that her practice runs in the chaser were getting smoother. The knowledge that her improvement had been noticed at all, let alone by the captain, filled Ilsa with a warm flush of satisfaction.

"He's been watching you." Tasha nodded. "Says you're a natural, and that if he didn't know better, he'd assume you were raised on the island." The harpooner grinned. "But don't let it go to your head."

"Wings! Wings on the horizon!"

The call rang out from above. Ilsa instantly forgot what she was about to say. From her perch in the lookout, little Nell waved and pointed off the port bow. Ilsa squinted in that direction, and her pulse immediately quickened.

Months of waiting, and now there they were.

Ilsa could make out five or six of them flying above the water, but she knew from her studies that there would probably be close to a dozen more just below the waves. As the dragons swooped and dove, their long, lithe bodies caught the sunlight and sparkled like jewels above the sea.

"What did I tell you?" Tashtanna grinned. She tossed back a final handful of muesli before pocketing her pouch. "Always trust the whales."

"I'll go tell the captain," Ilsa said. She rushed to the hatch that led below. "Mobius, go to bed."

She didn't have to tell him twice. After sighting the dragons, the tammer was more than eager to scamper below and curl up in his nest of blankets in Ilsa's cabin. As her heart pounded in nervous anticipation and her breathing struggled to catch up, Ilsa halfway wished she could join him.

Ilsa rapped her knuckles on the door to Captain Chase's quarters. For a moment, she thought she could make out voices in there, but whatever she'd heard fell silent at her knock.

"Yes?" An edge of irritation lined Chase's voice.

"Captain, dragons in sight!"

The door swung open. Captain Chase stepped out, already pulling on his overcoat.

"Very good, Miss Starling," he said. "Ready the chasers and prepare to pursue."

"Aye, sir."

When Ilsa reached the single-masted pursuit boat—a fast, agile craft built for quick maneuvering—Yuri was already there, rigging the jib. His iron spear rested against the starboard gunwale.

"Ready?" He asked, flashing his black, pointed grin.

"Or not!" Ilsa replied, a little breathless. She didn't let herself hesitate as she scrambled to her post at the back of the boat. She unlatched the small compartment under her seat and drew out a sealed glass jar of shimmering, iridescent oil. There were three of them, packed tightly between strips of wool to prevent jostling against each other. Ilsa rearranged the remaining two, making sure they were secure before she closed up the case. If one of the vials were to break, the consequences could be deadly.

With deliberately slow movements, Ilsa uncapped the vial and strapped it into its place on the boom. She inserted the thin wicks of rope into the oil, screwed in the control valve, and replaced the cap. If she'd done it right, the oil would seep up the ropes and into the sails, giving the chaser the lift it needed to get skyborne. She'd practiced this process many times in the last few weeks, sometimes supervised, sometimes by herself, but she still triple-checked her arrangement to make sure she hadn't missed some crucial step.

"Best of luck, greenhorns!" Tashtanna called out from the other boat. She waved her harpoon above her head in a wild salute. "Don't be too heartbroken when I bring in the first dragon of the voyage!"

"I put my spear through that beast before you are even in range." Yuri laughed at her. "Your arms are half the size of mine, so you only throw half as far."

"We'll see about that," Tasha retorted. She winked at Ilsa.

"Launch chasers!" ordered the captain from the deck.

"Chasers away!" Ilsa shouted in response, twisting the valve on the oil vial. Immediately, the oil began to flow up the wicks and into the sails, and Ilsa was struck once again by how active a liquid it was, as if some of the vitality of the dragon it came from still lived on in the oil. A bright sheen rippled across the chaser's mainsail, and the boat began to rise.

Their sails caught the wind, and *Relentless* fell away below. A short distance away, the second boat manned by Tashtanna and

Bones climbed skyward as well.

"Be safe, Hunters!" Nell called from the lookout. Her round, freckled face flushed with excitement. Yuri reached out to her as the chaser sailed past the ship's mainmast, and their fingertips brushed.

Ilsa threw a final glance back below toward the ship. Captain Chase watched from the deck, his spyglass in hand. He'd be tracking every moment of the hunt.

Although it was her first time, Ilsa felt a terrible need to prove herself worthy of her post, despite the fact that Captain Chase only hired her to spite Mr. Edwards. She would prove to him that while she may have joined this crew by accident, it was not by mistake.

Perhaps she wouldn't keep her bargain with Tasha, after all.

"Full sails, Yuri!" Ilsa called, letting out the mainsheet with one hand and grasping the tiller with the other. "Hang on!"

The chaser surged forward, climbing higher and higher above the waves. Ilsa had piloted small craft before, many times, but no landing boat or dinghy could compare with the sheer exhilaration of dragonsail. The chaser felt alive; the oil was its beating heart, and Ilsa was as much a part of this boat as the sails or the tiller. Together they raced along, a predator in pursuit.

They gained on the drakes, closing the distance fast. Now at closer range, Ilsa could tell that the beasts were flying higher than the boat, so she adjusted the valve on the oil regulating mechanism, easing more of it onto the sail. The chaser gained altitude, coming level with the dragons. These creatures were far smaller than the dragon on display in Edgewater, with heads about equal in size to those of horses, but their nimble frames and sharp-toothed jaws lent them a formidable appearance regardless.

Ilsa caught snatches of shouts to her left as Tasha hollered at Bones to go faster, to keep up the pace. By contrast, Yuri stood in the prow of his boat, silent and focused as a statue, his spear at the ready and a smile on his face.

It was a beautiful, surreal thing to weave in among the herd of dragons as they skimmed the water's surface. The drakes took no notice of the hunters, or if they did, they hadn't yet recognized the threat.

Not for much longer.

"Taking aim." Yuri called, raising his strong arm for a strike.

"Ilsa, you traitor!" Tasha yelled as Yuri let his spear fly. She needn't have worried; the spear glanced off the beast's flank, sending up a glittering spray of scales. The dragon didn't even dignify the strike with a glance in Yuri's direction as it dove back toward the waves.

"You'll have to do better than that!" Tasha shouted across the gap between the boats. Her face was alight with the thrill of the hunt.

Yuri laughed at her as he hauled his spear back in. "Just warming up."

"Look out below!" Bones's shouted warning broke into the harpooners' lighthearted banter.

Ilsa had little time to respond before a large drake burst from the surface of the sea directly below her boat, charging upwards with teeth bared.

Ilsa hauled in on the mainsheet, and the chaser dove out of the way, barely clearing the beast's head. The dragon shot past the boat, close enough to touch. Shimmering oil gleamed beneath its ice-blue scales.

"Well done, *Yil'saa*," Yuri said, and his calm voice was the only thing keeping Ilsa's shaking hands steady on the tiller.

"Too close, Yuri. We almost—"

"Tashtanna, you are in trouble?" Yuri called out, cutting her off. Ilsa whipped her attention to the other boat. It was reeling, tilting wildly in the air.

"Clipped us with its horn," Tasha yelled back. She tossed her harpoon aside and yanked feverishly on the sails alongside Bones in an attempt to stabilize the chaser.

The dragon whirled in the sky, turning back on the boats. Its wide wings batted the air, gaining momentum.

"He's coming again. Bones, take us down!" Tasha shouted to her pilot, but the Sylacian sailor was still fighting for control of the boat. It was all he could do to keep it upright. Tight maneuvers were out of the question.

"I'm going to help them!" Ilsa shouted to Yuri, yanking on the tiller. But the dragon beat her to them.

A shattering crack rang out as the beast rammed the little boat. The chaser reeled with the impact. Bones clung to the gunwales, holding on with a death-grip as the boat flipped over.

Tashtanna was not so lucky. She flung backward, over the side of the boat, and plummeted towards the waves.

With a crash of spray, the harpooner vanished into the churning white water.

"Tash!" Ilsa shouted in alarm. She leaned over the side of her boat. *Where is she?*

After a breathless moment, Ilsa caught sight of a bright flash of coral-colored silk bobbing among the waves. Tasha's headscarf.

"There!" Ilsa pointed as another wave swept over Tasha, obscuring her from view.

"Orders, Miss Starling?" Bones shouted.

Orders? The question shook Ilsa. She was the first officer. No time to assess the situation pragmatically; no spare seconds to wonder what the captain would like best to be done. Something had to happen, and fast, and she had to be the one to make the decision.

The surface of the water churned fifty feet below the chaser boats. If Tasha had landed right, the fall wouldn't have killed her. But a few minutes more and the cold just might.

Not to mention a sea full of agitated dragons.

As if on cue, a screech like rending metal tore through the skies above Ilsa. It was a bone-chilling sound, designed to carry for miles underwater, but its effect was far less majestic in thin air. The dragon circled directly overhead. Its shimmering wings angled downward, preparing to dive back toward its attackers. If they paused to fight the beast off, they'd lose all hope of saving Tasha. But attempting to evade the beast's attack might prove deadly for them all.

A split-second choice was Ilsa's only option.

"Yuri, go after Tash. She may be hurt. Bones, to the surface to pick them up. When you've pulled them out, return to the ship immediately. Get them warm. I'll hold that thing off."

"Alone, *Yil'saa*?"

"Those are my orders. Go. Now!"

The chaser reeled drunkenly with the change in weight as Yuri leapt from the bows. Ilsa scrambled to retain control. She didn't fear for him. Yuri's athletic body knifed cleanly into the sea, and Ilsa knew that in an instant, his powerful eyes would seek out Tasha, even in the dark, churning water.

A half-second later, Bones cut off the flow of oil to his sails, and the second chaser dropped through the air toward the waves. Bones's maneuver held little grace—Tasha had been right about his style of piloting—but Ilsa was grateful for it in that moment. He wouldn't waste time getting to the surface and pulling their shipmates to safety.

Another screech from above, louder this time. Ilsa glanced up. The dragon was a blurred silhouette against a pale sun.

Now to take care of you.

Ilsa's hands were strangely steady as she laid aside the tiller. Her heart was calm, and her breaths came evenly. Even her mind was clear and peaceful. Crouching for balance, she stepped to the bow and grasped Yuri's spear. The iron was far heavier than Yuri made it look when he carried it.

She'd never be able to throw it.

The dragon beat its shimmering wings and started to dive. Its jagged maw opened in another war cry. It was close enough now that Ilsa could feel the heat of its breath on her cheeks, standing out in stark contrast to the frigid sky.

Gripping cold iron with both hands, Ilsa braced the spear against the gunwale, pointed upward toward the beast. She was ready. Even if she didn't kill it, with any luck, impacting the spear would be enough to dissuade the dragon from circling back for another pass at her friends.

The dragon reached Ilsa's boat. Its ice-blue foreclaw tore through her mainsail, and its talons gashed at the starboard gunwale. The aged wood splintered at the impact, sending a tremor through the little boat.

Ilsa heaved the spear upwards, jabbing at the beast's underside as it swooped overhead. A shower of scales and a mist of blood mixed with oil told her that she'd at least hit her mark, but she hadn't struck the dragon anywhere near deep enough to down it.

The dragon recoiled from the blow, then rounded on her, readying itself for another pass. Ilsa felt the injured chaser boat groan with the effort of keeping skyborne; she didn't think it could withstand another hit. But she hoisted the spear to her shoulder, ready for whatever might come.

She looked down at the ocean below, just in time to catch a glimpse of Yuri tossing Tasha into Bones's boat, then hauling himself aboard after.

Safe.

Ilsa turned back to the dragon, a contented calm seeping through her, even as she stared into its open jaws. It was going to be all right. Yuri would look after Mobius; of that she had no doubt. Tashtanna would step in as first officer. The voyage would proceed as planned. And perhaps someday, years from now, the news would find its way back to Phillip. Perhaps he would understand.

And perhaps he would forgive her.

"Starling, get down!"

The shout from came from behind her. Instinctively, Ilsa ducked, a mere instant before an explosive blast of violet light shot over her boat. The ball of crackling energy streaked through the sky and struck the charging dragon in the eye.

The beast screamed. Its serpentine body writhed as it somersaulted backwards through the air.

Ilsa swung around to see where the blast had come from. A chaser boat, one of *Relentless's* two spares, whipped through the clouds to her stern. And standing braced against the single mast was Captain Chase, holding a smoking flintlock pistol.

"Captain, what—?" But the rest of Ilsa's question was drowned out by a thunderous whirlwind of pounding wings as the dragon herd, spooked by the explosion and the defeat of their leader, burst from the sea and took to the skies as one.

Ilsa dropped to her knees in the bottom of the boat, shielding her head with both arms as beating wings impacted her battered craft and showered her with seawater runoff. It reminded Ilsa of the time Mobius had startled a nest of roosting bats and had been caught in their panicked swarm as they attempted to escape. His fur had needed nearly an hour of grooming to get back to rights.

Except, Ilsa suspected the chaser would not recover as Mobius had.

"Get off!" Chase's shouted order jerked Ilsa into action. She scrambled up from where she'd been huddled against the barrage on her boat to find that the captain had pulled his own chaser alongside hers. The dragons were beyond her now, already vanishing into the cloudy distance, but their damage had been done.

The jib was shredded beyond salvaging, and the mainsail wasn't much better off. The glistening light of the oil cell sputtered, and the chaser gave another creaking groan. Using Yuri's spear to balance, Ilsa mounted the rail to board the captain's boat, only to find that she'd already lost enough altitude that he was out of her reach.

Her boat was going down.

"Starling, jump!"

The chaser's bow nosed toward the sea. Ilsa almost lost her footing. In a desperate effort, she hefted Yuri's spear with both hands and swung it over her head. The weapon struck true. The backward barb bit into the captain's port rail, hooking Ilsa to the skyborne boat just as her own broken chaser finally snapped in two and fell away beneath her.

For a frozen instant, Ilsa felt everything: the strain in her arms as they fought to cling to her lifeline. The slip of her hands against the spray-slick iron. And most of all, the frigid emptiness of open sky beneath her.

The captain grabbed the spearhead and hauled her upward. Ilsa grasped at his arm, clinging to him as she scrambled aboard. The iron spear clattered to the sturdy planks at the bottom of the boat, and Ilsa wished she could do the same. Her chest heaved with the effort of pulling air into her tightened lungs. She gripped the side of the boat with white knuckles.

The wrecked chaser boat crashed into the whitecaps far below.

"Brace yourself!" The captain's shout rang out the exact instant the boat hit the water. His warning was nearly too late. With a bright flash, the downed chaser exploded.

The shockwave rocked the skyborne boat, and a shower of sea spray and splintered wood rained down on Ilsa and the captain for a few seconds before the sky fell silent. Ilsa gaped down at the ruined remains of the boat she'd been piloting only moments ago, reduced to nothing but flotsam on a churning sea.

"Oil cells shattered," the captain said in answer to her unvoiced question. He swiped a hand over his pallid forehead, pushing his dark, sweat-damp hair out of his face.

"Captain..." Ilsa's voice shook as she looked down at her trembling hands, rubbed raw and bloody from the hunt. "I... I don't know what to say."

Thank you? I'm sorry? Here's my resignation?

"Do me a favor, Miss Starling." Chase grunted. He sat down in the boat's stern and stretched out his ivory leg. His pale face twisted in a tight grimace. "Seeing as how we set out with a mere four boats aboard *Relentless*, I'd advise not making a habit of breaking them in half and blowing them up."

Ilsa looked away, unable to do more than nod.

So much for being his best sailor, she thought bitterly, gritting her teeth.

"Shall I take us back down, Captain?" Ilsa asked, already reaching for the lines to redirect the boat toward *Relentless*. The captain didn't answer. Ilsa glanced over her shoulder, waiting for orders. But she didn't get any.

Captain Chase sat slumped against the tiller, white-faced and unconscious.

CHAPTER EIGHT

A Kinship of Suffering

ILSA LANDED TOO FAST. The chaser missed its mark on its docking station; its hull scraped against *Relentless's* deck with a jolting scream of wood against wood.

"Blast it all, Starling!" Bones shouted at her. "Are you trying to wreck *another* boat?"

Ilsa ignored the jab. She tossed the lines aside, not bothering with proper docking procedure.

"Brigid!" she called to the clustered crew on deck. "Quickly; it's the captain."

"What happened?" Bones asked, his frustration with Ilsa's shoddy landing forgotten.

"I don't know." Ilsa shook her head.

Chase lay crumpled in the bottom of the boat. Ilsa had managed to shove him aside after he'd lost consciousness in order to take over the tiller and bring the boat down, but beyond that, she could do nothing for him as long as they were skyborne.

Bones and Radney Steelkilt each took hold of one of Chase's arms, pulling him from the boat and laying him out on the ship's deck.

"I'll get my things and take a look," Brigid said, but it was Tashtanna who dropped to her knees beside the captain.

A wave of relief washed over Ilsa to see Tasha safe and sound, even though she looked pale beneath her dark complexion. Her colorful headscarf hung limp and tattered over one ear. She'd changed out of her wet clothes, at least, and now wore an oversized shirt that Ilsa recognized as one of her own. It hung past Tasha's knees. She had a blanket tossed over her shoulders, and an unmistakable red jewel hung around her neck, pulsing with contained firelight.

"He just dropped? No warning?" Tasha asked. She slipped a hand on the side of the captain's neck, feeling for a heartbeat.

"Is he all right?"

"He will be. He's only fainted. Pain and overexertion, by my guess." Tasha glanced up. "Someone hand me that bucket. And Yuri, there's a sachet of herbs in my hammock; go get—"

The captain's body spasmed and he gasped as he came sharply awake.

"Easy." Tasha soothed, sweeping his sweat-soaked hair off of his forehead in a surprisingly tender gesture.

"Fine, I'm fine," Chase muttered, pushing her touch away. He got an elbow underneath himself and sat up quickly. Too quickly.

Ilsa could almost feel the dizziness overtaking him. The captain fell backward and would've dropped hard against the deck if Tasha hadn't broken his fall. With a low grown, Chase curled to one side and wretched. Ilsa averted her eyes, hating how invasive it felt to watch the captain's dignity being shredded.

"All right, that's enough now," Ilsa said, raising her voice and directing her attention to the gathered crew. "Captain's going to be fine; there's nothing more to see. Back to your duties. Radney and Pippin, reset sails to resume our course. Nell, get aloft. Bones, see to it that the chasers are restocked and set for the next hunt. Yuri, man the helm."

"Thank you," Tasha mouthed to Ilsa as the crew scattered to obey the orders.

Ilsa turned away. She stumbled a little as she reached the hatch. Brigid, returning from fetching her medical supplies from the sick bay, stopped Ilsa on the stairs.

"Hard hunt, Miss Starling?" the old woman asked drily, looking Ilsa up and down.

"On the contrary—" Ilsa gave a tight smile. "—I've never been in one that's gone better."

Brigid rolled her eyes with a snort.

"You'd best take a moment and look after yourself," Brigid said. "This ship needs at least one able-bodied officer, so you and the captain had better work out a schedule to accommodate each other's infirmities."

"Just see to the captain," Ilsa ordered brusquely, straightening her shoulders. She brushed a stray strand of hair away from her face in an attempt to make herself appear more professional. Brigid may have been out of line, but she was right. As long as the captain was incapacitated, Ilsa was in charge. *Relentless* was relying on her.

But as Ilsa staggered down to her cabin, a weight of doubt pressed in, tighter even than the pain that began to coil its tendrils around her lungs.

ILSA'S HANDS SHOOK as she untied her boot laces. With a sigh, she eased her swollen feet into the bucket of seawater she'd hauled down below deck. The cold took her breath away, but after a moment, the first glimmer of relief spread through her feet and ankles.

"I made you some tea."

Ilsa looked up to see Tasha standing in the doorway of the

ship's dim galley, a tin cup cradled in her hands.

"Really? That was kind." Ilsa reached for the cup. She took a slow breath of fragrant steam. The scent was earthy and bitter, reminiscent of fresh-turned earth and growing things.

"It's willowbark," Tasha said. "Known to help with pain and ease swelling."

It was hard to ignore the pointed glance Tasha sent toward Ilsa's bucket. Ilsa forced a light smile.

"Tash, aren't *you* the one that fell into icy waters today? Shouldn't you be taking it easy and letting the rest of us wait on you?"

Tasha shrugged. "It wasn't the first time I've taken a tumble in a hunt," she said. "And that hot stone of Yuri's did wonders. Warmed me up quicker and got me back on my feet faster than anything I've worked with before. I'll still be wickedly sore in the morning though."

"I don't doubt it." Ilsa grimaced.

"You will be too." Tasha raised an eyebrow. "Yuri told me what you did. Hence the willowbark."

Ilsa took a sip of the tea, savoring its tingling warmth.

"That's very nice," she said. "How you do everything that you do is beyond me."

"As a girl, I was apprenticed to my clan's herbalist," Tasha said.

"That's useful."

"Mmhmm, it is—when you live somewhere with dirt you can actually grow herbs in. Out here..." Tasha trailed off with a chuckle. A tired smile was the best Ilsa could offer to join in.

"You know," Tasha said, tracing a finger up and down one of her beaded braids. She looked at Ilsa with cautious understanding in her sparkling black eyes. "When people advise going to the seaside for the sake of health, I don't think this is exactly what they have in mind."

Ilsa opened her mouth, a denial already taking shape on her lips, but she didn't get the chance to voice it. Mobius swooped in the door and alighted on the galley table in between Ilsa and Tasha. His prim chin tilted upward with an unmistakable air of importance. He dropped a small, folded scrap of paper on the table and nudged it toward Ilsa.

Ilsa picked it up and glanced over the cramped writing.

"Message received," she murmured, patting Mobius's head. He looked up expectantly, but once again, Ilsa was unprepared to reward him. At this point, he'd have to start a tab to keep track of how many treats she owed him if he ever was to be compensated for his efforts.

"I need to go. Captain Chase is asking for me," Ilsa said, trying not to sound too relieved about Mobius's interruption. She gathered up her boots and left Tasha in the galley, leaving a glistening trail of wet footprints behind her.

Ilsa hurried to her cabin and changed into dry clothes, not pausing to re-braid her hair. She wasn't sure what the captain needed, but his summons set her nerves on edge. The hunt hadn't gone well, and she, as first mate, was the one to answer for that. She didn't know if she could bear a difficult conversation. Any energy she'd had had been used up in the hunt. But she didn't have a choice; she had a duty.

Nothing else to do but face her mistakes head-on. Steeling her nerves, Ilsa made her way to the captain's quarters and knocked on the door.

"Yes?"

"It's Starling, Captain."

"I'm in the stateroom."

Ilsa let herself in, stepping carefully through the captain's personal office. Captain Chase was half-reclined on a chaise lounge that sat to the port side of his chart table. Ilsa had trouble making him out as her eyes adjusted to the stateroom's dim light.

"You wanted to see me, sir?" Ilsa paused inside the doorway of the low-ceilinged room.

"Miss Starling," he responded, his words slightly slurred. "Yes, do come in."

The captain's dark hair hung loose about his shoulders. He'd tossed his overcoat onto the table, leaving him in just his canvas shirt and breeches, as if he were a common sailor rather than a mighty captain. His dragonflame pistol—the one he'd used to save her life this morning—hung limp in his hand. It was strange enough to see him so informally dressed, but then Ilsa's eyes caught on his leg—or at least where his leg was supposed to be. Chase had unstrapped the ivory peg, taken it off, and cast it aside a little way from the chaise lounge.

Ilsa stopped and looked away. Heat crept to her cheeks; seeing him without the false leg felt like she was trespassing on something private. The sense that she was intruding grew as Chase took a slow sip of some kind of overly sweet-smelling liquid. Ilsa had spent enough hours in sickrooms to instantly recognize that smell: a pain-numbing drug, and a strong one at that.

"Should... should I come back later, sir?"

The captain coughed out a harsh laugh. "Oh, so *now* you're concerned about my dignity, Edwards? We both know you've seen me worse than this."

Ilsa blinked, stranded for a moment in awkward silence.

"Um, it's not Edwards, Captain." she ventured cautiously. "Ilsa Starling, remember? I'm your first mate?"

Chase looked up; his expression twisted in confusion. In all the weeks since setting sail, Ilsa had never seen him look so lost. It didn't last, though; the captain shook himself and sucked in a deep breath.

"Yes. Of course you are," he said. Though his words carried

confidence, a trace of uncertainty lingered in his voice.

"Should I come back later?" Ilsa repeated, still not sure the captain was completely with her.

"No, no." Captain Chase waved away her concern and motioned with the pistol toward the wing-backed chair beside his desk. "Please, sit."

Ilsa obeyed, perching stiffly at the edge of the seat. Not wanting to meet his eyes, she instead glanced around the darkened room. Her eyes caught on an oil painting that hung on the wall just above the captain's desk.

The subject was a massive sea dragon, wings spread and jaws gaping, hovering in the sky over a stormy sea. From where Ilsa sat, it appeared that the dragon was looming directly above the captain, as if watching everything that happened in the stateroom. Something about the painting seemed ominous, almost alive, like the beast could escape the canvas at any moment. Why Chase had chosen such a thing for decoration, Ilsa couldn't guess. She looked away.

"Normally I would ask for a more formal report of a hunt," the captain began, his voice stronger now. "But since I saw most of what happened today, I just need you to update me on the state of things now. How is Tashtanna?"

"Settled," Ilsa replied, shifting uncomfortably in her chair. "Yuri got her warmed up and Brigid looked her over. She took a hard fall, but from all appearances, there's no lasting damage."

"Appearances." Chase grunted. "Those can be deceiving. Check in on her later, won't you?"

"Of course."

Chase took a long, careful sip of his drink. He grimaced as he swallowed, then exhaled sharply with a shudder.

"It's not your fault." He sighed. Though he meant it kindly, Ilsa almost wished he would be a little angry about the hunt. This cold, grim acceptance was difficult to read. "You handled your boat beautifully. Bones is a fine processor—the best we've got. He was never meant to pilot a chaser."

"He does what he can, sir."

"That's going to have to be enough, this time around," Chase murmured, more to himself than to Ilsa. She wondered what he meant by the statement but didn't want to ask.

The captain shoved a shaking hand through his thick hair, skewing it wildly.

"It wasn't like this last time. You should've been there, Starling," he said, leaning his head back and blinking at the ceiling, staring past the wooden planks and into the past. "Our last voyage. Ah, it was a sight to behold. Four strong teams of chasers. Edwards, always leading the charge with his harpooner, a valiant old devil they say carried the blood of the stars in his veins. Then close behind were Stubb and Flask in their boats, trying not to let Edwards steal all the glory. And Tash and I—" Chase cut off with a grimace that he hid in another drink.

"She said the same thing," Ilsa said slowly, starting to put the pieces together. Tasha and the captain. There must've been something deeper there than mere professional camaraderie. Something that neither of them had forgotten.

"What?" The captain's head snapped up, and his eyes flashed. "What did she say?"

Ilsa shrank back in her seat at his outburst.

"Just that..." she scrambled for an honest way to smooth this over. Whatever might've happened between them, it was clear that it was a delicate subject. "That she wishes you were piloting her chaser, not Bones. She seems to think you were very good."

Chase eyed Ilsa; then, as if satisfied with the answer, he let his expression soften.

"Well," he said. "You don't get to be a Hunting captain at my age if you don't know your way around a chaser boat. We *were* good. Incredible, even. If dragons kept histories, we'd be legends. Tash and I felled sixteen of the brutes on our own. Sixteen, in one voyage! Can you imagine that? Would've been more if we'd had the chance to finish our route."

He didn't try to disguise the bitterness from his tone.

"I heard that Mr. Edwards had to make a difficult decision," Ilsa said softly. She glanced at the captain's stump of a leg. What drove him to take the pain medication—the physical wound, or the sting of everything he'd lost?

"Difficult." Chase snorted. "So that's what he claims. I doubt he deliberated long, though."

"From what I can gather, the choice was clear to him."

"No, of course," Chase scoffed. "Why *would* you give much thought to it before condemning me to lifelong pain and exile from the life I loved? He always thought he knew what was best for me. I think he really does believe he saved my life."

"Didn't he, sir?" Ilsa frowned in confusion. Edwards reported that the captain would have died from his wounds if they had tried to finish out the voyage. The fact that she was even talking to Chase now was a testament to the wisdom of the former first mate's actions.

"Do I look saved to you?" Chase snapped, gesturing toward his missing leg.

His question caught Ilsa off guard. To her, he had always looked strong and capable, daring the world to hit him with its best shot, in spite of his handicap. But now that she saw him with his defenses lowered, Ilsa saw that she had misjudged him. Adam Chase was barely holding together.

His grim, determined face was thin and drawn with pain he couldn't hide. He bore the marks of a deep, internal suffering—a look Ilsa knew all too well. She saw it often enough in the mirror.

Did he really look saved to her?

Eventually, Ilsa shook her head. "No, sir."

"Hm. No indeed." Chase said, then, surprisingly, he smiled. It was a small, wan smile, but it was the first she'd seen on his face.

"You know, you're the first person who's ever been honest about that." The captain took a deep, ragged breath. "Everyone else says I should count myself lucky. That it's ungrateful to be angry. Well, you could be dead, Adam! Is that what you want?" He laughed bitterly. "Why are those my only choices? Dead or broken, take your pick, and be thankful."

"I read Edwards's report of your injury." Ilsa confessed. "I'm sorry if that was overstepping. But for what it's worth, I really do think he meant well."

"Edwards was a narrow-minded fool." Chase closed his eyes, leaning his head back against his couch. "But you know, if he had swallowed his pride and come with me this time around, I might've forgiven him for dragging me back home, broken and disgraced." Chase paused, then tilted his head to look at Ilsa. "Of course," he mused. "Then I'd never have met you."

Ilsa glanced sideways at him, trying to decide if he was joking. "That would be no great loss for you, Captain Chase."

"Is that so?" he said. "You dropped into my life out of nowhere exactly when I needed you. You're everything I want in a first officer. Smart, capable, supportive, a quick learner..." Chase shrugged. "Not to mention, considerably prettier than Mr. Edwards."

Ilsa narrowed her eyes at the glass in his hand. "How much avimene have you had?"

"Hardly a question to ask your captain," Chase remarked, arching an eyebrow at her.

"I happen to know that particular drug well." Ilsa suppressed a shudder, trying to block out the memory of the stale-aired sickroom. But it came anyway.

Dust dancing on the streams of light that leaked in from the edges of the drawn drapes, a taunting reminder of a world beyond that kept on turning. Worried voices—always hushed—from just outside the door. Phillip's hand in hers. *I'm here, darling. Stay here, darling.*

"All I meant was," Ilsa said, pulling herself back to the present. "If you're not quite...yourself, I want to protect you from saying anything you'll regret."

"Very shrewd, Miss Starling." Chase gave a hoarse chuckle and looked away. "I can respect that."

A few moments passed in silence. Just as Ilsa was beginning to think she should leave, Chase looked up at her again.

"How'd he die?" he asked without preamble.

Ilsa blinked in confusion.

"Sorry, what?"

"Oh, come on, everyone on this ship has you figured out." Chase rolled his eyes. "You may not dress like it, but from the day I met you I had you pegged as a widow. You've got all the marks of it. And you obviously have some knowledge of medicines. Put two and two together and I must assume your man died of some long, painful illness."

"If he had," Ilsa sputtered, coloring. "What on earth made you think *that* was a good way to broach the subject?"

Chase laughed harshly and swirled his drink around in his glass.

"Sorry," he said. "My manners do grow a little dull the more of this stuff I take. But as long as I'm speaking without inhibitions, it's time you knew you're not fooling anyone."

"I..." Ilsa stammered. Her heart started to race, and her breaths grew shallow and sharp. "What?"

"Starling, I knew the truth from the moment you walked onto my ship with a white harbinger on your shoulder." The captain shrugged.

"What's Mobius got to do with it?" Ilsa asked, pushing past the sudden dryness in her throat.

"I may not be Central Melvian gentry, Miss Starling," Chase said. "But I *can* read. It's not exactly lofty academic knowledge that those animals are supposed to be red. They change color when their masters die."

Ilsa looked down at her hands, squeezed tight and pale in her lap.

"Well, no, not exactly," she countered, feeling like her own voice was coming from far away. "The color change has to do with the well-being of their bonded partner. Tammers bond in pairs, you see. Occasionally with their human masters, but far more commonly with other members of their own species. A mate, or littermate, or even just a good friend from the same aviary."

"You're avoiding the question, Starling."

"Yes, they're born with deep auburn fur," Ilsa said, squaring her shoulders. "And it's true that we've learned to interpret the tammer's color as a sign—or, in the archaic terminology, a *harbinger*—that the other member of the bonded pair needs special veterinary care."

"But once it's turned white, it's too late for care, isn't it?"

"Why does this concern you so much, Captain?" Ilsa snapped. She hated how cornered she felt. "Whatever you have to ask me, you can ask it outright."

"I suppose I will." Chase looked Ilsa in the eye. "What are you doing here?"

Ilsa frowned, wondering if the captain's confusion was returning. "You...you summoned me, sir."

"No, no." Chase waved his hand dismissively. "What are you

doing *here*. On my ship. On this voyage."

"You offered me a job, and I took it." Ilsa folded her arms over her chest. "If you're reconsidering that offer after today's hunt, then I'd be happy to discuss—"

"Listen, Miss Starling," Chase interrupted. "I know the nature of Hunting crews better than anyone alive. Sailors get on ships bound for the Edge for a few rather particular reasons. We've got a nice sampling of them among our crew. Some do it because they're islanders. Born and raised on Map's End. It's the only life we know. That's me and Nell."

Ilsa wanted to redirect the conversation, steering it safely away from territories she didn't want to explore, but the captain went on without giving her a chance.

"Some do it because they've got something to prove. Brigid, for instance. Bones too, originally." Chase shrugged. "But now I think he's just here because he's too set in his ways to leave. Others are in it for the experience. The adventure. The novelty of seeing the Edge."

"Yuri." Ilsa supplied, thinking back to Yuri's explanation of his ten-year pilgrimage.

"And Tashtanna," the captain added with a slight nod of acknowledgement. "And the Steelkilt boys are fugitives who judged life on a Hunter to be easier to face than answering for their deeds on land. That motive is more common than you'd think."

Chase looked straight at Ilsa again. The intensity in his eyes made his gaze impossible to hold for long.

"That leaves you." Chase narrowed his eyes. "So I'll ask you again, Miss Starling: why are you here?"

Ilsa had to stop herself from fairly sagging with relief. That was all the explanation he wanted?

"I'm a born sailor, captain," she said, her voice much steadier now. She was confident enough in her rehearsed answer; she'd almost been able to convince herself of it. "I belong at sea. I tried to build a life inland, and it didn't work out. So here I am."

But the captain shook his head.

"If that were all there was to it, you'd have gone back to the South Ardan Isles," he said. "But you didn't. You chose the fiercest seas. The most grueling test of a sailor's will. You sought out a Hunter."

"Captain..."

"You gave up, didn't you?" Chase pressed. "You don't intend to make it home from this voyage."

Ilsa stiffened, already shaking her head. "If this is about me taking on the dragon myself while sending Yuri to save Tasha, then I can explain—"

"Blast it all, Starling, I don't *care* about the dragon!" Chase shouted. "I don't care about the hunt! I want the truth! I have to know: is this why you joined my ship's company? Did you come out here, on purpose, to try to get yourself eaten by a dragon?"

Ilsa stared at him, openmouthed, unable to verbalize a defense against his accusation.

"Let me be very clear on something, Miss Starling." Chase leveled a pointed a finger at her. "You are not expendable. Stop acting like it."

Ilsa pressed her lips together and looked down. "Aye, captain."

"No matter what you left behind on shore, it isn't worth throwing your life away out here." Chase looked away, speaking more to himself than to her. "Not on this voyage, at least."

No matter what you left behind... Ilsa studied her hands, tracing a finger over the spot where her sapphire engagement ring used to rest. What had Phillip done with that beautiful jewel? She'd left it on top of her bureau the night she disappeared. Had he found it? Or was it still sitting where she'd set it down, collecting dust?

Chase eyed her, giving Ilsa the uncomfortable sensation that he could see right through her carefully constructed front.

Tell him.

Ilsa was startled at the intensity of the thought. Tell him? But she couldn't! He'd brought her on his ship, entrusted her with a position of leadership on this voyage. She'd promised him she was a match for the responsibility. The truth would capsize her good standing on *Relentless* and break the trust she'd built with him.

But as she met Chase's intense, searching gaze, she knew that the truth was the only story he would believe. An idea took hold. She could remove the mask and tell him the truth—or nearly so.

The truth, with one important alteration.

"You were correct, captain," she murmured, letting the lie slip out softly. "He died."

"I'm sorry," Chase said. "Was it painful?"

"It was."

It still is.

"Two weeks before we were to marry," she said. "He was taken gravely ill with sunburst fever."

Chase frowned. "Isn't that a childhood illness?"

"He never had it as a child." She shook her head. "If he had, it probably would've been mild. But in adults who never had the chance to build up a resistance to it..."

"Ah." Chase nodded his understanding. "We see that sometimes in islanders who spend their early years at sea, isolated from other children."

Ilsa swallowed hard. Already he'd found a thin place in her story: Phillip hadn't been raised at sea, away from other children.

Ilsa had.

But if the captain had noticed the slight discrepancy, he didn't let on.

"He fought hard for months," Ilsa said. "At last, we thought he'd beaten it. Progress was slow and painful, but he did begin to regain his strength. And then, like you guessed, Mobius's color started to fade."

"Why? If he was getting better?"

"The fever permanently weakened his heart." Ilsa fiddled with the end of her hair ribbon. "He would never get better. Little by little our future was stolen from us. First, the doctors told us we'd never be able to have children."

Pitying looks that burned like embers. Whispered conversations that hushed when she entered a room. "You know she can't give Phillip an heir, Herman. For the estate, the title..."

"Then it became clear that before long—" Ilsa's voice dropped. "That wouldn't even matter. He'd become a complete invalid, unable to walk or even leave his bed most days. And then, he'd be gone. It could happen in a year, two, five if we got lucky, but it was inevitable."

"Lucky? No. It would be torture. Five years of that kind of life... life with a broken body," Chase murmured. Ilsa glanced at him, surprised at his understanding, but his attention wasn't on her. He traced a hand over an empty space on his couch as if rubbing a leg that wasn't there.

"It wasn't fair to him." Long-suppressed anger tightened in Ilsa's chest, and her words tumbled out on top of each other, unchecked. "It wasn't fair at all. Why did the Creator even let me survive the fever if it was just to be a weak, depressed invalid—the object of everyone's pity and whispers, doomed to fade away slowly—"

Ilsa bit her tongue. She'd slipped. She'd admitted the dreadful truth to the captain, despite her efforts to misdirect him. Had he noticed? A hard knot formed in her stomach as she watched his thoughtful face. It was impossible to guess what thoughts were passing behind his distant eyes.

After a heavy pause, Chase looked up at her.

"I know," he said. He sat up straight and drew near to Ilsa, clasping her hand earnestly in both of his.

"Ilsa—may I call you Ilsa?— listen to me: I *know*. I understand exactly. Your life was stolen from you. And now, you've thrown yourself to the mercy of the sea in an attempt to take it back, haven't you?"

Ilsa pulled back, startled by the intensity in his eyes, the fire in his tone.

"I don't know, Captain," she stammered. "I...I shouldn't have said any of that."

"But it's true, every word of it," Chase insisted. "You and I are victims of the same sort of misfortune. And we've both come here seeking to mend it."

Ilsa shook her head with a weak smile. "There's nothing left to mend, Captain. It's gone."

Chase studied Ilsa with an unreadable expression. But whatever he was weighing, he must have decided in her favor; he sat up abruptly.

"Come, there's something I must show you."

Chase snatched his crutch and pulled himself up. He hobbled across the stateroom to his chart table. Ilsa hesitated, just for a heartbeat. But when the captain turned back and reached for her hand, she gave it to him. Though she couldn't guess what he meant to show her, she let him draw her to his side. That same pull towards him surged through Ilsa, just as it had back in Map's End the first time she saw him in the Hunter's Chapel. She knew what it was now, even if she hadn't then: a kinship of suffering, an invisible bond as deep as their wounds.

"Now I know it truly was Providence that brought you to my ship," Chase said, sweeping a chart out of the way. He shuffled through a stack of maps before finding the one he wanted. He spread it on the table before him. "Edwards couldn't understand. Or perhaps he refused to. But you... You!" Chase smacked his palm down on the chart for emphasis. "You, Ilsa Starling, have felt my fury. You've been dealt a blow. And only through that are you strong enough to join me in my quest."

Ilsa gave him a quizzical frown. "Quest, Captain Chase?"

"It's time you knew." Chase tapped the map, his finger tracing along its outermost edge. Beyond the storm band. Right at the edge of the world. "Somewhere out here lurks the beast that dismasted me. The ancient white dragon, Avatheon." He spoke the name with something like reverence in his tone. "It's a deadly specter fiercer than any monster on land or sea or sky. Twice the size of *Relentless*. White as death, wings like a hurricane."

Captain Chase's face hardened with determination and his voice dropped to a whisper.

"I'm going to find it, and I'm going to bring it down."

A chill ran through Ilsa at his words. Attempting to kill a dragon like that was a fool's errand. It was impossible. But she knew, deep within her, that Adam Chase fully meant to do it, or die trying.

"It isn't about revenge," the captain murmured, more to himself than to Ilsa. "Revenge on a brute beast is nothing. That's no justice."

"So why do it at all?" she asked carefully. "If you're not trying to avenge yourself?"

"Oh, but you misunderstand. I most certainly am trying to avenge myself. But it isn't about Avatheon." Chase shook his head, flicking a strand of hair out of his eyes. "It's about Map's End, my home that betrayed me. It's about Edwards, and everyone else on my crew who turned their backs on me. It's about the physicians who wouldn't clear me for sailing, and the investors who refused to finance this voyage. It's about Providence itself."

In a violent motion, Chase threw back the last swallow of his pain-numbing drug, then hurled the empty glass at a framed mirror that hung on the wall above his charting table. Both the glass and the mirror shattered in a spray of a thousand glittering pieces. Ilsa flinched, frightened by his passion.

"I will defy the hand that was dealt to me." Chase spoke through clenched teeth. Fire flashed in his eyes. "I will show the world it was wrong about me. I will revel in glory so bright they will never see me as wounded again. I will become a legend!"

Looking at him in that moment, Ilsa found it impossible to doubt the truth of his words.

"And when the light is streaming off our sails," he said, his tone softening as he again took Ilsa's hands in his. "You will be beside me, at my right hand. We are not broken, you and I. We can fight fate, and we'll fight it together."

Ilsa couldn't speak. Chase was so earnest, so convinced, that she could almost let herself imagine that he was right. But she shook her head. It was a beautiful fantasy. Nothing more.

"Don't doubt me, Ilsa." Chase's voice was a rough whisper. "Please."

"I don't, Captain."

I doubt me.

"Do you want to go back?" Chase asked.

"Back? To Map's End?"

"No." Chase clenched his fist over the empty expanse of ocean on his map. "Back to how things were before."

"Captain..." Ilsa shook her head. It wasn't worth going down this path. She should know; she'd walked it often enough to know it was a dead end. "That's impossible."

"Everything was impossible once. Until it wasn't." Chase

straightened, resolve stealing over his features. "I think it's time I entrust you with the rest of my reason for hunting this beast. Do you know all the uses for dragon oil?"

"Um, energy, mostly," Ilsa replied, trying to keep up with the sudden shift in conversation. "Light, heat, transportation. Dragonsail, of course. And weaponry, sometimes, though it's more of a novelty than it is practical."

"Comes in handy in a pinch, though." Chase gave a wry smile and reached for a gilded box that sat on the table. He unlatched it, placed his dragonflame pistol on the interior velvet lining, and closed the lid. "You've obviously done your homework before setting sail."

"I'm a schoolteacher, captain," Ilsa said. "Old habits die hard."

"Indeed. What other uses can you tell me about?"

"Well..." Ilsa pondered a moment. "There are some who use the oil medicinally. It's experimental, untested. But the results are promising. With time and research, it could revolutionize medicine."

"Precisely." The captain's features hardened with determination. "And what do you know about the oil's potency?"

"As a general rule, the bigger the beast, the stronger the oil. More valuable, too." Ilsa glanced down at the map, its broad brushstrokes depicting a great barrier slicing across the sea. "That's why Hunters cross the storm band. The closer you get to the Edge, the bigger the dragons get..." Ilsa trailed off as she began to connect the pieces of the captain's puzzle.

A giant ancient dragon. Medicinal oil use. A quest for the impossible. And a broken man.

"You don't mean," Ilsa gasped. "But that's—"

"I do mean it." Chase cut her off. "A beast that size. I have it on..." he hesitated for an instant, but then recovered himself. "I have it on good authority that oil from that monster could work wonders like nothing we've ever dreamed."

Ilsa glanced down, her gaze lingering on Chase's stump of a leg. *Impossible.*

But hadn't she heard an offer like this before, back in Edgewater? The temptation of dragon oil's power, the tantalizing offer of the impossible?

Strength from weakness. Life from death. Health from frailty.

The memory of the ghostly stranger's words ran through her mind. She couldn't ignore how similar they sounded to the captain's proposition.

"Healing, Ilsa," he whispered, reading her thoughts. "Total, complete restoration. Just think of it."

But she shook her head, not daring to hope that such a thing was possible.

"I'm not sure I believe in magic, Captain."

"Psh. Magic, science, Providence, it's all the same thing." Chase waved away Ilsa's protest. "What you call it depends on what you want to believe about it."

"I don't know what I believe," she admitted, stepping back, away from him. "But I know that Providence moves in ways we aren't meant to understand. All my life I've been taught to accept blessings and trials each in their turn. Is it right to attempt to reverse a hardship that is beyond our control?"

But Chase held up a hand, cutting her off.

"Please, Ilsa, don't preach at me," the captain said. The open, inviting tone was gone from his voice; the moment of vulnerability and honesty had passed. He took his crutch and limped back to his chaise lounge. "I'm tired." Chase sighed, sinking back onto the couch. "Take over for a bit, will you, Miss Starling?"

"Of course, Captain." Ilsa stood to go, but she hesitated before she reached the door. A cold trickle of unease had seeped into her mind, though she couldn't quite explain why. Chase believed the oil from an Edge dragon could work a miracle; that much was clear. But Ilsa had only seen someone ingest dragon oil once before, and it was not a memory she particularly cherished. She couldn't shake the feeling that there was some distasteful connection between the shadowy stranger who knew things he'd never been told, and the captain's belief in the impossible.

All at once she knew what was troubling her.

"Captain Chase?"

"Mm?"

"I can't help but wonder... what were you doing in the chaser boat today? You were there when I needed you, and for that I'm grateful, but by all accounts, you shouldn't have been out there at all." Ilsa squeezed her arms tight against her chest.

"Perhaps it was Providence." Chase chuckled, leaning his head back against the couch.

"Or perhaps it was something else?" Ilsa pushed, unsatisfied. He couldn't have known she would be in trouble. He wouldn't have had time to react, to launch his boat and be skyborne in time to save her. Not unless he'd somehow predicted what would happen before it started. And how could such intuition be explained, unless...

"What sorts of...side effects are known to accompany the use of medicinal dragon oil?" It felt foolish even to hint at it, but Ilsa couldn't pretend that something wasn't adding up.

"That is a conversation for another time." Chase shook his head. "Please see to your duties on deck now, Miss Starling."

"Captain..."

"You play your cards very close to your chest, Miss Starling." Captain Chase cut her off. "So forgive me if I occasionally elect to do the same."

Chapter Nine

Dragons in Our Midst

"You may be triple her size, Yuri, but she will murder you for this."

Yuri's glowing yellow eyes sparkled as he grinned at Ilsa from the dimness of the storeroom. Mobius perched on top of his head, looking comically like an oversized, fluffy hat. The tammer peered down, watching with sparkling eyes as Yuri worked his mischief. Tashtanna's treasured harpoon, its polished oak handle covered in dozens of tiny notches from her knife—one representing every dragon she'd felled—was in the Stoneman's massive hand.

"Trust me," he grunted, reaching beneath a cask to feel around the floorboards. "In my homeland, this sort of thing is how we show love."

"So you've said. But don't think for an instant you've fooled me." Ilsa rolled her eyes as Yuri went back to rummaging around in the darkness for a place to hide the harpoon. "Though, being an absolute pain in the neck is a common trait among older brothers everywhere, regardless of culture, so it doesn't come as too much of a surprise."

"Oh." Yuri glanced up at her and cut a sly smile. "I am pain in the neck? Not you, making a deal with Tash to help her slay more dragons than me?"

"Listen, I've told you *both*," Ilsa retorted, tossing her braid over her shoulder. "I'm not taking sides in your silly rivalry."

"But you *can* be bought."

"I don't know what you could possibly be referring to." Ilsa hid a smile behind a sip of spiced wine from Yuri's travel flask. He told her he'd been hanging onto it for such an occasion. And he was right; Ilsa's loyalties could be temporarily won over for the right price.

Ilsa smiled and shook her head. It was a relief to be doing something foolish and lighthearted after the tensions following last week's botched hunt. Ilsa had hardly seen the captain at all; he'd taken the better part of a week to recover his strength, leaving the command of the ship to her. And his disappearance had not gone unnoticed. More than once in the last few days, Ilsa had overheard snatches of discontented murmuring from the forecastle. The crew had seen their captain falter, and the seeds of doubt had taken root. Though Ilsa had dispelled those whispered conversations with a stern warning that that sort of talk wasn't to be tolerated on this ship, she'd be lying if she claimed her own heart hadn't echoed the same sentiments.

Yuri gave his deep, rumbling chuckle and turned back to his mischief.

"I have paid for your loyalty this time." He reminded her. "Your job is to make sure she does not catch me."

"Mmhmm. I'll do my best, but you and I both know Tash will win in the end."

"Yuri T'Berris!" Tasha's shriek was so loud that it could probably be heard in every corner of the ship. "Where are you, you big, dumb lump of rock?"

At the sound of Tasha's shout, Mobius sprang from his perch, abandoning Yuri. Ilsa laughed as the tammer took his place on her shoulder and did his best to look uninvolved.

"Mobius," Yuri said. "It appears you are... what do they say? A friend in good sunshine?"

"You mean a fair-weather friend?" Ilsa asked.

"Yes, that." Yuri wagged a finger at Mobius. "I thought better of you. Quickly, check the hall. I must hide this."

Ilsa stepped out of the storeroom and swept the companionway with a glance. Tasha wasn't there yet, but her shouts were growing louder. Yuri probably had half a minute before Tasha would burst in on him with the rage of a wet cat.

"I hope you've planned your funeral." Ilsa chuckled, stepping back into the storeroom to pat Yuri's shoulder. "Shall I go distract her, or would you like to make your last stand here?"

No response from her partner in crime.

"Yuri?" Ilsa repeated. He still knelt beside the stack of casks, but Tasha's harpoon had fallen from his hand and lay forgotten on the floor.

"Yuri, what's wrong?" she shook his shoulder. Even Mobius could sense the game had ended; he bounded to the ground next to Yuri and nudged his stony elbow with a concerned squeak.

"Look at this, *Yil'saa*," he said, without looking up at her. Ilsa peered over his shoulder to see that he held a folded stack of papers, covered in writing, sketches, and diagrams. Yuri handed her the top sheet.

Ilsa's eyes widened. "Where did you find this?"

"Stuffed under a loose floorboard, under that crate," he said. "Someone took great care to make sure it was hidden."

Ilsa squinted in the dimness at the paper. A jagged, toothy grin stared back from the largest of the drawings.

"That looks like the dragon skull from Edgewater."

"I thought the same," Yuri said. "What does the writing say?"

Ilsa frowned at the scribbled, cramped handwriting. It was difficult to make out, like whoever wrote it was working hurriedly. Or maybe in the dark.

"It's...a bunch of notes, it looks like," she said. "Measurements, calculations. Why do you suppose...?" her question died on her lips as she turned the paper over. She drew a sharp breath. She knew that handwriting. She saw it every day when she updated the ship's logbooks.

"What is it?" Yuri asked. "Ilsa, what's wrong?"

"It's a letter," she answered. "From Captain Chase." Ilsa looked up at Yuri. "It's a contract of employment with someone named Vandraak Seafang." Ilsa frowned as she scanned the page. "It looks like he's promised this Vandraak almost the entirety of the profits from this voyage."

"Someone he owes a debt?" Yuri proposed.

"Maybe." Ilsa nodded, hoping that's all it was. "He did say he had to finance the voyage on his own, without the support of investors."

Her eyes caught on the last line of the letter:

Strict confidentiality is the utmost imperative. No one among the crew must suspect your involvement, especially not my first officer.

"Surely he means Edwards," Ilsa murmured to herself, trying to ignore the cold weight of dread that settled in her chest.

"Yuri!"

Yuri and Ilsa both startled at the shout. Tasha stood in the doorway, fists on her hips and face like a thundercloud. She pointed at the harpoon, still lying next to Yuri.

"Hand it over, Stoneman, and pray to the Creator I don't skewer you with it!"

"My apologies, Tashtanna," Yuri said. All former mischief was gone from his face. He passed the harpoon to Tasha without further comment. Her fiery expression melted into concern.

"Hey, are you two all right?" she asked. "You look like you've seen a ghost."

"Tash," Ilsa said, folding the papers away. "Do you know if the captain is associated with anyone called Vandraak? An old crew member, perhaps?"

Tasha pursed her lips and squinted in thought.

"No, that doesn't sound familiar," she said. "Why?"

Ilsa glanced a question at Yuri, and he shrugged in response. But before Ilsa could explain, a call came from the deck above.

"Wings! Wings on the horizon!"

"To your boats, Hunters!"

The three of them only hesitated a moment; they knew their duty.

"Go on to bed now, Mobius," Ilsa said, nudging the tammer toward the door. "I'll find you when the hunt's over."

Yuri took the folded papers back from Ilsa, carefully replacing them under the floorboards. He was one step behind her as they jogged to the deck and readied the chasers for the hunt.

Icy wind bit Ilsa's face and snatched at the loose strands of her hair as she and Yuri darted their chaser through the sky. There was no herd this time—the dragon was a lone male, following the migration patterns of kelp rays. The absence of a herd simplified the hunt; they had only one target. But that target was young, strong, and dangerous.

"Come and get me, lizard!" Tasha yelled at the dragon from the other boat.

The unfortunate ending of the last hunt didn't seem to plague her much. She stood in the bow of her chaser, harpoon held high and braids streaming behind her.

The dragon turned on her, sending out a warning blast of blue fire. Bones ducked the chaser out of the way just in time, darting beneath the beast's left wing.

"Flank it, Starling!" he shouted, waving the other boat forward.

"Swinging to starboard." Ilsa called the warning to Yuri before she hauled away. He braced himself, and Ilsa brought the boat about.

The maneuver drew the dragon's attention, and it bared its teeth. Yuri balanced his spear on his shoulder, waiting for the right moment to strike.

But the dragon saw him coming, and with an ear-splitting roar, it darted upward, corkscrewing through the sky as it made its escape. Its razor-finned tail whipped over the boat, and Ilsa ducked down, narrowly avoiding a deadly slash.

"It's no good!" Tasha shouted over to the companion boat as the dragon darted skyward. "Can't take down a young buck like this with two chasers. It's hard enough to keep skyborne, let alone get in close enough to strike."

"We've got to try," Ilsa called back. Maybe they'd get lucky. But Tasha's doubt wasn't encouraging. The harpooner had more hunting experience than anyone on the ship, barring the captain, so if she thought it wasn't possible, then Ilsa didn't hold out much hope.

"He's making a run for it!" Bones called, pointing upward. The dragon's wings beat the sky as it climbed, then it somersaulted in the air, nose down. It flattened itself, preparing to knife through the waves.

"Hang on!" Ilsa shouted to Yuri, cranking hard on the valve that regulated the flow of oil. Power flooded the sails, and the chaser surged forward in a burst of speed.

The dragon lunged, and Ilsa was not fast enough to cut off its escape. She briefly lost sight of Bones, but then caught a glimpse of wood and sail on the opposite side of the dragon. He'd pulled in close to the beast, too close for comfort, and was racing along with it in a risky attempt to cut it off before it could reach the water. The chaser darted into the dragon's path and turned sharply, charging straight for the beast. The dragon veered out of the way with a screech of rage, barely avoiding a head-on collision.

"What was *that?*"

Ilsa startled at the closeness of Tasha's voice. She turned, shocked to see that Bones and Tash's boat had pulled up behind, level with her own chaser.

"I thought it was you!" Ilsa said.

Tasha shook her head, wide-eyed as they both came to the realization at the same time: a third chaser had joined the hunt. A glance back towards *Relentless* revealed that the spare boat was missing from its storage on the ship's deck.

"What in the..." Tasha's eyes narrowed as the dragon whirled out of the way, giving her a clear look at the third boat. "That had better not be who I think it is."

But it was, of course. Captain Chase gripped the tiller of the chaser, his mouth set in a hard, grim line.

Tasha spit out a word in Eelni. Ilsa didn't have to understand the language to comprehend its meaning.

"He *promised* he wouldn't do this again!" Tasha groaned, shaking her head at the captain. Chase's ivory leg was strapped to the side of the boat, anchoring him in place, but it was clear even from a distance that he was fighting through severe pain. His jaw was set in a tight grimace; sweat streaked his face despite the chill.

"Who is the harpooner?" Yuri frowned.

Ilsa shifted her attention to the form in the prow of the captain's boat—a bony person draped in a threadbare black cloak.

Her blood ran cold at the sight of him. She knew the answer to Yuri's question without being told. She'd seen him before; his white, sickly face and dragonish features had lurked in the corners of her nightmares ever since. The figure's smile—the haunting, thin smirk—was exactly the same as it had been back in Edgewater.

"Vandraak." Yuri and Ilsa spoke the name at the same time.

The captain's boat turned, surging forward toward the others.

"Blast it all, Adam, what are you doing?" Tasha's shout was nearly lost among the crashing of the waves.

"Regroup!" Chase ordered, ignoring her. "We're taking this monster down today. Bones, to port. Starling, cut off his escape." He surged his own boat forward. "I'll get in close."

Tasha hesitated a second more, looking as though she had a few more choice words she'd like to share with Chase. But then, her features hardened. Ilsa saw the moment Tasha made her choice.

"You heard the captain, Bones!" she barked at her pilot. "Hard to port!"

Bones yanked on the tiller and the chaser pulled away, headed towards the dragon's left flank. Ilsa's boat darted forward, racing to whip around and face the dragon head-on.

The dragon tried to dodge out of the way, but with the captain's boat blocking its escape, it had nowhere to go. The beast screamed its frustration into the sky, then tried to dash past Ilsa and Yuri's boat.

"Yuri, now!"

Yuri's spear was a streak of shining sunlight as it flashed through the air. His aim proved true. The dragon roared, then fell, thrashing in the sky as it plummeted toward the sea. A spray of icy seawater erupted as the monster's body crashed into the churning waves.

"Dragon down!" Tasha cheered. "And fairly won, Yuri! Haul the brute in!"

"Taking us down." Ilsa twisted the valve to cut off the flow of oil. She grasped the mainsheet, and the boat began the swift descent to the surface.

The chaser splashed down next to the dragon's massive form. Yuri leaned over the gunwale and caught the beast by the horn, looping a line over it to tie it off. Bones and Tasha's boat landed alongside and they did the same. It would take both boats to tow in a monster of these proportions.

"Well done, Hunters."

The rasping voice made Ilsa's skin crawl. She turned to see the third boat approaching to starboard. A pair of bony white hands grasped the gunwale as the captain's chaser eased in next to Ilsa's. She couldn't suppress the chill that ran through her at the sight of him.

As unsettling as it had been to meet Vandraak on a dark night in Edgewater, it was far worse to see him in the sunlight. At least in the fog, his shrouded, ghostly features had been well-suited to his surroundings; here, his twisted form was exposed for what it was.

"Stay back, *kulaaniwa*," Tasha snapped, leveling her harpoon at the stranger's boat. "We don't want your kind here!"

"Tashtanna." The captain's voice carried a low warning. "He is a member of our ship's company, and as such is under my protection."

"Since when?" Tasha demanded. She did not lower her weapon.

"Since we left port, obviously." Chase did not raise his voice to match her challenge. Ilsa thought she could see anger simmering behind his eyes, but the captain held back. "We're in the middle of the ocean; where else would I have picked him up?"

Ilsa shuddered. The dragonish stranger had been nearby all this time? Out of sight, but ever present, like an invisible disease.

Vandraak reached over the side of his boat and dipped a clawlike hand into the slick of oily dragon blood that pooled on the surface of the sea. It washed over his hand, staining his talons red. He smiled.

"So, you've been hiding him aboard, have you?" Tasha whipped her glare from Chase to Vandraak. "What barrel of moldy hardtack did he stuff you under, devil?"

"That is enough!" the captain shouted. Whatever restraint he'd been trying to exercise was gone from his tone. "Rein in your tongue, sailor, or you will be charged with insubordination."

Tasha flinched, a flicker of hurt crossing her face. But she shut her mouth and looked away, swallowing whatever retort she might've been planning.

"I've had enough of this. Take us back to the ship," Chase instructed. He leaned heavily against the mast, turning the tiller over to Vandraak. "Starling, I trust you've got the situation well handled."

"Aye sir," Ilsa responded reflexively, but it was a lie. No one—especially not Ilsa—knew how to handle the situation.

As soon as the captain's chaser pulled away, headed back to the ship, Tashtanna let loose.

"What on sky and earth and sea has possessed that man?" she demanded. "Letting an abomination like that aboard our ship? What, does he want to get us all killed?"

"Easy, girl," Bones said. "Just do your job. It's what we know to do."

Tasha scowled at him, but she took his advice and resumed work on the fallen dragon—though a steady low muttering in the

Eelni language betrayed her frustration.

"Yuri." Ilsa kept her voice low. "What did Tasha call that thing?"

"*Kulaaniwa,*" Yuri repeated, his somber gaze following Vandraak's retreat. "A cursed one."

"Horrible, disgusting affront to nature!" Tasha spat on the floor. "I hate the very sight of it!"

"Not in my galley, girl," Brigid swatted at her with a spoon. "Get a rag and clean that up."

"It's an evil thing to have aboard," Bones muttered, running a hand across his grizzled white beard. "No good will come of it, mark my words."

"Never seen anything look quite so dead and still be livin'." Radney Steelkilt shuddered. Pip nodded mute agreement.

"It frightens me," Nell said in a small voice, hugging her thin arms around herself. Her freckles stood out sharply against her pale face.

"Courage, little one," Yuri said, placing a heavy hand on the girl's shoulder.

The small knot of crew members had gathered in the galley. They'd spent all day doing the dirty work of boiling down dragon scales, skimming off the oil, and carefully packing it away in the hold. All day, Vandraak hovered, never quite engaging, but never out of sight. His eerie grin and pale eyes followed everything that happened on board. Ilsa couldn't help but imagine how much he'd been watching unobserved, long before they knew he was there.

"What on earth could the captain want with something like that?" Ilsa wondered aloud. "Surely he wasn't *that* desperate for sailors."

"You'd have to be more than desperate to willingly keep company with that dragonblood filth." Tasha muttered.

"You called him cursed," Yuri said, turning to Tasha. "What did you mean?"

"He's a dragon cultist," she said. She grimaced, as if the words tasted bad in her mouth. "They worship the beasts, striving to make themselves as dragonish as possible. They were human once, before they began injecting dragon oil straight into their blood."

"They worship and serve the creature more than the Creator," Yuri mused. "In my homeland, there are great beasts, firebirds, that live in seismic lakes and magma vents. Most of my grandfather's reign was spent dissolving firebird cults." Yuri shook his head. "We were not made to worship lesser beasts."

"That's evident enough in the fate of dragon cultists. The oil destroys them." Tasha grimaced. "Eating away at their humanity until there's nothing truly left. They're just beasts themselves."

"They crave the oil. They *need* it." Bones shook his head. "I wouldn't be surprised if that's part of the deal. The captain is feeding this dragonblood's need for a steady stream of oil in return for his services."

"But why?" Ilsa pressed. "What could he be offering the captain?"

"From what I've heard rumored, oil gives the cultists dragonish power." Brigid shrugged. "Uncanny strength, long life, heightened senses. Some even claim they have the gift of foresight. Others swear they've heard them speak directly into their minds. Not sure how much of it I believe, though."

Ilsa thought back to the day they'd set sail—how she saw the cloaked figure in the fog, and thought she heard a voice... a voice that Yuri didn't hear, though he stood right beside her.

"I don't care what Adam has him doing here. I won't stand for it!" Tasha stamped her foot. "And neither should any of you." She added, sweeping the rest of them with a scathing glare, as if daring anyone to defend the dragonblood.

"He can hire whoever he wants. He's the captain, Tashtanna," Brigid said with a significant glance at the incensed harpooner. "You'd do well to remember that from time to time."

Tasha waited for Brigid to turn away, then made an ugly face behind her back.

"Captain or not, it was bad form to hide it from us," Bones muttered.

"He knew we would not like it," Yuri said. "He did not want to lose his crew when there were already so few of us."

"I'm sure the captain has a good explanation for what he's doing," Ilsa said, feeling the need to come to Chase's defense. "There's got to be more to the story."

Even as she said it, a splinter of doubt lodged itself in Ilsa's mind. She was the first mate; it was her job to reinforce the captain's authority. But defending the captain to his crew when she didn't agree with his actions felt like a betrayal of something deeper than her position aboard the ship. And at what point would she decide that Chase had gone where she couldn't follow? What would happen then?

"Talk to him, Ilsa." Tasha begged. "Find out what on earth he was thinking, and then talk him out of it. Tell him to stop taking advice from that snake, or better yet, toss the brute overboard." A note of sadness crept into her voice. "He'll listen to you."

Ilsa looked around at the circle of faces, each etched with varying degrees of uncertainty and fear.

These were her shipmates. Her responsibility. Her friends. Ilsa took a deep, fortifying breath.

"I'll do what I can."

ILSA FOUND CHASE AT THE HELM, staring intently at the horizon as his hands rested on the spokes of the great wheel. Vandraak was nowhere to be seen, but that didn't give Ilsa any great comfort. He'd more than proven his ability to remain present but out of sight.

"Captain." Ilsa cleared her throat. "The crew has some concerns."

"Of course they do. I knew they would." Chase replied without looking her way. A hard smile flickered across his face. "You ought to tell Tasha that the next time she wants to challenge me, she ought to do it herself and not send you to do her dirty work."

When Ilsa didn't answer immediately, the captain sighed.

"I had hoped to keep him hidden for a while yet," he said. "At least until his expertise was needed at the Edge. But after the last hunt, it was clear we needed a third chaser."

"Anyone could learn to pilot a chaser, Captain. What expertise is so valuable that you'd take council with the likes of him?"

"The kind you can't get from respectable sources." Chase glanced sideways at Ilsa. "You said yourself that my quest is impossible. When attempting the impossible, it's best not to have qualms about what resources you may tap."

Ilsa looked away, frowning. The captain softened his tone.

"To tell you the truth, Miss Starling," he said. "There are a lot of things I've done to get to where I am today. I'm not proud of all of them, but I did what I had to do. And I plan to keep doing what I have to until I get what I want."

"There are those aboard your ship that would argue that some things are too vile to be justified," Ilsa replied. "And that harboring a dragon cultist crosses that line."

"Mm." Chase nodded. He rubbed a weary hand along the side of his haggard face. Ilsa couldn't help but notice that it trembled a little. "Did you see the Cliffs of Edgewater?"

The question came out of nowhere, but Ilsa knew Chase well enough now to take his abrupt questions in stride. He would make his way to his point in his own good time.

"I sailed from them to get to Map's End," Ilsa answered. "Yuri and I set out from the cliffside docks."

"A month before I set sail on this voyage, I went to Edgewater myself," Chase said. His gaze wandered the horizon, then up into *Relentless's* sails. "I was barely more than a dead man. I ventured out to the cliffs one night." He turned his head and looked straight into Ilsa's face. "My intent was to throw myself from them."

"Captain, I—" Ilsa stammered. Her face flushed, and she looked down. She couldn't meet his eyes, not after he'd voiced such a thought in that frank manner. It was shameful—wicked, even—to entertain such a notion, let alone to speak it aloud. Or so she'd always been taught.

"Think what you must about me, but that is the truth." Chase sighed. "And you must know it if you want to understand why I've done the things I have."

"What saved you?"

Chase laughed bitterly. "There's that word again. Saved."

"You know what I mean, Captain," Ilsa said. "Why didn't you...you know...?"

"Take my own life?" Chase supplied for her. Ilsa flinched at his brazen tone, but the captain didn't notice. Or simply didn't care.

"Because that's where I met him. Vandraak."

Chase said the name like it left a bad taste in his mouth. But he shook himself and continued. "He made me an offer."

Ilsa's mind filled with the memory of Vandraak's crooked hand, dripping with dragon oil as he stretched it out toward her.

An offer.

"I was desperate. Hopeless. But he gave me something to live for, Miss Starling. Something that made me walk away from those cliffs and start planning for the future again." Chase shifted his weight, leaning heavily on his good leg. "Say what you will about Vandraak, but he brought me back. He gave me a taste of healing. I could hardly stand up on my own before I met him. But with his help, I've grown stronger. I'm even able to pilot my boat again."

The realization of his meaning hit Ilsa like a cold splash.

"You're using oil on yourself?" she choked out.

In answer, Chase unbuttoned his cuff and pushed his shirtsleeve up to his elbow. Ilsa's breath caught. The captain's forearm was covered in neat rows of tiny white scars, some not quite healed over. At least one—a red, barely scabbed one— glistened with traces of a telltale iridescent shine.

"It was Edwards that started me on it, whether he fully understood what he was doing or not." Chase explained. "He used some experimental oil-based compounds to dress my wound and fight infection when I was first injured. He claims it kept me alive. But it got the stuff in my blood." Chase glanced over his shoulder, then swiftly pulled down his sleeve, hiding the cuts. "The methods Vandraak uses are not so cautious. But they're far more powerful."

"Does it help?" Ilsa asked, pushing the question past the dryness in her throat. She remembered what Edwards had reported: a year ago, Chase was half-dead. If the oil was what had brought him back, then it couldn't be all bad, could it? A strange emotion lingered on the fringes of Ilsa's mind; she realized, with some surprise, that it was envy.

Chase shrugged. "In all my years of hunting them, I've never seen a one-eyed dragon, no matter how many times I've blinded one with my harpoon." He rubbed absentmindedly at his scarred arm. "That regenerative power is there, but we're still learning to harness its potential. And since we can only use so much at a time, it's hard to see results."

"What do you mean, you can't use much at a time?"

"The stuff is practically poison." Chase shuddered. "But if you build up protection from it little by little through repeated exposure, you can reap its benefits without the dangers. My body can only handle it in very small, controlled doses, dripped into my blood. Vandraak's been at it for so long that he's able to drink it raw and straight, right off the scales."

A shock like lightning ran down Ilsa's spine at his words. She looked at the captain, wide-eyed.

"He offered it to me."

"What are you talking about?" Chase asked, frowning at her.

"In Edgewater," Ilsa said, her words tumbling out over each other. Her hands grew slick with cold sweat. "I met him, before I met you. He knew who I was. He spoke my name. And he offered me a drink of raw, untreated oil."

And I nearly took his offer.

But Chase shook his head.

"That...that doesn't make any sense," he said. "Vandraak wouldn't have done that. Raw oil ingested as a first exposure would kill you outright. You must be remembering it wrong."

"I know what I heard, captain. If Yuri hadn't been there—" Ilsa began, but Chase cut her off.

"I understand that you don't like him." He put a firm hand on Ilsa's shoulder. "Frankly, I don't like him either. If he wasn't the only one who knew the deepest secrets of the dragons, I wouldn't deal with him at all. But though he may be distasteful, he's not a murderer. Besides," Chase continued. "If he knew who you were, then he would already know better than to cause you harm. He needs you as much as I do."

Ilsa shook his touch off and stepped backward, gaping at the captain.

"It's not as bad as it sounds." Chase grimaced and spread his hands out to her in an imploring gesture. "You have to understand, Vandraak has the gift of foresight—among other, er...unique abilities. Byproducts of his nature."

"It isn't *nature*, Captain. It's quite the opposite."

"That's fair." Chase conceded with a half-smile.

"So, what has he foreseen?" Ilsa demanded, hugging her arms tight against her chest. The shiver that ran through her had nothing to do with the cold sea breeze. "And what on earth does it have to do with me?"

Chase pressed his lips together and looked out to sea again. He was quiet for so long that Ilsa wondered if he'd forgotten she was there. When he finally spoke, his voice was low and somber.

"I needed to know it was worth it," he said. "I cannot survive another failure. So, before I could set sail, I asked Vandraak to promise me that this venture would succeed."

"What did he tell you?" Ilsa's question was barely above a whisper.

"That I cannot count any loss too great a sacrifice in pursuit of my purpose." Chase closed his eyes. He recited the words with ease, like he had repeated them over and over to himself many times before. "I must harden my heart and my will. Any trace of doubt or weakness on my part, and I could doom us all."

"That doesn't sound like a promise of success, captain."

"That wasn't all." Chase studied her face. "The clearest, most certain prediction he could give me was that my first mate will kill the dragon."

"Me?" Ilsa's heart skipped a beat. "Captain, you can't be serious."

"I'm afraid I am." Chase shook his head. "Trust me, I'd have it another way if I could. I'd rather this rested on my shoulders alone, but Vandraak's prophecy was unquestionably clear. He said, word for word, 'the hand that rests on the helm in your stead is the hand that will dispel the threat and set all to rights.'"

Ilsa couldn't speak. It was ludicrous, laughable, even. She looked at her hand. Thin and frail. The hand of a dragon slayer?

Not likely.

Chase chuckled, shaking his head. "Why do you think I was so desperate to get Edwards to sail with me? I make a point not to beg, not for anything, but I begged Edwards. I thought I needed him for the success of the venture. But as it would turn out, I need *you.*" Chase placed both hands on Ilsa's shoulders and looked directly into her eyes. "*You're* the one who will kill the dragon, Ilsa Starling. Remember when I told you that you aren't expendable?"

Ilsa nodded mutely, unable to speak around the tightness in her throat.

"Please, Ilsa. I need you by my side," Captain Chase said. "I need you to believe in me. The crew will doubt. That's to be expected. They don't know what you and I do. All they can see is what they hate about Vandraak. And for good reason," Chase added with a grimace. "But in the end, no one will remember him. Try to see beyond him. Look to the bigger picture, to our goal. Will you do that for me?"

"I..." Ilsa hesitated, torn between instinct and empathy. She knew deep inside that Vandraak was not to be trusted. Her more rational mind screamed at her to have nothing at all to do with him or his schemes. But Chase's earnest expression pulled at her heart. His hope was infectious. And if he was right... then everything could change. She could feel strong again. She could have a future. She could go home.

Home to Phillip.

"I will try, Captain." Ilsa heard herself say.

Chase's face broke into the most genuine smile Ilsa had ever seen him wear. "And for that, you have my thanks, First Mate Starling."

The captain extended his hand, and Ilsa took it. Something about the handshake felt solemn, like an oath. When she let go, she found that a sense of grim resolve had settled over her heart.

"The helm is yours, Miss Starling," Chase said with a slight smile. His hand lingered on the wheel next to hers for a moment longer than was necessary as he turned its control over to her. Ilsa knew the prophecy echoed in his mind as clearly as she felt it in her own: *the hand that rests on the helm in your stead...*

Chase limped down the steps to the lower deck, leaving Ilsa alone. She closed her eyes and took a deep, slow breath. Trying to calm the whirlwind of confused thoughts that darted through her mind, she focused on the bite of the freezing air and the methodical dip of the waves.

Hear the waves, my girl? Grandfather's comforting voice echoed in Ilsa's memory. *Our Creator holds them all in the hollow of his hand. When you hear their song, remember that he holds you too.*

Ilsa straightened her shoulders and exhaled, grateful for the memory. But when she opened her eyes, the momentary sense of peace shattered.

There, at the mast, with his paper-thin lips peeled back in a skeletal grin and his lidless eyes unblinkingly trained on her, stood Vandraak.

CHAPTER TEN

The Brewing Storm

TOWERING STORM CLOUDS LINED the horizon, drawing a black veil between sea and sky. Ilsa stood at the bow with Mobius on her shoulder. The tammer's ears lay flattened back against his skull, a sure sign of unease. Ilsa couldn't blame him; her own breath caught as she took in her first glimpse of the perpetual storms that bordered the far seas, a wall around the world.

For centuries, sailors thought that the wall of storms was impassable. It might as well have been the utmost edge of the world. It wasn't until the age of the Fellwings, a dynasty of pirates nearly as infamous as the dragons themselves, that ships first dared to attempt to cross it. Even then, most who entered the storms never returned.

But the Hunters of Map's End, assisted by their precious commodity, changed that. A thousand years in the future, that might well still be their legacy—the sailors who breached the storm band and sailed beyond. It was a death-defying, legendary feat, and yet to Hunters, it was merely another part of the job: make it past the storms, hunt the Edge, go home. Do it all again on the next voyage.

"Breathtaking, isn't it?"

Ilsa turned to see Captain Chase standing beside her. She stiffened, but relaxed when she saw that he was alone. His eyes were trained on the horizon, and there was something open and honest about his faraway look. Maybe it was the fact that Vandraak was nowhere in sight—a rare occurrence in the three weeks since his presence aboard the ship was discovered—but whatever the case, Chase seemed more like himself at the moment.

The past few weeks had been relatively smooth sailing, the undercurrents of unease among the crew notwithstanding. *Relentless* had brought down a handful of dragons, filling her hold with oil. And though no one wanted to admit it, the hunting had gone much better with a third chaser, despite the nature of its second crewman.

"It is beautiful, in a way," Ilsa replied, pulling her cloak a little tighter against the cold. "Though I think I'd like it better if we weren't headed straight for it."

"It gets easier the more you do it. The first time I saw those towering clouds looming, I was so terrified that I had to be carried below, crying and screaming." Chase chuckled. "I was nine."

"I don't even know what to expect in there." Ilsa admitted. "I've read that it's days on end of hurricane-force storms."

"We'll make it," Chase said. "We always do. *Relentless* has weathered the band many times."

It crossed Ilsa's mind that every ship that had ever been wrecked trying to brave the storm band also had a perfect record up until the moment it went down, but she kept that thought to herself.

Mobius sat up straight, his glittering black eyes trained on the horizon. His velveteen nose quivered.

"What is it, Moby?" Ilsa followed Mobius's gaze to the wall of cloud. A white shape sat at the horizon, outlined sharply against the darkness. Mobius beat his wings and flew upward, circling the mast, evidently taking it upon himself to alert the lookout of his discovery.

"Do you see that?" Ilsa asked Chase, pointing toward the distant silhouette. "It looks like it might be a ship."

"It's not impossible." He squinted at it, then pulled a spyglass from his coat. "Have a look," he said, handing Ilsa the glass.

"Sail ho!" Nell's call from the top of the mast confirmed her suspicion before Ilsa could raise the glass to her eye. She peered through it to make out the details of the ship.

"*Millie Mae.*" Ilsa read the name on the prow. A flash of color lit up the approaching ship's deck, sent up by a dragonflame flare. "Looks like she's signaling us."

"I know *Millie*. She's a Map's End ship," the captain said. "Commanded by an old acquaintance. She'll want to talk." Chase paused, running a hand over his haggard face. "Actually, the trouble will be getting her to *stop* talking. Bring us about, Starling, cut sail, and prepare to be boarded."

Half an hour later, the *Millie Mae* was close enough to lower a boat. A small knot of sailors rowed across the waves and tied off alongside *Relentless*. Yuri dropped a rope ladder over the side of the ship and welcomed the visitors aboard.

The first one up the ladder was a round, rosy-cheeked woman, probably in her midforties, with tight brown curls cropped close around her ears. Her once-fine clothes looked thin and weather-beaten, as if they'd been worn around the world a few times.

"Fair sailing, Hunters!" she greeted, sticking up a hand towards Ilsa. "Captain Salina Faber, of Map's End. Our dear *Millie Mae* is two years out from land, and now homeward bound, blessed Creator be praised."

"Ilsa Starling, first officer," Ilsa replied, taking her hand and helping her aboard. "Outbound for the Edge."

"Bless you lass, but you're a sight for sore eyes after seeing none but my own crew for so long!" Captain Faber laughed, a jolly sound that set her curls trembling. "And what's this? A wee rabbit with wings like an albatross? Handsome little fellow, isn't he?"

Mobius ruffled with pride at the compliment, apparently electing to ignore the unintended slight.

Captain Faber glanced around the deck. "Has *Relentless* changed hands since I sailed from the island? Last I heard tell, young Master Chase was commanding this sturdy old tub."

"He still is, Faber." The captain's voice interjected from behind Ilsa, drawing the woman's attention.

Captain Faber looked Chase up and down, and her jaw went slack.

"Stars above, Chase!" She gasped. "What's happened to you, lad? You look like death!"

"It's good to see you too," Chase replied, giving her a wan smile that didn't reach his eyes. Ilsa hadn't noticed it before, but now that Faber had pointed it out, she had to agree with her; Chase did look bad. Ilsa glanced toward his sleeve, knowing what he concealed beneath. Was it the oil that was wearing on him? Or merely the tension of being so close to the storms?

"But look at you!" Captain Faber insisted, gesturing widely at his pale form. "Skin and bones! And looking like you've aged a decade! You're all eaten up from the inside out! 'Twould break your poor mother's heart to see you so, may the sea rest her memory."

"And you, dear Salina—" Chase grimaced. "Have not changed one bit."

"I don't make a habit of changing; you know that." She straightened her shoulders and pulled up the collar of her tattered coat, giving the distinct impression of a hen ruffling her feathers. "And that's why I'm still afloat."

"Fate doesn't care about your habits," Tasha muttered, scuffing the deck with the toe of her boot. "Sometimes change just happens."

"I see you're as bright a ray of sunshine as ever, Tashtanna," Captain Faber sniffed, looking down her nose at the harpooner before turning her attention back to the captain. "Where's Mr. Edwards? And the others? You've lost half your crew!"

"A lot has happened in the last year," Chase snapped. "Now, are you going to keep interrogating me or do you have anything important to say?"

Captain Faber stiffened a bit at the coldness of his tone. "You've been through this enough times; you know what I'm about. I'm here to negotiate offloading costs."

Ilsa had heard about offloading mid-voyage. It was an old hunting tradition, though this was the first time she'd seen it in practice. Ships returning from the Edge would buy the oil on outgoing ships and take it back to shore to sell. The practice kept outgoing ships light and agile, decreasing the risk of accidents in the storm band, and guaranteeing that at least some of the oil would make it home—even if the hunters didn't.

But Captain Chase shook his head.

"No, thank you."

"Whatever do you mean by that?" Faber made a face.

"I'm not planning to offload, Captain Faber."

The visiting captain's eyes widened. "But you've got to!" she sputtered. "There's no point in hauling so much oil through that nasty business." Faber jabbed a finger toward the looming storm clouds. "You're inviting catastrophe."

"I know." Chase's voice remained calm and measured. "But I plan to need every drop of oil in my hold, Salina."

Chase's stone-faced manner made Ilsa shiver. She felt like she ought to protest, or at least question his decision, but she held her tongue. It wasn't her place. Chase had made the crossing dozens of times, and she hadn't. The captain knew what he was doing; he had to.

The visiting captain, however, was not of a mind to keep her opinions to herself.

"What forever for?" Faber threw her hands up. "You'll only slow yourself down! Not to mention the risk of oil leaks! You know how fragile the stuff is. One bad turn in those storms, and you could lose this ship and everyone on it."

"How I run my ship is my business." Chase's tone was final.

"Your funeral," Faber muttered, sending a significant glance toward the wall of darkness on the horizon.

"Have you seen the white dragon?" Chase asked, abruptly.

"What's that got to do with anything?" Faber frowned.

"Just answer the question."

"Yes, we saw it." Faber shuddered. "And gave it a wide berth, you'd best believe. Straight out of nightmare, that. A hunter would have to be close to a madman to get anywhere near the beast."

"Tell me where." Chase's tone was even, controlled, but Ilsa could see the hunger flash in his eyes.

"But why..." Faber's question trailed off as she slowly made the realization. She shook her head firmly. "You're out of your bloomin' mind."

"Salina." Captain Chase's tone betrayed the fact that his patience was wearing thin. "Give me Avatheon's position or get off my boat."

Captain Faber pursed her lips, considering. Then she gave in.

"Show me your chart and I'll mark it out for you," she sighed. "But your blood's on your own head! I wash my hands of the matter."

"Thank you, Captain Faber. Come; I'll show you to my stateroom."

"I never liked that woman," Tasha murmured to Ilsa as they headed below, in a voice just loud enough that Ilsa was sure Captain Faber heard her, and just low enough to make it look like an accident.

Chase and Faber reemerged half an hour later. The visiting captain's face was a thundercloud as she huffed across the deck. Before she disembarked, she grabbed hold of Ilsa's upper arm and pulled her close.

"If you want out of this madness, Miss Starling, there's a berth for you and your rabbit aboard the *Millie Mae*. I'll treat you well and make sure you make it back to the homeland alive." She shot a venomous glance at Captain Chase, not seeming to care that she was attempting to poach his first officer right in front of him. "You seem like a nice girl. Get out of here while you still can."

Ilsa looked over at Chase, who watched with an impassible, steady gaze. For a moment, she was genuinely tempted to accept Faber's offer. The thought of stepping off of this ship, leaving its troubled captain behind her in favor of a safe, steady voyage back to shore, did hold some appeal. It would be a relief to be rid of Vandraak and his lurking grin. To be free of the looming sense of foreboding that followed *Relentless* like sharks in her wake. To untangle herself from the constant battle between her duty and conscience, two forces that ought to be united, but lately had been pulling her in different directions.

Mobius nosed the side of Ilsa's face. Ilsa looked up, surprised to find that Faber wasn't the only one awaiting an answer from her. Yuri and Tasha stood by the mast, watching. Tasha's face was twisted in an accusing frown; Ilsa knew if Faber's offer had extended to Tash, she would've rejected it without a second's hesitation. Yuri looked on, too, though his expression was more thoughtful. Ilsa met his eyes, and she knew what she had to do.

She would not abandon her shipmates, her friends who cared for her when she had so little to give them in return.

For better or worse, she had committed to this ship and its captain. A place on the *Millie Mae* would be only a temporary reprieve; as soon as she made port, Ilsa would be back where she'd started—nowhere to go, nowhere she belonged.

And maybe, just maybe, Chase was right. If *Relentless* succeeded in bringing down the white dragon, then home might be worth returning to.

The mere hope was enough.

"Thank you, Captain Faber," Ilsa replied, gently detaching herself from the captain's grip. "But my duty is to *Relentless* and her crew."

"I truly hope you live to regret that decision," Faber said, shaking her head. "It's better than the alternative."

An hour later, Ilsa stood beside the captain as the *Millie Mae* fell away to stern. Soon the homeward-bound ship was nothing more than a white smudge on the horizon.

"Why didn't you offload the oil, Captain?"

Chase turned his back on *Millie* and gazed toward the opposite horizon. His eyes were far away, as if he could already see his destiny lurking beyond the world's edge.

"You'll thank me when the time comes," was all he said in reply. It was becoming a common refrain with him:

You'll understand soon. You'll thank me later. You'll see.

Ilsa didn't dare say it aloud, but she was growing weary of all of his promises.

Ominous stillness enveloped the ship. The sails hung limp in the dreadful calm as *Relentless* drifted closer and closer to the dark wall of cloud. Mere hours stood between the ship and the storm band. Everyone aboard scurried about their duties in silence, speaking only when necessary and then only in hushed tones.

On her way to relieve Yuri at the helm, Ilsa paused before she reached the steps to the quarterdeck. Mobius sat on her shoulder. He hadn't left his perch all afternoon. Ilsa wondered how much he understood; did he grasp the gravity of their position, or could he merely sense the tension? Whatever the case, he straightened his spine, sniffing at the air. He unfolded his wings and gave them a few restless flaps, batting the side of Ilsa's face in the process.

"Do you mind?" she muttered irritably, sweeping the tammer down into her arms. "I happen to prefer my ears without your feathers in them, thanks."

Mobius whimpered in response. Or at least, Ilsa thought it was Mobius. But the tammer cocked his head to the side and glanced questioningly at Ilsa.

"Not you, then?" Ilsa asked. Mobius shook himself free of her grasp and flew toward one of the stored chaser boats. Ilsa followed, and as she got close to the boat, she caught a glimpse of dark braids dotted with colorful beads.

"Tasha?" Ilsa ventured cautiously.

The harpooner slumped between the dormant chaser and a coil of rope, her head in her hands. She looked up swiftly when Ilsa spoke and swiped a hand across her cheek—but she wasn't fast enough to erase the tear streaks.

"Oh, it's just you." Her voice was heavy with relief.

Ilsa sank to her knees on the deck beside her friend. Cold sea spray seeped through her skirt, chilling her, but she didn't care.

"Are you all right, Tash?"

"Fine as ever." Tasha attempted a grin, but failed. Her expression crumpled, and she dropped her face back into her hands, choking back a sob.

Mobius alighted on Tasha's buckled knees and nuzzled his pink nose against her forehead. Without looking up, Tash gathered Mobius into her arms and hugged him close, burying her tear-stained face in his plush white fur. Mobius, usually so prim about his fur not getting tousled, snuggled in and let her hold him without complaint.

Ilsa watched helplessly. Tasha was usually so strong, so unshakably good-humored, that it was hard to see her like this. Ilsa didn't know what to say. After a long, uncomfortable pause, she cleared her throat.

"Can I help at all?"

"You could pretend I'm not crying." Tash wiped her nose on her sleeve. She looked away, not meeting Ilsa's eyes. "That would be helpful."

Ilsa tugged at her hair ribbon.

"Did the *Millie Mae's* visit upset you?"

"No." Tasha wrinkled her nose. "Faber's an old bag, but she's mostly harmless." She picked up the end of one of her braids and twisted a bright orange bead between her fingers, absentmindedly mirroring Ilsa's nervous habit.

"Strange that the captain didn't offload, isn't it?" Ilsa ventured, hoping the question might give Tasha something else to think about, rather than whatever was troubling her.

"Heaven knows what Adam is thinking," Tasha muttered bitterly. "He didn't consult *me* about it, that's for certain."

Tasha swiped viciously at a fresh tear streak. There it was again. *Adam.* The name no one ever spoke... except Tasha.

"Tash," Ilsa said slowly. "About you and the captain... I've wondered for a while, but..."

Tasha dropped her head again, her braids drooping in limp coils on the deck beneath her. Mobius shot Ilsa a dirty look.

"I'm so sorry," Ilsa said quickly. "I don't mean to pry."

"No, don't be." Tasha sniffed. "You were bound to figure it out eventually. Can't live in close quarters for this long without learning pretty much all there is to know." Tasha gave a bitter laugh. "I'm violating the conditions of my employment by talking about it, though. Captain's orders."

"It's just me," Ilsa said. "And Mobius, but he won't tell on you."

Mobius twitched a long white ear in agreement.

"Right. Just *you.*" Tasha rolled her eyes. "Just the first mate, whose expressly stated duty is to enforce the captain's will and orders?"

Ilsa shrugged. "I guess I've never been very good at this job."

At that, a little bit of Tasha's genuine smile broke through.

"And I'm not very good at pretending to be something I'm not." Tasha admitted. "Truth is, I'm his. Always have been; always will be."

"You don't have to talk about it if it hurts."

"It hurts worse not to," Tasha said. "Adam and I met on my first voyage. He wasn't a captain yet, but we all knew he would be soon. He always had greatness in him—the kind of contagious greatness that made everyone around him want to do better too. Don't tell Yuri, but the only reason I ever attempted to learn harpooning is because I was trying to impress a boy."

"Of course," Ilsa said drily. "Because what every man wants is a woman who can stab him through the heart at twenty yards."

"Hey, don't knock it if it worked." Tasha rubbed Mobius between his ears. "You would've loved the old Adam," she murmured, almost to herself. "All that passion, that fierce intensity. He's always been that way. But he wasn't angry back then. Just dedicated. Determined, ambitious. When he set his mind on something, you could be sure he'd see it through." She sighed. "I guess the word for that is stubborn. *That* hasn't changed, at least."

"He broke it off with you, didn't he?" Ilsa knew the answer before she asked. "After his accident?"

Tasha wiped her cheek with the back of her hand.

"He insisted the injury ruined him. I couldn't talk sense into him. I tried my hardest." Tasha shrugged helplessly. "But you can't love someone hard enough to convince them they're worthy of love, not if they refuse to believe it themselves. Adam made up his mind that he was too broken for me, so he pushed me away. Said it was for my own good."

Ilsa shivered and looked away.

Please tell Phillip it's better this way...

"Course, he couldn't get rid of me that easy." Tasha went on, not noticing Ilsa's discomfort. "He may not let me love him, but he needs a harpooner. I'll stand by him, come what may. But it kills me to watch him do this to himself."

"What do you mean?"

"This voyage. I thought it would help him... you know... get better. Going back to sea, doing what he loves. Proving to himself and everyone else that he could still do it." Tasha shook her head. "I thought it would bring the old Adam back a little bit. But he's getting worse. Every day he sinks further."

Guilt drove Ilsa to look away. She couldn't bear the weight of the captain's dark secret. Surely Tasha had a right to know about the oil, didn't she?

No. It wasn't Ilsa's secret to share. The knowledge would only make Tasha angry. And that wouldn't help anything. Besides, if what Chase believed about the oil turned out to be true, wouldn't it benefit Tasha in the long run?

"It's that accursed dragonblood." Tasha went on, oblivious to the struggle that raged beneath Ilsa's silence. "I don't know what sorcery it worked on him, but it's gotten its wretched talons into Adam. I'm sure it was that devil that put the idea in his head to come out here in the first place." Tasha pounded her fist on the damp planks beside her. "Why can't he see? I don't want him to prove himself to me. I want him to wake up and realize what a fool he's been for trying to do it alone. I don't need him to fix what's broken; I just want him to let me walk through this with him."

He won't let you, Ilsa thought. *He can't let you.*

Her mind wandered back to that day in the captain's cabin, after the first hunt. Guilt brushed her conscience as she remembered the way he'd confided in her. How cruel, how unfair to bare his soul to a near stranger when the woman who loved him was yearning for him to let her in.

"Tash, you should know... Adam—the captain, I mean—"

But Tasha cut her off with a sharp shake of her head. "Please don't tell me, Ilsa. Whatever happened between you, it's not my business. He isn't mine. Not anymore."

"Oh, stars, no." Ilsa gasped. "Nothing like that. I only meant to tell you that I think he still loves you. He wants to believe it's possible to go back to how things were before, and I can't imagine that you wouldn't be a part of it." Ilsa shook her head. "And as for me, well...my heart is spoken for. I do care for the captain, but..."

But he will never be Phillip.

"I won't pretend I'm not relieved to hear it," Tasha said, giving her a weary smile. "But I wouldn't blame you if you did. Adam is very easy to fall in love with." She sighed. "But very difficult to love."

"You still do, though," Ilsa said. "Even though he pushes you away. Even though he's breaking your heart. You love him, Tash."

"And I always will." Tasha nodded. "There's no moving on from what I shared with Adam, not as long as there's breath in my body."

Tell Phillip to move on quickly, and to forget me if he can manage it.

"Tasha," Ilsa said slowly, afraid to give voice to the question but desperate for the answer. "What would you have done if he'd...just disappeared? Left without warning, without sending word. What would you do then?"

Tasha eyed Ilsa quizzically, studying her face. Shame drove Ilsa to look away. She couldn't meet Tasha's eyes, for fear she'd see Phillip there.

"I would move heaven and earth to find him," Tasha finally said. "And if that didn't work, I'd spend every day after that praying that the Creator would give him a good whack on the head, maybe knock some sense back into him. And most of all, I'd pray that he'd come home. But..." Tasha raised an eyebrow at Ilsa and gently touched her hand. "We're not talking about Adam anymore, are we?"

Ilsa swallowed hard. At last, she shook her head.

"I left him, Tash," she whispered, unable to blink back the hot tears that filled her eyes. At the sight of her tears, Mobius wriggled free of Tasha's hug and crawled onto Ilsa's lap. Ilsa stroked his ears, grateful for his touch. "With my health the way it is, I... I didn't want to be a burden to him, to his family. He deserved so much better. I couldn't watch him sacrifice his youth for a wife who could give him nothing in return."

"Nothing?" Tasha drew back sharply as if Ilsa had slapped her across the face. "I would give anything for the chance to care for and serve the person I love most. You call that *nothing*?"

Ilsa couldn't answer.

"I'm not going to tell you what to do, Ilsa," Tasha said. "But if you're asking about how it feels on the other side, well, all I can tell you is that if Adam were to come to his senses, I'd forgive him in a heartbeat."

"Miss Starling?"

Ilsa jumped at the voice that broke in. Pip Steelkilt stood a respectful few yards away, scuffing his boot across the deck.

"Sorry to bother you, ma'am," said the boy. "But the captain needs you in the stateroom. We're about to enter the storm."

"Thank you, Pippin," Ilsa said, pulling herself to her feet, relieved at the excuse to escape. "Come, Mobius."

"Ilsa wait." Tasha scrambled up too. She put out her hand and stopped Ilsa's retreat. "It's your first crossing, so I've got to warn you: the storm will test you." Her voice was as solemn as Ilsa had ever heard it. "Don't let it win."

CHAPTER ELEVEN

Tempest Tossed

CAPTAIN CHASE GAVE EVERY APPEARANCE of a man in command, but Ilsa couldn't overlook the whiteness of his knuckles, gripping the edge of his charting table as if his life depended on it. One ill-timed pitch of the ship would send him sprawling, and she wondered if he was more afraid of that indignity than of the storm itself.

"We're four days in," Chase said. Ilsa stood over the chart right beside him, and but she still had to lean in close to hear him over the howling gale. "So far, the wind has been with us. We're making good time."

Ilsa could only nod weakly, fighting another wave of nausea. The constant tossing of the ship for days on end had rendered her unable to eat. Some moments she could hardly stand up. The rest of the crew was no better off; even Tasha had been sick.

"Another two or three days of this and we should break through. We're getting so close—"

Frantic pounding at the door of his cabin interrupted him.

"What?" The captain shouted.

The door opened a crack, and Nell's pale face poked through. She was soaked and shivering, but then, so was everyone. After four days in the storm, there was not a dry thread to be found among the lot of them.

"Sorry Captain, Miss Starling," the girl said. "I don't mean to intrude, but—"

"Out with it!" Chase barked, and Nell ducked as though she expected him to throw something at her. She was right to worry. Everyone's tempers had grown short in the storms, the captain's more than most.

"Bones sent me." Though her voice quivered, Nell forged on bravely with her message. "He found oil pooling in the cargo hold. Said there's a leak in one of the casks somewhere, and that you ought to be notified immediately."

Chase pushed a hand through his thick hair in frustration. He cursed under his breath. Ilsa couldn't make out everything that he said, but she caught Vandraak's name mentioned in the angry tirade.

"Thank you, Nell," Ilsa said, taking pity on the cowering girl. "You can go."

She gave a relieved nod before slipping away, closing the door behind her.

"A leak?" Ilsa turned to the captain. *Relentless's* hold was dangerously full of the most volatile substance on earth. A leaking oil cask would be a grave discovery in the calmest sailing conditions. In storms like these... Ilsa didn't want to imagine it, but she couldn't help but remember the way her first chaser boat had exploded instantly when the oil cells shattered.

"Captain, in weather this rough, a leak could be deadly. And since you didn't offload—"

"That devil promised we were in no danger." Chase cut Ilsa off, though the words he muttered through gritted teeth seemed to be spoken more to himself.

"Sir? What should—?"

"Use your imagination, Starling!" the captain snapped,

smacking his palm down on the table. "If we're leaking oil, we've got to fix it. Send Yuri below to find the leak and stop it up. Now!"

Ilsa hurried out of the cabin.

"And send Vandraak to me!" Chase yelled after her. Ilsa pretended not to hear him. Whatever conflict the captain had with his dragonblood advisor, she wanted no part in it.

Ilsa headed for the main deck, pausing to tie herself off to one of the lines stored at the hatch before pushing it open. No one would dare to attempt walking on the open deck in such weather without securing themselves to the ship first. One bad wave to broadside and they'd never be seen again.

Ilsa braced herself, then opened the hatch to stagger out into the storm.

Rain lashed the deck in sideways sheets and the wind howled with the fury of a hurricane. Ilsa tried to shield her eyes from the blinding rain, but she would've had more luck trying to see through stone.

The helm stood unmanned, lashed tight. The spars were bare; any sail left up would've been shredded by the wind in a matter of minutes. The last spare chaser had been lost early on—nobody quite knew when—tossed overboard when the lines that tied it down had snapped.

Relentless had long since stopped trying to fight her way through the storm. Now she ran before it; the gale drove the ship where it willed.

Yuri stood at the mast, his broad back braced against it. Even in weather this foul, the crew took shifts standing storm watch, thirty minutes at a time. No one had the strength to withstand more than that, though Ilsa had caught wind of a rumor that Yuri and Tasha were trying to out-compete each other for how long they could bear it.

"Yuri!"

His head turned toward Ilsa, but if he spoke a reply, it was lost to the gale.

"Come below! Captain's orders!"

Shielding his face from the punishing wind, Yuri staggered to the hatch.

"Tashtanna, the deck is yours," he shouted over his shoulder.

"Oh, thanks a lot, Yuri!"

They hurried down the steps and let the hatch slam shut behind them. The ship reeled and tossed, but the difference between standing exposed on the open deck and huddling in the enclosed companionway was profound. Ilsa's hands shook as she gathered up the heavy, soaked fabric of her skirt and attempted to wring it out.

"Captain promises another day or two and we'll be through it." Ilsa tried to be encouraging, but her voice came out strained.

"Ah, and then we will have peace?" Despite it all, a twinkle lingered in Yuri's eye. Ilsa smiled weakly and shook her head. Everyone knew what lay before them after the storms: the Final Sea, and the mighty dragons that stood guard over the edge of the world.

Still, after days in this storm of storms, Ilsa would rather face the dragons.

"Why did you call me?" Yuri asked. "Though," he added with a smile. "I do not complain. I was tired." He paused, glancing up toward the dripping hatch. "But do not tell Tashtanna I said so."

Ilsa shook herself, forcing her thoughts back to the matter at hand. The intensity of being on deck was so severe, she'd almost forgotten what she'd been sent up to do.

"There's a leak in the hold," she told Yuri. "Oil. Bones found it, but we don't know where it's coming from."

Yuri's face instantly sobered.

"Captain wants you to find out where it's coming from and patch it." Ilsa beckoned him forward. "I'll help."

"No, you won't."

Ilsa paused, startled by the finality in his tone.

"What are you talking about? I'm fine." The lie felt sticky in her throat. "Yuri, please, I don't want you to do this alone."

Her friend shook his head.

"You forget—I too am a leader," he said. "If I am to be king of my people, I must decide what is best for those I am sworn to protect. You stay."

Ilsa opened her mouth to protest again, but the concern in his eyes stopped her. His words were firm and steadfast, but his strong voice trembled as he spoke. Ilsa couldn't remember ever seeing Yuri look quite so afraid. She wasn't sure which it was—fear of his perilous task at hand, or fear for her safety—but whatever the case, it proved contagious. Cold dread slipped its icy grip over Ilsa's heart.

"Please, *Yil'saa.*" Yuri placed a stony hand on her shoulder, heavy and firm. "Stay."

"All right," she conceded, looking down at her boots. She fiddled with the end of her braid, squeezing a few cold seawater tears from the drooping ribbon.

When she raised her gaze again, Yuri was gone.

"Thirty minutes out there is about twenty-nine minutes too long." Tasha shivered. She unfastened the clasp of her oilskin and let it drop to the floor. She looked at the dripping cloak, then shrugged, too weary even to pick it up.

"Try to get some sleep." Ilsa stooped to pick up the cloak herself and hung it on a hook on the galley wall. It was a futile gesture. The cloak wouldn't dry before Tash needed it again; the sea had been too rough to risk lighting the stove for days.

"Here, warm up a bit before you go." Ilsa offered her a blanket. It was damp. Everything was.

"Thanks." Tasha pulled the blanket around her shoulders. She looked half asleep already. When the ship first entered the storms, Ilsa had been incredulous. How could anyone even dream of getting rest while the ship was heaving and rolling without reprieve? But she'd since proved herself wrong. The small snatches of sleep she was able to steal here and there between watches were the only relief available.

"And you should probably try to eat something," Ilsa added. The advice was a bit hypocritical; the thought of food turned her stomach.

"All right, *mother*," Tasha said, rolling her eyes. "But I can never eat during the crossing. I'll only—"

A trembling roar, louder even than the storm, tore through the ship. Every plank and board seemed to shudder. *Relentless* careened unnaturally to starboard, against the roll of the waves. Ilsa was unable to hold herself back from being flung forward; across from her, Tasha barely caught hold of the table's rim in time to avoid being tossed to the floor like a sack of flour.

"What now?" Tasha gasped, scrambling for balance.

"Something rammed us!" Ilsa exclaimed, breathless, but Tasha shook her head.

"That's impossible! Dragons never surface in the storms."

"Then what could've—" Ilsa cut off. The blood drained out of her face. A wave of nausea hit her at the same time the realization did. The leaking oil must've exploded, and that meant...

Yuri.

Ilsa had never moved so fast. One moment she was standing in the galley with Tasha, and the next she was flying, her feet pounding down the stairway to the cargo hold.

The ship reeled wildly, throwing off her balance, but Ilsa pressed through it, fueled by a fear like none she'd ever felt.

Please. Her mind screamed over and over. *Please, please, please.*

When she reached the storeroom that housed the oil kegs, Ilsa's burst of strength ran out. Pain shot through her chest, and she pitched forward, unable to keep her footing. Her hands thrust out reflectively, and she caught herself on the door. But the latch was unsecured, and the door swung open under her.

Ilsa tumbled into the storeroom with a jarring blow that sent a white-hot shock up her arms. She rolled onto her back, gasping for breath. She couldn't move. Throbbing pain pulsed through her whole body, and each breath stung.

The air was hot and thick, and heavy with an acrid smell like burning metal. A purple haze hung in the darkness around her, emitting a pale shimmer of its own but not strong enough to illuminate anything else.

He needs you! The voice in her head was merciless. *Yuri needs you and you're failing him!*

"Yuri!" she tried to call to him, but she was unable to produce more than a strained whisper. With monumental effort that she felt in every bone, Ilsa pulled herself to her hands and knees. "Yuri, can you hear me?"

Fighting waves of dizziness, Ilsa crawled forward, deeper into the hold amid the kegs of oil. She groped blindly along the floor; Yuri hadn't brought any light with him. He wouldn't need it, not with his specialized vision, but it was costing precious seconds now.

I should've been there. I should've come with him. I should've ordered him to let me help.

Something jagged and wooden blocked Ilsa's path. She wrested it aside, and her eyes locked onto a dull red glow, gleaming in the darkness beyond like a pinprick of hope.

Yuri's stone.

"I'm coming!" Ilsa's hand slipped against something slick on the floor as she scrambled forward, following the red gem's glow to her friend's side.

Yuri sprawled on the floor, facedown and still, but that was all Ilsa could make out in the darkness. She couldn't even tell if he was breathing.

A pale bloom of light appeared in the doorway behind her, but its scattered beams were rendered useless by the thick haze.

"Miss Starling!" a voice came from outside the hold. "Are you in there?"

"Brigid!" Ilsa gasped. "Thank God. I need help!"

"Get out of there, girl!" Brigid shouted. "Those fumes are poison!"

Ilsa buried her face in the crook of her elbow, muffling her nose and mouth with her damp sleeve. Even if Brigid wouldn't risk breathing the oil fumes to come help, Ilsa wouldn't leave.

Not without him.

"Out of my way!" There was a scrambling sound, then someone dropped to the floor in the darkness beside Ilsa.

Tasha. Dear, loyal Tasha.

"I'll get one side, you get the other," Tasha said, sounding like she was trying to hold her breath. Ilsa didn't hesitate. Together, they managed to roll Yuri onto his back. Ilsa didn't pause to check if he was breathing. She couldn't bear to.

"Come on!" Tasha grunted. The tiny harpooner strained under Yuri's weight, but she didn't waver. With all the strength she could muster, Ilsa managed to throw one of Yuri's massive arms over her shoulder. Tasha did the same with the other, and step by grueling step, they staggered out of the hold, dragging Yuri along with them.

They had barely cleared the doorway when Tasha's knees buckled under her, and she collapsed over the threshold. Ilsa couldn't hold Yuri on her own, and she crumpled to the planks beside him.

Now free of her weighty burden, Tasha jumped up and slammed the door to the hold. She pressed her back against the door and slid down into a heap on the floor, panting.

"Pair of fools if I've ever seen one." Brigid glared at Ilsa and Tasha. "You could've gotten yourselves killed, and where would we have been then? Down a harpooner and a pilot, not to mention the first mate!"

"Yuri," Ilsa whispered, ignoring Brigid's scolding. "Please don't be gone."

Raw, angry burns marred Yuri's face, neck, and chest. His stony skin was nearly white. Ilsa put a shaking hand on his cheek and wiped a trickle of dark blood away from his mouth.

Yuri groaned, a low, wet rumble. His head turned weakly to one side, and a grimace of pain flickered across his brow.

"He's alive!" Ilsa choked on a relieved sob. "Brigid! He's alive!"

Tasha helped Ilsa to her feet and they stepped back, letting Brigid crouch next to Yuri. Ilsa leaned heavily on Tasha's shoulder; she could feel the harpooner shaking.

After what felt like an eternity, Brigid looked up. Her mouth was a tight, grim line.

"Well?" Tasha demanded, unable to bear the tense silence any longer.

"It's not good." Brigid shook her head. "Even without the force of the shockwave hitting him full-on, the burns alone could be enough to kill him. Not to mention he's got a good bit of debris embedded in him."

"And who knows how much of the fumes he breathed in," Tasha said. Her chin quivered as she looked at Yuri's still face.

"He's got the worst luck I've ever seen," Brigid said. "Somehow he managed to be right on top of the oil when it blew."

Realization wrung Ilsa's heart. It hadn't been luck.

"He threw himself on the explosion," she whispered.

"What?" Tasha gasped.

"Yuri must've seen it was about to blow, and he got to it just in time." Ilsa shook her head. Her eyes filled with tears as she looked at her friend, lying still and broken. He'd done it for her, and she knew it. "If the explosion had set off the other kegs, it would've torn straight through the hull. We'd have been sunk. But he took the impact himself. Yuri saved the ship."

"You have to save him, Brigid," Tasha said, grasping at the older woman's hand. Brigid shook her off.

"And just how do you expect me to do that in these storms, Tashtanna? Treating wounds like this would be delicate under the calmest conditions. In this weather..." Brigid threw her hands up with a frustrated huff. "I'm not a miracle worker. Best I can do is try to keep him stable, and reassess when we're through the storms."

"But that'll be days!" Tasha shouted. "We can't leave him like this! Surely there's something we can do *now*!"

"Pray," Brigid said, hauling herself to her feet and wiping her hands on her apron. The finality in her voice chilled Ilsa to the soul. "But don't hold your breath."

CHAPTER TWELVE

The Pistol

"Captain, we've been in this gale for ten days."

"Tell me something I don't know, Starling." The captain's voice sounded every bit as ragged as Ilsa felt. He bent over his charting table, head down, staring blankly at a crumpled map. Behind him, ever-present but just beyond the reaches of the light, lurked Vandraak.

"The crew is exhausted, sir. Their morale is shredded. It slips away more and more every day we spend in these accursed storms. Even those who have been through the band before are beginning to lose hope."

"It's part of the job."

"Yuri is dying."

Chase finally looked up at her. His limp, unwashed hair hung in scraggly strands over his red-rimmed eyes.

"Blast it all, Starling, what do you want me to do about it? We can't run a hospital in a hurricane."

"Then get us out of the hurricane!"

"And how do you suggest we do that?" Chase snapped. "I thought we'd be through it by now. It's impossible to tell how far off course we are. Navigation is useless here. We're doing all that we can."

"No, not all, Captain," Ilsa countered. *"Relentless* has the capability to more than double her speed. I know that Edwards was able to use oil reserves to hasten the voyage home after your injury. It saved your life. Perhaps we could do the same to save Yuri's."

Vandraak stepped from the shadows, coming up behind the captain. His bony fingers curled over Chase's shoulder.

"That would expend much precious oil," he said, his thin voice rasping close to the captain's ear. "You can't afford it. Not after the loss from the accident in the hold."

"A loss *you* swore wouldn't happen." Chase shook him off.

"Perhaps..." the dragonblood drew out the word with a hiss. "Perhaps it was not fully an accident. The Stoneman was the only one present at the time of the explosion, yes?"

"How dare you?" Ilsa gasped. "Yuri is the least likely sailor on this ship to attempt—"

"No one is accusing Yuri of anything." Chase cut her off. He glared at Vandraak. "By all reckoning, he saved us all from much greater disaster."

"Yes, yes." Vandraak conceded. "A shame to lose him, really."

"That's enough, Vandraak," Chase said.

"The crew is looking to *you,* Captain," Ilsa said through clenched teeth, refusing to look at Vandraak. She squeezed her shaking hands into tight fists. "And every day that you stand by as one of your best struggles to survive...well, they are beginning to doubt that you have their best interests at heart."

"Be careful what you insinuate, Ilsa Starling," Vandraak said. "Mutiny is a capital offense, you know."

"I said nothing of mutiny."

"No, of course not." Vandraak's smile was icy. "But if the crew were to decide Captain Chase was not serving them well, then who, do you suppose, would take command in his place?"

The hand that rests on the helm in your stead...

"That's *enough,* Vandraak!" Chase repeated. "Miss Starling knows her duty. You will give us a moment alone."

"As you wish, captain."

Chase watched the dragonblood go. Ilsa might have imagined it, but it seemed that the captain breathed a little easier once Vandraak left the stateroom.

"I'm sorry, Ilsa," Chase said, rubbing a hand over his shadowed face. "Vandraak was out of line to speak of Yuri like that, but I do agree with his stance on the oil."

Ilsa bit back a sharp reply as Chase went on.

"I have no idea of our position relative to the storms. If we add a burst of power, it could merely take us further west, along the band. Or worse, we could backtrack and end up on the wrong side of the storm. Even if we did manage to get out, there is no guarantee that Yuri will fare any better." The captain stepped forward and put a hand on Ilsa's shoulder. "Your suggestion was kindly meant. But I cannot burn through our stores on such a narrow hope."

"This whole venture hangs on a narrow hope!" Ilsa's voice shook. "Does Yuri's life mean so little to you that you would trade it for profit?"

"Profit? When have I ever cared about profit? No, we need the oil to face the White Dragon. Every drop. Why do you think I didn't sell to Faber? If we're going to have any chance against Avatheon, we have to follow Vandraak's plan and—"

"*Vandraak's* plan?" Ilsa jerked backward, away from his touch. "That's your reliable source that's going to help you slay the dragon? His promises have already failed you once. What makes you believe it will be any different next time?"

"Vandraak's word is the only hope I have."

"Then you are betting our lives on a lie!"

For an instant, the captain looked so fierce, his face contorted into a dragonish snarl, that Ilsa braced herself, thinking he might hit her. But the flash of anger was momentary, and Chase instead turned his back to her and limped across the room. He clasped his hands behind his back and stared up at the painting on the wall. The brush-stroked dragon loomed over him with open jaws.

"What do you know about the life cycle of a sea dragon, Starling?" Chase asked, his voice strangely calm, a lull in the storm.

"Sir?"

"It's every bit as brutal as you might imagine to be fitting for such creatures. Dragons abandon their eggs in shallow waters. Some of their laying grounds are not far from Map's End. When I was a boy, my schoolmates and I would search for egg fragments along the coast after storms. They were beautiful... so sharp..."

The captain held up his hand and looked at it. From where Ilsa stood, lamplight danced across the creases of his palm in thin streaks, reminiscent of bright ribbons of blood.

"Left to fend for themselves, the immature hatchlings are easy prey for nearly everything in the sea. Ironic, isn't it, that the greatest monsters of the deep start out their lives abandoned and vulnerable?"

"I suppose there's a reason you're telling me this?"

"Didn't you teach literature?" The captain chuckled. "You've been away from your books too long if you can't see the parallels. I was born at sea. My mother fought hard for a few months, but she died two days before we reached port. Drink and neglect claimed my father less than a year later. Do you see it now?"

"I would not take much pride in likening myself to a dragon, sir."

"Perhaps not. But juvenile dragons and Map's End orphans are cut from the same cloth," he said. "The hatchlings have barely left infancy when they begin their great pilgrimage to the edge of the world. It's a perilous journey, one they pursue with a monomaniacal passion. Some never even stop long enough to feed, and so starve themselves on the way. No one really knows why; the Edge is a forbidding nursery. Young dragons are swept away by the hundreds, falling to the fathomless depths below. Only the strongest can fight it long enough to grow. Only the strongest," Chase murmured, repeating the words to himself with an almost prayerful reverence.

Ilsa clenched her teeth, biting back sharp words that she knew would have no effect. She wished she could take him by the shoulders and shake him until it roused him from this dark dream. If she thought it would help, she would have done it in a heartbeat.

"Once the dragons have developed enough to survive the seas, most leave the Edge." Chase went on, oblivious to her growing anger. "But some... some never do. It's the most punishing place in the world to survive and yet there they are, stubbornly staking their claim, growing stronger daily not in spite of the hardship, but because of it. The Edge cannot defeat their fury; it only feeds it."

"Captain—"

"I am bound for the Edge," Chase said, his voice stronger now. "I have set my course. And so help me, I will not retreat. That dragon, that all-destroying but unconquering fiend—I will spit my last breath at it."

Chase clenched a fist.

"Every Hunter knows you must kill a dragon all at once, or not at all. Wound it—" he shifted, leaning heavily on his good leg "—and you've done nothing but awaken a greater monster. A rage that cannot be snuffed out by anything but death. To let a wounded dragon live is a mistake for which there is no forgiveness."

It was impossible to miss his meaning. Adam Chase, the wounded dragon. Who, then, was he blaming for letting him live? Not Edwards; the former mate had merely picked up the pieces as best he could. No, it was Providence that had spared Chase's life in the critical moment. The Creator could have let his story end in the dragon's jaws, and only by his will did Chase survive.

Providence let the wounded dragon live; the Creator made a mistake.

Chase's accusation was nothing short of blasphemy.

A sharp rebuke rose to Ilsa's lips, but she stopped before she could give it voice. Hadn't she secretly harbored the same thought? The memory of her own words haunted her:

Why did the Creator even let me survive the fever if it was just to be a weak, depressed invalid—the object of everyone's pity and whispers, doomed to fade away slowly...

Chase's anger, Ilsa's despair. They were not so unsimilar after all.

Ilsa swallowed hard, pushing the thought away. Now wasn't the time for this. Yuri needed her to fight for him, and she couldn't let him down.

"I am not interested in philosophizing about the fortitude of dragons, Captain," she said, her voice ragged.

Chase finally turned to look at her. The sharp shadows cast across his wan features made him look otherworldly.

"I cannot count any loss too great a sacrifice in pursuit of my purpose," he said, repeating Vandraak's words like a mantra. "I must harden my heart and my will. Any trace of doubt or weakness on my part, and I could doom us all."

"You're already dooming one of us."

"I do not want Yuri to die, Ilsa."

"But you are going to let him." Ilsa's voice broke. "You will sacrifice him. You would sacrifice any of us—all of us—if doing so would ensure you'd kill that dragon."

Chase did not answer. He didn't have to. His grim, hard eyes said it all.

"If that's all you had to report, Miss Starling," he said. "Then you may return to your duties."

Chase gestured toward the door, and Ilsa caught sight of a dark crimson stain on his sleeve.

"You're bleeding, Captain."

"I often do." Chase folded his arms across his chest quickly, hiding the stain, but not before Ilsa saw an unmistakable shimmer intermingled with the blood.

"You've increased your oil usage, haven't you?"

"I use only what I need to sustain my strength."

"And Vandraak?" Ilsa challenged. "I suppose you're giving him what he craves as well?"

"What I pay him is none of your concern!" Chase shouted. "Don't you see? I need him! Without him I'm as good as dead."

"What could he possibly have promised you to make you think that?"

"Everything." Chase's voice was a fierce whisper. "Strength from weakness. Life from death. Health from frailty."

The very words that had once seemed so alluring to Ilsa now sickened her.

"If you think your value comes from your physical strength, Captain, then you're sorely mistaken."

"Don't lie to me, Tasha—" The captain cut himself off as he realized what he'd said. He turned away with a stricken look on his face. He hung his head, looking so lost that Ilsa wanted to reach out to him, but she couldn't.

"If you were honest with yourself for once in your life," Chase said quietly, his teeth clenched. "You know you would do the same. If you could have everything back—everything that was stolen from you restored—you wouldn't hesitate to make any necessary sacrifice."

Everything that was stolen, restored?

For a moment, Ilsa let herself linger on the thought. Suppose it was possible? Suppose it could be put to rights? Ilsa closed her eyes, and the storm-tossed Hunting ship and its troubled captain faded to mist in her mind. She could feel warm sunshine on her face as she walked arm in arm with Phillip across the lush green grounds of Baywood Estate. A rosy-cheeked child scampered gleefully after Mobius, and another lay cradled in her arms. The dream was full of light and laughter—laughter unhindered by the ever-present tightness in her chest or the weakness in her limbs. She was well; she was whole. And everything, *everything*, was perfect, except of course...

"No!" Ilsa shouted, snapping herself from the fantasy. Chase startled, but Ilsa didn't heed him.

"A perfect future bought with the blood of my friend is a future I want no part of." Ilsa lifted her chin and looked her captain directly in the eye. "And a captain who would sacrifice his crew to his own ambition is not one that I can follow. It is my duty, as first officer, to inform you that you are unfit for further service, Adam Chase."

"Unfit? Unfit!" Chase staggered backward. "Look at *you!* There are days when you can hardly stand! And I am the one who is unfit?"

"Yuri is fighting for his life while you continue to poison your body and mind and take orders from that murderous snake. Every day you become more like him; you're turning into a madman—"

"Stop talking!"

"I will not!" Ilsa shouted. "While I have breath in my body I will not stand by and allow your blind ambition to kill us all!"

"Why can you not see how much I need this?" Chase threw up his hands. "I need to be healed."

"Yes," Ilsa said. Her throat tightened and her eyes stung with angry tears. "Yes, you do, Captain. But the healing you need has nothing at all to do with your leg."

White fury overtook Chase's face.

"Vandraak was right about you, you mutinous, defiant—" Chase lunged forward, snatching the gilded box that rested on his table. "I trusted you! You were supposed to stand by my side. And now you would destroy everything I've worked for."

Before Ilsa fully realized what he was doing, Chase had the dragonflame pistol in his hand. The weapon he'd once used to save Ilsa's life, he now leveled at her heart.

A shock of grief tore through Ilsa, so sharp and strong that for an instant she was certain the captain had already fired the gun. Even as he threatened her life, she didn't feel frightened, only sad. Deeply, unspeakably sad.

"I am not the one who will destroy you, Captain," she whispered. "You will destroy yourself."

The captain held her gaze for a breathless moment. Then his fierce expression crumpled. His shoulders sagged, and he lowered the pistol.

"Get out of my sight," he ordered, throwing the weapon down on the table. "Before I change my mind."

"I think we got on the wrong ship, Yuri."

Ilsa knelt by Yuri's straw pallet and laid a hand on his feverish cheek. The close, damp air in the infirmary was thick with the earthy aroma of herbs, but it couldn't mask the smell of death that hovered in the shadows.

Mobius dropped from Ilsa's shoulder and onto Yuri's bed. He nuzzled Yuri's shoulder, then looked up at Ilsa with eyes full of somber understanding. He knew death. He'd smelled it before.

Yuri's eyes fluttered open. Their golden glow was dim.

"*Yil'saa.*" Yuri's once-strong voice was nothing more than a strained rasp, barely audible through the howl of the storm.

"Don't speak," Ilsa whispered, squeezing his hand. "Save your strength."

"There...is nothing to save it for."

"Don't say that!" she urged him. "You're strong, Yuri. Tasha's herbs will help you heal. You're going to get well."

But Yuri's eyes drifted closed, and he shook his head slowly, weakly.

"I go to rest with my forefathers. My mother. And my..." he gasped a shuddering breath. "My little sister."

"No." Ilsa took his chin in both her hands and made him look in her eyes. "No, not your sister. I'm right here, Yuri. Stay here. Stay with me."

"You are my sister, but not sister by blood." His voice dropped to a ragged whisper. Ilsa had to lean in close to catch his words. "I lost her long ago. A scar on my heart that never healed. But the Creator gave me you, to love and protect in her place, and for this I am forever thankful."

Ilsa pressed her lips together and squeezed her eyes shut, but it did nothing to stop the wave of sorrow that rushed over her. She could feel Yuri fading, and she could do nothing to keep him.

"Yuri, we're going to get you through this. Remember, you have to go home. You have to take your father—" Ilsa choked back a sob. "Take him the Eelni spices, remember?"

Mobius looked from Yuri to Ilsa, as if unsure who to comfort. Yuri's gaze fell on the tammer, and the ghost of a smile flickered across his lips.

"You will take care of her for me, yes?" he whispered to Mobius.

Mobius sat up straight and looked Yuri in the eye. Though his ears drooped with sorrow, he raised his paw and placed it solemnly on Yuri's chest. A promise.

"*Yil'saa*, you make me a promise, too."

"Anything, Yuri," Ilsa said.

"I am born of earth. When I am gone, do not let my body rest in the sea."

With monumental effort, Yuri slowly lifted his hand and laid it over the gem that rested on his chest and pulled the cord free of its clasp.

"Take," he said. He placed the stone in Ilsa's hand.

"This firestone...a blessing from my people. It was born in sacred flame and contains the shadow of a firebird. The great beasts of my land, as dragons are of yours. I have carried this stone many years, and now it must at last carry me." Yuri drew a long, ragged breath.

"When I am gone, break the stone. Release the firebird. And let it carry me away."

"Yuri, I can't—"

"Promise."

Ilsa clasped the firestone's living warmth to her heart, unable to speak. Yuri murmured something that she couldn't make out, and then he fell silent. His breathing was shallow but persistent as he slipped into a fevered sleep. Mobius curled up at his side, lending comfort for as long as he could.

"I'll make you a promise of my own," Ilsa whispered. She tied the cord around her neck; the stone pendant rested heavily against her chest. "I won't stop fighting for you, Yuri. I'll do whatever it takes."

GRANDFATHER'S WATCH, its crystal face illuminated by the firestone's red glow, told Ilsa it was nearing three. The witching hour, some called it, when darkness was at its thickest and human hearts were weakest to its pull.

Outside, the wind shrieked like demons and the thunder threatened to rip the sky in two. *Relentless* shuddered as if in the throes of a fever.

Ilsa tucked the stone into her blouse, hiding its light. She felt her way through the darkness of the corridor until her outstretched hands brushed against the smooth wood panels of the captain's door. The creak of hinges was lost among the constant groaning of the ship. She slipped inside, silent as a shadow.

A single moonstone lantern hung from the ceiling, swinging wildly with the tossing of the ship. Twisted shadows lurched across the stateroom in a drunken, eerie dance. A glimmer of pale light flickered unnaturally across the shards of the broken mirror, glancing off its jagged edges like a flash of lightning.

By its light, Ilsa could make out a shadow in the center of the room; Captain Chase lay slumped over his charting table, his face buried in his arms.

Ilsa froze, biting back a gasp. The captain was deathly still. It wasn't until she could make out the steady rise and fall of his hunched shoulders that Ilsa was even sure he was breathing.

As Ilsa stepped cautiously closer, she discovered the explanation. The stateroom was thick with the heavy, sickly-sweet aroma of Chase's pain-numbing drug.

"You scoundrel," Ilsa breathed. Ice-cold fury seized her chest. His crew was fighting for their lives. Yuri was dying. And the captain was here, drowning his own suffering.

All at once, Ilsa realized she hated him. She hated him with a rage stronger and fiercer than any she'd ever felt.

"Selfish, weak fool." She no longer feared waking him; she knew it would take far more than the sound of her voice to rouse him from his drugged slumber.

The pistol he'd threatened her with still lay on the table, loaded and within her reach. Possibilities raced through her mind as it rested in her hand, heavy with cold finality.

Had she really reached for it?

Kill a dragon all at once, or not at all...to let a wounded dragon live is a mistake for which there is no forgiveness.

Ilsa squeezed her eyes shut and her heart began to race.

Chase would die instantly. Painlessly. Upon his death, command of the ship would pass by default to his first officer.

The hand that rests on the helm in your stead is the hand that will dispel the threat and set all to rights.

All it would take was a single moment of heartless resolve.

With full command of the ship and its resources, she could change the course of this voyage for everyone. No more Vandraak. No more mad rush to the edge of the world.

She could save Yuri's life.

"The greatest threat to this ship is no dragon, captain." Ilsa raised the pistol slowly. Her hand felt like it wasn't her own; her voice sounded like it was coming from somewhere dark and distant. "And by this hand that threat will be dispelled. I will set it all to rights."

A blast of thunder like a gunshot exploded through the night. A flash illuminated the stateroom as lightning momentarily flooded the darkness with searing light. Ilsa startled, biting back a cry of alarm. She threw a panicked glance over her shoulder, and her eyes caught on the mirror's broken reflection. It wasn't her own face that stared back from the marred glass.

Through the mirror's crooked shards, Adam Chase's haunted eyes met hers. Then the light flickered out, leaving them both adrift in darkness even thicker than before.

"Captain?" Ilsa whispered, hardly daring to breathe. The pistol dropped to her side. She pressed it against her leg, concealing it between the damp folds of her skirt. "Adam, are you awake?"

No response.

She stepped closer to the table and laid a hand on his shoulder. Chase didn't stir. She shook him, but in his drugged state, he didn't so much as groan at her touch. He was as responsive as a corpse.

Ilsa let out a tight breath. She wiped cold sweat off of her temple with a shaking hand. She was so sure he'd looked up, so certain she'd seen his bloodshot eyes flicker with fear in the split second he'd seen her standing over him with a gun.

You're only imagining things. You have to do this. You have to set it to rights.

Ilsa shook herself. Her fingers tightened around the pistol and she raised it again—though this time it felt much colder and heavier in her hand.

"The hand...the hand that..." Ilsa's whisper quavered despite her attempt to bolster her shaken resolve. "That...raiseth the stormy wind, and lifteth up the waves thereof..."

Ilsa froze, the words dying on her lips as she realized what she'd said. Vandraak's prophecy, interrupted by the Creator's promise. Words hidden so deeply in her heart that she'd hardly noticed when they surfaced.

The rest of the Sailor's Prayer flooded her mind unbidden:

Their soul is melted because of trouble. They are at their wit's end. Then they cry to the Lord in their trouble, and he bringeth them out of their distresses.

Ilsa stared at the pistol in her hand, wrestling with her choice. If she didn't kill the captain, he'd kill himself and the whole crew with him. Chase's mad ambition would destroy everyone on this ship, but Ilsa had the power to stop him. In fact, she had a *duty* to stop him. Didn't Vandraak say—?

Whose words are you going to listen to, Ilsa?

The question was a deathblow.

Ilsa sank to her knees in surrender. The captain's pistol clattered to the floor beside her, and she buried her face in her hands. Tears long stifled streamed down her cheeks. For the first time since leaving home, Ilsa let herself cry.

Then they cry to the Lord in their trouble, and he bringeth them out of their distresses.

"Oh God, help me," she gasped. "Help us all."

The only answer was the sound of a shuddering breath as Captain Chase stirred in his sleep. Ilsa sat upright. How long had she been here? She wasn't sure, but she needed to get out.

Ilsa staggered to her feet and backed away from the table, leaving the pistol on the ground. Chase groaned in a fitful dream as Ilsa slipped out of the captain's quarters and closed the stateroom door softly behind her.

She nearly collided with someone in the corridor just beyond the door.

"Ilsa!" The light of a moonstone lantern danced merrily across Tasha's grinning face. Both her shout and her smile were jarring after the intensity of the last few minutes.

"What? What's wrong?"

Tasha took no notice of Ilsa's panic, as if there was nothing at all unnatural about meeting outside of the captain's quarters at three in the morning.

"Don't you feel it?" the harpooner grabbed Ilsa in a tight hug. "Don't you *hear* it?"

"I don't hear anything."

"Exactly!" Tasha laughed. "No wind, no rain! We made it! At long last, we made it. The storm is over."

PART THREE

The Edge of the World

A. Chase, Owner, Captain, and Commander

H. V. RELENTLESS OF MAP'S END, OUTER MELVIA

Let this account serve as a formal indictment against one Ilsa Starling, sometime first officer aboard the same.

I do solemnly swear and testify that in the course of our voyage it became necessary for the health of the ship to remove Miss Starling from her position for reasons stated below:

- She has allowed personal concerns to interfere with her duties as an officer

- She has repeatedly insinuated that my need for medical treatment renders me less than able to lead our crew

- She has displayed open animosity toward my trusted advisor on multiple occasions

- She has ascribed false motives to my actions, making me out to be at best, ignorant of the dangers that lay ahead, and at worst, a willful murderer of my own crew

All of this I might have overlooked, had Miss Starling not taken a direct and immovable stand against my position as captain, and then encouraged the crew to do the same. She left me with no choice but to take preventative action before she compromised the very integrity of my ship and its authority structure.

The decisive incident arose over a disagreement concerning the proper course of action while crossing the storm band. Hot words were exchanged between Miss Starling and myself, which by my reckoning were merely the natural result of the tense situation and should not have been regarded with much significance. However, upon reaching the peace of the Final Sea, Miss Starling again challenged my authority. This time she staged her defiance in front of the crew, using the arguments we'd had in the storms as evidence of my inability to command my ship. She advocated for my immediate replacement—presumably with herself.

Let it be known that my crew was, without exception, loyal to me. That in itself should speak volumes about the legitimacy of Miss Starling's slanderous claims of my ineptitude.

Considering the forewritten account, and in accordance with the laws of Outer Melvia and the articles of this ship, I do hereby charge Miss Starling with contempt of authority, insubordination, and conspiracy—in short, mutiny.

Far from all jurisdictions but that of the heartless sea, I was advised by some to execute immediate justice by my own hand. I elected to refrain from exercising that right—though I doubt either Her Excellency the Magistrate or our blessed Creator would have faulted me if I had. As it stands, Miss Starling is confined to quarters for the remainder of the voyage and will be surrendered to the proper authorities when we make port.

*S*IGNED,

Adam Chase, Captain

*W*ITNESSED,

Vandraak Seafang, First Mate

CHAPTER THIRTEEN

The Final Sea

"You've got ten minutes. After that, I can't cover for you anymore."

The muffled voice from the other side of the door roused Ilsa from a shallow sleep. She sat up stiffly and rubbed her bleary eyes. A metallic creak announced a key in the lock; she didn't have time to smooth her matted hair before someone on the other side pushed the stubborn hinges open. A shaft of light spilled into the dank storage closet that had served as Ilsa's cell for the last three days, leaving her blinking against the sudden brightness. Then a tall figure stooped through the doorway, blocking the glare.

"Yuri!"

Ilsa couldn't muster the strength to rise from the damp straw pallet, but she didn't have to. Yuri dropped to his knees beside her and gathered her into an embrace. She crumpled into his stony arms. Tears of relief flooded her vision as she pressed her face against his broad, carved chest. He was a little paler than she remembered, a little thinner, and his chest and face bore the lingering marks of his wounds. But each of his thundering heartbeats served to hammer in the reassuring truth: he was alive.

"I hadn't heard, nobody's been allowed in to tell me—" Ilsa gasped between sobs. "I was so worried."

"The Creator did not will my time to be over yet," Yuri

rumbled. "Though perhaps he considered it a little longer than I would have liked."

"What are you doing here? How did you even get in? I haven't seen anyone at all since—"

"*Yil'saa.*" Yuri held her at arm's length. He tilted her chin upward and studied her face with concern etched into his brow. Ilsa couldn't imagine how dreadful she must've looked. Her strength had waned rapidly since she'd seen him last. Or perhaps it only felt that way since she no longer had any reason to push herself to perform through sheer force of will.

"I am sorry I have been sick," Yuri said. "You should not be left with no one to look out for you. You get into trouble."

"Yes, Yuri, this is all your fault, of course." Ilsa looked away with a self-conscious chuckle. She reached up to tug on her ribbon out of habit, forgetting that it had long since been lost. Her tangled hair hung loose over her shoulders. If Phillip's mother could see her now, she'd never make another sideways comment about Ilsa's braid again.

"Is it true what they say?" Yuri asked. "You led mutiny against the captain? When Tashtanna told me, I feared I had passed from this life and woken in much stranger one."

"'Led a mutiny' is a very generous description for what I did." Ilsa rolled her eyes. "Who phrased it like that, Radney? He's got a talent for blowing things out of proportion."

"That does not answer what I asked."

"If you're asking whether or not I told the crew that I think Captain Chase is no longer fit to command this ship, then yes. I did. And for the record, I did it in a respectful and diplomatic manner."

"It is clear to me that the captain did not feel respect."

"No, I suppose not."

"You have not yet told me why."

"He's not in his right mind, Yuri," Ilsa said. "He's so hell-bent on killing that dragon that he can't see that he's killing himself. Vandraak has got him mixing raw oil into his blood. He's drugging himself just to be able to stand. Don't tell me you can't see a difference in him."

"He is not the only one I see change in."

Was that a bit of pride in his voice?

"What news from on deck?"

Yuri grimaced. "The crew is nervous. No one likes taking orders from Vandraak. They sense trouble, but do not quite know why."

Ilsa closed her eyes and leaned her head back against the planks.

"I wish I could've stopped it all," she murmured.

"I would have stood beside you."

"I know you would."

"Tashtanna did not?"

Ilsa shook her head. "You know she won't oppose the captain directly, even when she disagrees with him."

Yuri grunted agreement. "Mobius misses you."

"You can tell him the feeling is mutual," Ilsa said. Her heart twisted at the thought of the tammer, anxious and restless without her nearby. But she wouldn't wish him here with her, confined in a tight, dark hole.

"One thing I do not understand," Yuri said. "Tashtanna tells me you charged her with Mobius's care before you challenged the captain. You did not think you would succeed?"

Ilsa shrugged. Of course she'd known her chances of deposing Chase peacefully were close to nonexistent. It would take more than unease to make a Map's End crew turn on their captain.

"But you did it anyway, knowing this?" Yuri asked.

"I didn't like my other option," Ilsa said.

Yuri frowned, an unspoken question written on his face.

"I almost killed him, Yuri," Ilsa whispered, hating to admit it aloud, even to him.

The Stoneman's eyes widened, but he did not interrupt.

"In the storms," she went on. "I made up my mind to kill him and take command of the ship by force. I had the perfect opportunity. His pistol was in my hand. I aimed it at his skull."

Ilsa shuddered at the memory.

"It felt like... like I had nothing to lose. And that maybe if I did it, I could fix it all." Ilsa looked up and met Yuri's eyes. "But I couldn't take his life."

"You did well."

"No, I did nothing. I simply *didn't* do something wrong. That wasn't enough," Ilsa said. "When all this is said and done, I don't want to be remembered as someone who was complicit by my lack of action."

"So you told the crew he was unfit to lead, and tried to get him removed from command?"

"You asked me why I challenged him, and that's why," Ilsa said. "I'm at peace with my decisions."

"They hang mutineers," Yuri said.

"I suppose that's true."

"You are not afraid?"

Afraid? No. If Captain Chase wanted to have her killed, he could've done it already, and no law would stop him. Ilsa didn't know why he'd spared her, but she hadn't had much energy to waste on fear.

"It's a long voyage back to shore," she said.

"You are unwell, *Yil'saa.*"

"Mm," Ilsa agreed. "I have been for a long time."

"But it is worse now," Yuri said. "You need sunlight. Fresh air.

Your kind was not made to live in the depths. I speak to the captain."

"Don't get yourself into trouble on my account."

"Perhaps I should have said the same to you?" Yuri raised his eyebrows.

"Fair enough." Ilsa gave a weak smile. She reached up and pulled the firestone pendant over her head. "Here. I kept it safe for you. Thank God, we won't need it after all."

Yuri looked at the gemstone in his palm for a long moment before speaking again.

"Before I give you that stone, I never ask anything of you."

That was true enough, and secretly Ilsa had always been grateful. It was difficult to disappoint someone who never expected much.

"You believe you are not worth it," Yuri said. "You do not want to be loved, for you fear you have nothing to give in return. You are wrong. You have been wrong since the moment you left me in the Edgewater inn."

Yuri's gentle words stung. Ilsa dropped her face to hide her tears.

"Don't tell me your life wouldn't be easier if you'd never met me," she whispered.

"It would be, yes. But what gives you idea I want ease?" Yuri lifted her chin. "You are a burden, *Yil'saa.* But my Creator made me with strong arms. I count it an honor to spend my strength to carry you."

Ilsa crumpled, and Yuri pulled her back into his embrace.

"Do not despair," he said. "Do not give up. Forget this lie that your life does not matter. I want you to live. If you cannot do it because it is right, then do it for me. For Tasha and Mobius and all those who love you. You are worth it to us all. Live."

Ilsa nodded through tears. She could try, for Yuri. For Tasha and Mobius.

For Phillip.

"Sail ho! All hands to stations!" The muffled cry came from above.

Yuri looked up. "I must go. Tashtanna will be in trouble if it is known she let me in here."

He squeezed her hand in parting.

"Stay strong, little sister."

"WHAT'VE WE GOT, CAPTAIN?"

Chase looked up as Tasha dropped from the rigging and stood beside him. She'd stayed closer to his side more than usual in the last few days, though neither of them mentioned it. As much as he wished he could order her away, he had to admit, at least to himself, that he needed her help. Chase may have made Vandraak his first officer in Ilsa's stead, but the dragonblood still preferred to spend most of his time lurking in the shadows rather than assisting with any real duties on board.

Ilsa Starling's tammer scampered up, just a few steps behind Tasha. Ever since being separated from his mistress, he'd dogged Tasha's steps wherever she went. Chase turned away, not wanting to look at the ever-present reminder of Ilsa's betrayal.

Chase pointed into the distance, squinting against the cold, pale sunlight. The sky to the south was a solid wall of black cloud. But it was in their wake. Now the only thing standing between *Relentless* and the Edge was the Final Sea, a pale, shallow stretch of ocean whose tranquility belied its danger.

That, and the Map's End ship that sat low in the water on the eastern horizon.

"It's the *Shepherdess*," Chase said, snapping his spyglass shut with a growl of disgust. Stupid name for a Hunting vessel; he'd always thought so. Far too pastoral and nurturing a name for a ship exiled to the most savage seas in the world.

"That would be Abel Hawthorne's boat, wouldn't it?" Tasha's question was unnecessary. They both knew the captain of the familiar ship.

"Unless by some mercy he's sold the blasted thing, yes."

Tasha arched her eyebrows at Chase, but he deliberately turned away. He was in no mood for her judgment, and she ought to know better than to push him now. A rough go in the storm band always shortened his patience, but after the trouble with Ilsa, his temper had been particularly raw.

A streak of purple light shot up from the *Shepherdess*. The dragonflame flare arced across the sky before fizzling out in a puff of shimmering smoke.

"Looks like she's hailing us, sir."

"I have eyes, Tashtanna," Chase snapped.

Tasha shook her head as she bent to scoop Mobius into her arms. "Hawthorne's about to get eaten alive," she muttered under her breath.

Barely a minute after the flare went up, a chaser boat launched from the *Shepherdess's* deck.

"Wasting oil in a place like this?" Chase muttered as the little boat streaked toward him through the sky. Only a fool would get skyborne for a distance that could easily be rowed.

The wind was with the chaser, and its pilot—and lone occupant, Chase noted—was generous with the oil he cranked onto its sails. He came in for a swift landing on *Relentless's* deck.

"Chase! Thank God." Abel Hawthorne, a burly, bearded sailor

whose build and manner Chase had always thought would be more suited to a fishing trawler than a quarterdeck, leapt from his boat the moment it touched down. "When we saw your sails break out from the storms a few days past, we knew the Creator was with us."

"Perhaps he's been so busy attending to your troubles that he's forgotten to do anything about mine," Chase growled.

Hawthorne raised a bushy eyebrow. "Hard crossing?"

"We had an explosion in the hold," Chase said. "We lost a good bit of oil, and it nearly killed a crewman. It took three times what I estimated to get through. And no sooner had we escaped the storms than I had to quell a rebellion against my leadership."

"Sounds like your woes have been...relentless."

Chase glared at Hawthorne.

"Right. I forgot." Hawthorne chuckled. "This is why we aren't friends. Forgive the jest, Adam."

He clapped Chase on the shoulder. Chase fought the urge to recoil from the friendly gesture. Abel Hawthorne's propensity for making jests at inappropriate times was not the only reason the two weren't friends, but it certainly didn't help his chances. Ever since they were boys working together on the same ship, Chase had hated the way Hawthorne would make light of even the darkest circumstances. In fact, the more dire the situation, the more likely it was that Hawthorne's foolish laughter would make an appearance.

"*Relentless* does seem a bit worse for wear. Bring the old girl over and tie off alongside," Hawthorne said. "My men can help you repair and regroup from the storms. We'll make a regular gam of it, like the old days."

"We don't need your charity, Hawthorne."

"Perhaps not." Hawthorne frowned, then looked over his shoulder, back toward his own ship. "But we need yours."

"What do you want?" Chase's patience was waning. "Say it outright and be quick with it."

"It's my wife, Mary. She's with child, and the baby's coming. It's not her time yet, and Mary's been in hard labor for over a day—"

"I'll get my things," Tasha said. She leaned her harpoon against the mast and started off belowdecks.

"Await orders, Tashtanna."

"But I can help!"

Chase waved a hand to silence her. Tasha turned on her heel and stomped to the hatch, with Mobius bounding away after her. Chase's ire rose at her obvious snub to his orders, but he didn't call out after her. Not in front of the likes of Abel Hawthorne. The last thing he wanted was to hear Hawthorne's opinions on his relational tension.

"Why do you need my help?" Chase asked Hawthorne. "What happened to your surgeon?"

"Mary *is* the surgeon."

Of course she would be.

"Your first mistake was conceiving a child at sea. A Hunting ship is no respectable place to give birth."

"Stars above, Adam," Hawthorne swore. "You act as if I planned it particularly to spite you. It's been two years since I left port. I wasn't even a married man when we set sail. You of all people know that life goes on during long voyages. Weren't you born belowdecks yourself?"

"Precisely why I believe that sort of thing can wait until you reach port."

"Forgive me for not consulting you first!" Hawthorne burst out in a peal of nervous laughter. There it was; of course he was laughing at a time like this. Chase fixed him with a hard stare until his grin melted off of his face.

"Oh stars, you're really serious. Please, Chase," Hawthorne begged. "I need help. My wife and child—we need your help. I don't know how much longer she can fight like this on her own."

"How early is the baby?"

"About a month."

Chase shook his head.

"I can't help you, Hawthorne. Go and comfort your wife."

"Adam!"

Chase ignored Hawthorne's cry and turned to address his crew.

"Radney, Pippin, get aloft. Full sails and make ready to heave to."

"Curse your stone heart, Adam Chase!" Hawthorne shouted after him.

"And somebody get that man off my boat," Chase added.

Tasha reappeared, stuffing her herbalist's kit into a woven bag she'd slung over her shoulder. She glanced from Hawthorne up into the rigging at the Steelkilt brothers, climbing to the spars.

"You're not setting sail!" she exclaimed. "Adam, you can't—"

"A child born that early might survive if he was born on a fine estate and handled with kid gloves by a team of the best physicians money could employ," Chase said. "But to be born in the bowels of a Hunter at the Edge with only a half-trained herbalist's apprentice to care for him? Not a chance."

Pale anger washed out Tasha's features.

"To blazes with the chances! You're not seriously going to keep me from helping them!"

"Tell me what good it would do!" Chase snapped. "Meanwhile, we have an actual reason to keep on toward our goal without needless delay—"

"Are you the Creator of life, that you think you can choose when it no longer matters?"

"You're not saving them any suffering."

"If you can't see the value in taking a stand for what's right even when you know you won't be able to change the outcome—" Tasha fumed. "Well, then maybe you should ask Ilsa Starling. I'm sure she'd be happy to explain it to you."

Her words struck Chase like a blow. Never once since his confrontation with Ilsa had Tash so much as hinted that she might disagree with him. Had she secretly harbored thoughts that Ilsa was in the right this whole time? The thought was frightening. Tasha's fierce Eelni loyalty, the one thing Chase had never imagined losing, was slipping away.

"If you defy me," he said. "Then you can prepare to join her! Get out of my way; I've got a ship to command."

But Tasha did not back down.

"The man I married would never have left a mother and child in need of—"

Anger and pain surged over Chase like a tidal wave. He grabbed Tasha by the shoulders and shook her, cutting off her words. He'd told her never to speak of their short-lived marriage, not in front of the crew. How dare she weaponize it against him now?

"I am no longer the man you married!" He shouted. "The man you married is dead, Tashtanna! How many times do I have to tell you that before you'll realize it?"

Chase let go, shoving her away from him. Tasha stared at him for a frozen moment, stricken.

"I think that was the last time, Captain," she said at last. Tears filled her eyes and her lower lip trembled, but she held her head high. She stepped over to her chaser and retrieved her harpoon, then held it out to him. "Please accept my resignation."

A stab of pain like a firebrand shot through Chase's heart. He did not take the weapon.

"I refuse it."

"Then feel free to press charges for my desertion when you're back ashore," Tasha said. She dropped the harpoon. It clattered to the deck before him and rolled against his boot. "You're going to have to start a list soon if you keep up at this rate."

"If you walk away from me now, you turn your back on everything we've worked for—"

"Captain Hawthorne!" Tasha called, not letting him finish the threat. "I'm coming with you. No, Mobius, you stay—"

"That creature is no longer welcome here." Chase interrupted, glaring at the tammer.

"You don't mean that," Tasha said, gathering Mobius into her arms. "Be angry with Ilsa, be angry with me, but Mobius hasn't done—"

"Get that infernal rat off of my boat before I have it tied in a sack and drowned." Chase growled. Tasha pressed her lips together, looking like she might argue. But a glance at the *Shepherdess* off the starboard bow seemed to remind her that there were more important issues waiting for her. Tasha swept the deck with a final look, seeking out Yuri.

"You'll tell Ilsa?" she asked him.

The Stoneman nodded solemnly, and Tasha turned away.

Chase stood, rooted to the deck, unable to stop her as she boarded Hawthorne's chaser. His chest felt hollow, as if Tasha had torn out his heart and taken it with her. He wanted to call out, to plead with her. He wanted to grab her, hold her back.

You can't leave now! His mind screamed after her. *We're so close. Just give me a few more days... I'll fix it.*

But he said nothing. He merely stood by as she slipped from his life. Tasha looked back once, only after she was settled in the bow of Hawthorne's chaser with Mobius on her lap. Captain Hawthorne loosed the oil valve, and the chaser shuddered to life.

"Goodbye, Adam."

Then she was gone. Chase watched mutely as the skyborne boat raced off, back toward the *Shepherdess*.

Chase turned away, and his ivory peg caught on Tasha's harpoon, the one she'd carried on every hunt of her career, the one that bore carved testament to every dragon she'd felled.

And she'd thrown it all away.

She'd thrown him away.

Chase stooped and snatched the harpoon by its iron barb, blinded by fevered fury. With an animal cry of rage and pain, he swung the weapon at the mast with all the might he could muster. The harpoon's wooden shaft splintered on impact. Chase flung the broken pieces down, breathing hard.

"Orders, Captain?" Brigid's cautious question brought his attention back to his own ship. Chase looked up to see his few remaining sailors watching him with alarm.

"They have already been given." Chase spoke through clenched teeth. He turned his back on the *Shepherdess* and set his face to the north. "Full sail to the Edge. We go on."

CHAPTER FOURTEEN

White Devil

RELENTLESS LAY AT ANCHOR in the shallow sea, a silhouette against the full moon. The ship was silent as a coffin; a lone figure stood watch on the deck.

Adam Chase stared at the empty horizon, stiff and unmoving. Sleep evaded him that night, as it often had for the past nine.

Nine days. Nine days since Hawthorne's sails had disappeared astern, taking Tashtanna with them. Nine days of his crew tiptoeing around him like he was a leaking oil cask, liable to explode at any moment. Nine days of patrolling, back and forth, slowly, cautiously, as close to the eternal drop as he dared. And for what? Nothing.

Nothing, nothing, nothing.

Chase clenched a fist. Vandraak's promises rang hollow. Faber's charts proved useless. No sight of so much as a fish in these barren seas.

A whisper of a breeze passed over the reefed sails. It was barely more than a breath, but on a night so still, it was enough to draw his gaze up through the sails and spars. The lookout's perch on the maintop stood empty, but for a moment Chase felt as though he could almost see a small figure sitting there—a boy, with two legs and big dreams, gazing at the mysteries beyond the edge of the world for the first of many times.

Chase shuddered, and the ghost of his memory vanished, leaving behind a void he could only describe as longing. How many times had he sat at the lookout, settled amongst the rigging so naturally that he felt a part of the ship itself? He'd watched more sunrises from the maintop than he'd ever spent in a pew. How many whispered prayers had risen to heaven from that holy perch? There he'd dreamed of greatness. There he'd hidden his boyhood tears. There he'd whispered lovers' vows. There he'd been at peace.

Perhaps, up there...

Chase glanced down at his stump of a leg, weighing his odds.

He cursed under his breath. He hated the need to pause and consider whether he should attempt something so trivial, something he'd taken for granted all his life. He shoved his doubts aside and took hold of the ropes. He swung himself upward, straining his arms and letting his ivory leg drag limply behind.

The climb was agony, but Chase pushed through. He'd pay for it later, he had no doubt, but no matter. He had strength to waste, and more where it came from. He swallowed back the bitter bile that rose in his throat at the thought of leeching toxic oil into his veins later.

He wouldn't be dependent on it forever. That's what Vandraak told him. Just until he could gain enough strength that his body would be able to heal on its own. It didn't matter if he had to take a little more now to make that happen. He could reclaim it in the end. He would take it back.

Panting with effort, Chase finally gained the summit. He found himself face to face with a carving at the top of the mast. He didn't need to get closer to read it; he'd put it there himself, on a night that felt a thousand years past. *Adam loves Tash.*

Anger flared in Chase's heart at the sight of it. He had loved her, once. He probably still did.

But some things were unfixable, even with magic.

Chase turned sharply away. The lookout's perch was nothing but a scrap of weathered wood that would afford him a marginally better view of the sea. Anything else he'd attributed to it was nothing more than sentiment, and sentiment was weakness.

The captain took a stiff seat and set his face toward the horizon, a sentinel in the darkness.

Silent hours slipped by as the moon sank deeper into the rippling sea. Its silver light had almost vanished when Chase was roused from his stillness like one broken out of a trance. He shook himself, haunted by the suspicion that something had happened, and he'd missed it, like a dream that vanished before it could be recalled.

What had caught his eye?

Ignoring the pain that shot through his leg, Chase pulled himself upright. He stood at the edge of the platform, gripping the spar above him to steady himself. His eyes strained against the darkness, trying to recapture whatever it was that had been different a moment ago.

But after a few silent minutes, the thrill faded. Only a lingering trace of moonlight, magnified by a rolling wave. That's all it could have been.

Chase grunted and stretched his stiff muscles. It had been foolish, coming up here. Now he had to get himself down, and he didn't relish the thought of that undertaking. But he'd sooner fall to his death than call for help, especially now that—

There.

Chase whipped his attention back out to sea. There it was again, about three or four ship-lengths to his stern. On the water, pale against the blackened deep, rose a shape like the slope of a great white snowhill rising from the sea.

Chase's blood ran cold. He gripped the spar and leaned out as far as he could without losing his balance. A shiver trembled through his shoulders.

The shape was unmistakable. He'd seen it hundreds of times. It was a dragon.

Chase didn't dare to take a breath as the dragon slowly surfaced. The beast's nostrils broke through the water first with a sharp hiss. Two parallel jets of steam shot skyward as dragon's hot breath met the frozen night air.

The rest of the dragon's head followed, moving slowly, smoothly, through the dreamlike stillness of the sea. Chase half wondered if it was a hallucination, a mirage conceived by his desperation and desire. But the moment the dragon's slitted eyes appeared above the surface of the sea, his doubts faded. He could never forget what it felt like to look into those eyes. White as death, gleaming with a pale light of their own. A piercing, hypnotic stare that was horrible to meet but impossible to ignore.

Chase shut his eyes and clenched his jaw, but he wasn't quick enough to shut out the memory that overtook him like a waking nightmare. Clinging to the monster's face just below that achromatic lens as the dragon writhed and spiraled in the sky beyond the Edge, trying to throw him into the fathomless abyss.

"Not this time," Chase swore. He sagged against the mast, sweat-soaked and shaking.

And still the dragon glided ever nearer. Its great wings unfurled, slicing silently through the ink-black sea. For an instant, the dragon was directly beneath the ship. From his vantage point, Chase could see its full form: head and neck extending past the bowsprit, a wing each to port and starboard, and its tail stretching far beyond the stern. Chase's ship looked no more significant than a small, dark scar above the monster's back.

Avatheon passed under *Relentless*, a specter beneath the waves. The ship groaned as the dragon's back scraped along the hull.

In a heartbeat, the monster had passed, its highly specialized wings and tail propelling it far faster than any man-made vessel could hope to imitate. Once it was beyond the ship, the dragon surfaced again to breathe. Then, with a low, sonorous moan that Chase felt reverberating in his own ribcage, it turned downward and began to dive. The spines on its back arced above the waves as its lithe body made the turn. At last, all that remained visible of the monster was its broad-finned tail, which fanned skyward in a somber salute to the stars.

IN THE HEART OF THE SHIP, Ilsa was praying.

Something had awoken her deep in the dead watches of the night; she didn't know what, but it didn't matter. At first, she'd tried to go back to sleep, but soon gave up the effort. A looming, heart-pounding dread took hold inside of her and kept her from settling.

And so, she prayed.

At first her words were faltering; it had been so long since she'd tried to form anything close to a petition to the Creator. It never seemed to do any good. Prayer only served to plant hope that would inevitably shrivel in the drought of divine silence. Just a waste of precious breath.

But as the night wore on, her prayers came faster, her words more earnest, like a torrent of rain on parched ground.

There was plenty to pray for; the stream of news that Yuri whispered through her door in the evenings had grown bleaker with each passing day. Ilsa prayed for the voyage, for what was to come. She prayed for Mobius, no doubt having a restless night of his own so far from her. She prayed for Abel Hawthorne's wife and child, though she doubted she would ever learn their fate.

And she prayed for Adam Chase.

"He's so lost," Ilsa whispered in the darkness. "Why can't he see that in his desperation to heal his body, he's destroying everything that's worth saving?"

Ilsa rubbed tears from her eyes with the heel of her hand.

"Please, God. I don't ask for my own healing. I can accept the path you've set me on, and I can learn to be grateful. But please, for his own sake...for Tasha's...for us all...please save Captain Chase."

No sooner had she spoken the captain's name than a sudden jolt interrupted her. *Relentless* shook with a long, scraping shudder, as if something had raked across the bottom of the ship, just on the other side of the hull from where Ilsa lay. She sat upright with a start. Had the ship run aground? No, that couldn't be it; they weren't even sailing. She remembered hearing the order to drop anchor given early in the evening.

Before she could run through more possibilities, a deep chord vibrated through the hull—a long, sad note that pierced her heart with a thousand pangs of longing, yearning, and regret. The sound faded to silence, like the last vibrations of a funeral knell, but it was a silence completely unlike it had been a moment ago. Where there had been restless anticipation and dread, now only hollow resignation and acceptance remained.

A click of a key in the lock broke the spell.

"Miss Starling."

Captain Chase stood in the doorway.

It had been nearly two weeks since she'd seen him, and the time had not been kind. Dark shadows sagged beneath his hollow eyes and his skin seemed stretched across his bones. His once-glossy hair was tangled and matted, and a scraggly, untended beard clung to his chin. Pale silver light from his moonstone lantern washed any color from his haggard face, giving him a corpselike pallor eerily reminiscent of Vandraak.

"You look terrible," Chase said.

"Thank you."

"Come with me. I need to show you something."

That was it? No further explanation? No mention of the fact that she was imprisoned for mutiny by his orders? Ilsa hesitated, a twinge of fear crawling along the back of her neck.

But when the captain put out his hand, she took it. Chase helped Ilsa to her feet, and even put out a steadying hand when she stumbled.

Ilsa followed in silence as Chase limped up the companionway stairs to the open deck. She breathed deeply of the cold night air, savoring its freshness. Whatever he meant by bringing her out here, Ilsa didn't care. It was enough to be grateful for that moment.

Chase led her to the starboard bow and passed her his spyglass, just as he had so many times before. Ilsa took it without question and raised it in the direction he pointed.

At first, she saw nothing in the inky sea. Chase steadied the glass, directing it toward a slightly elevated roll in the waves a few furlongs away. Ilsa focused on it. For a moment, she thought she could see a slight splash.

"That's him," the captain said in a voice completely matter-of-fact and devoid of emotion.

"Him?"

"The dragon."

His simple statement cast a chill over Ilsa's heart. She lowered the glass and looked at Chase, but the captain's gaze was fixed beyond, toward the sea.

"We've come twenty thousand miles for this moment," Chase said.

"I didn't imagine it being so quiet."

"And I will not be denied my destiny." He went on, as if he hadn't heard her. "You will stand as witness to it, whether you help me or not."

"I do want to help you," Ilsa said, and she meant it. She meant it more than she'd ever meant anything in her life.

Chase looked at her with such hope in his eyes that it nearly broke Ilsa's heart.

"Just... tell me one thing, Captain," she said, gently laying her hand over his on the railing. "If we succeed, what then? We kill the dragon. We live to tell the tale. Vandraak's promises prove true, and you get your strength back. You walk off this ship on two legs, fully restored." Ilsa took a deep breath, then spoke her question into the still night air. "Will it be enough?"

"Why would you ask me that?" Chase said, jerking away from her touch. "If I don't have that hope, I have nothing. If I cannot kill this dragon, I am not going home. This is my last chance."

"No, there is so much more for you. Please don't throw your life away."

"What, like you threw yours away?" Chase rolled his eyes at her.

"What?"

"You led a mutiny, Starling, and you knew it would fail before you started. If that's not the work of someone with a death wish, I don't know what is."

"I'm sorry it came to that," Ilsa said. "But I couldn't stand by and watch you destroy this ship and its crew without at least trying to stop it."

"What does it matter to you?" Chase spat. "You're dying anyway."

Ilsa had often wondered how she would feel when someone finally spoke the truth aloud. Now that it came to it, she didn't feel much. Tired, mostly, and a little relieved to drop the lie, but that was it.

"Everyone's dying, Captain," Ilsa said. "Some of us are just... going about it a little faster."

"I knew it," Chase muttered.

"When?"

"I pointed a pistol at your heart, and you didn't even flinch." Chase gave a short laugh. "I had my suspicions before, but that was my confirmation. Stars, if you'd shown even a little fear, I might've pulled the trigger. But you just looked at me."

"I came on this voyage expecting not to make it home," Ilsa admitted. "Whether that meant my heart failed...or a dragon ate me... or you shot me...it didn't seem to make much difference."

"You're a piece of work, Ilsa Starling." Chase shook his head. "I'm tempted to admire you for it."

"Don't; I've changed my mind."

"Oh? What brought that about, may I ask?"

"You did."

Chase cut a questioning glance at her.

"I looked in the mirror and saw you," Ilsa said. "We're two sides of the same coin, you and I. You, too proud to surrender to Providence. And I, too despairing to see the purpose in pain. You, fighting to be healed at the cost of everything that would make that healing worthwhile. And I, trying so hard not to burden anyone with my own pain that I only made it worse for those who wanted to stand beside me."

"Neither one of us getting what we wanted," Chase said.

"Because what we want isn't what we need." Ilsa put her hand over his. The captain flinched, but he didn't pull away. "You don't have to do this, Adam. Call off the hunt. No matter how things end with that dragon, it won't fix what's broken."

"I know."

The whispered admission took Ilsa by surprise. She'd never seen Chase look so honest.

"If I could go back—"

The captain cut off as a shadow fell over his face. Ilsa looked up and saw a familiar, haunting figure stepping up from behind them, looking as though he'd simply emerged from the darkness.

Vandraak.

"Dragon in sight, Captain," the dragonblood hissed, pointing a clawed hand out over the waves. His eyes glinted with bloodlust and his smile bared his fangs. "What are your orders?"

Chase shook himself. He looked at Ilsa, then out at the rolling sea where the white dragon lurked. A stony resolve overtook his face.

"Wake the crew, and ready the ship," he said without looking at Ilsa. "We're going after that monster tonight."

Chapter Fifteen

Chase, the Legend

Ilsa had never witnessed a crew of sailors hoist anchor and set sail so quietly. Smothering dread lay like a pall over their hurried activity; it almost felt as if their movements were happening in a dream. Any sound that broke through the silence—a slight groan of the ship, chink of anchor chains, flap of canvas, or whispered order—seemed exaggerated and deadly, like the creak of a floorboard under a burglar's boot.

At last, *Relentless* surged forward through the roll of the waves. The dragon still swam ahead, only visible as an occasional glimpse of white against the inky sea. But the power of its presence was inescapable. Every eye on the ship was trained on it, every heart pounding with mounting anticipation.

As a pale dawn seeped across the open sky, the distance between hunter and hunted shrank, like the tightening of a noose.

Ilsa stood beside Chase at the helm. His death-grip on the spokes was tight enough that the veins on his hand were visible.

"So close," he whispered. "So bloody close."

Ilsa pressed her lips together and breathed a wordless prayer. Anything that could've swayed him from his course of destruction had already been said.

A clatter of steel against wood cracked like a gunshot over the ship as a belaying pin, sprung free of the bulwark, hit the deck. Any other day it would have been a nonevent, merely something to be resecured and then forgotten. But today, it was a signal. The first blast fired in a great battle.

Ilsa started forward to retrieve the pin, but Captain Chase held up a hand.

"It doesn't matter. He's heard us."

The water before the ship began to boil. Up in the sails, Radney Steelkilt let out a shout at the sight of it. His brother clapped a hand over his mouth, but he was too late to smother the noise.

"Heaven protect us," Brigid breathed, staring wide-eyed at the sea.

"What is it?" Nell's small voice teetered on the edge of panic. "What's out there?"

Before anyone could speak, Avatheon, the monster of legend, erupted from the sea of white foam. When its great wings unfurled, they seemed to fill the sky.

The dragon reared its head. Ilsa gasped. Twice the size of *Relentless*, isn't that what Chase had told her about this beast? He'd woefully underestimated. Its skull alone was over half the length of the ship.

The dragon swung its head around and fixed its colorless gaze on them. Ilsa could've sworn it looked at each of the huddled sailors in turn, sizing them up.

"So it begins," Chase murmured.

The dragon surged from the sea and took to the skies. It beat its wings, and a spray of seawater droplets flung in all directions, sparkling like falling stars.

The beast whose dreadful shadow had loomed over the voyage since they'd first weighed anchor was now in full view. It turned its head skyward and let out a scream that rent the clouds.

"Should we ready the chasers, captain?" Bones asked, his whisper hoarse.

"We won't be needing them," said Chase. "Not this time." He turned to Vandraak. "Make ready!"

"As you wish, Captain," Vandraak said. "Bring oil! Everything that's in the hold."

A few confused glances passed amongst the crew, but they moved to obey. The sailors hauled up cask after cask, piling the precious cargo at the base of the mast.

Vandraak grinned at the amassed oil.

"Good. Now," he said. "Douse the sails."

"This is madness!" Bones exclaimed. "Don't you know how live this stuff is? Captain, you can't be serious."

"Do as he says." Chase ordered. The captain's face was a wall of stoney resolve.

Ilsa looked on, breathless, as Yuri lifted the first cask into the rigging. The others followed, and soon the air was full of the sharp, bitter smell particular to the oil. She watched the Steelkilt brothers soak the mainsail in shimmering liquid, so carelessly, so opposite to the way she'd been trained to handle the oil in the chasers. No wick attached to a vial, no valve to control the flow. They simply dumped the volatile substance all over the ship with reckless abandon.

Ilsa recalled Chase's repeated insistence throughout the voyage: *We need the oil to face the White Dragon. Every drop.*

So this was it? The grand plan to bring down Avatheon?

As if sensing her doubts, Chase turned to Ilsa.

"We lost to him before because we were no match for him in the sky." Chase clenched his fist on the railing. "What is a chaser to a dragon like that? Barely an annoyance, a gnat to be swatted away. But if we take the whole ship up, we're a force to be reckoned with. Vandraak knows more about this fiend than anyone. His plan will work."

"Captain—" Ilsa started, but Chase cut her off.

"We'll be his match in speed, if not strength." Chase went on, more to himself, it seemed, than to Ilsa. "Put enough force behind the blow, and we'll ram the devil right out of the sky. I'll impale his soulless heart on my bowsprit."

"You're planning to crash your skyborne ship directly into—"

A lurch forward stole Ilsa's words. The ship shuddered, then began to rise. The sea fell away beneath the hull as *Relentless* lumbered skyward with an unnatural groan.

"*Relentless* shall be our chaser," said Chase. "The first of her kind to sail the skies. And she shall be true to her name. From this moment on, we do not turn back."

The crew, perhaps too stunned to protest, stood in mute acquiescence to Chase's declaration.

The white dragon turned north, and *Relentless* followed close behind. The ship climbed steadily higher in pursuit.

"We approach the Edge, sir," Yuri reported. Ilsa joined him at the railing and stared.

There was no horizon. Where the sea ended, there was... nothing. Water poured endlessly over the Edge, falling for an eternity into a colorless, shapeless void. All that lay ahead was sky, mist, and a dragon shaped like a legend.

"Full sail," Chase ordered.

"Captain, are you mad?" Pippin Steelkilt exclaimed. "We can't follow—he's gone right over!"

Chase drew his pistol and aimed it at the boy's head.

"I said," Chase repeated, with ice in his tone. "Full sail."

"You heard the captain, lad." Bones grabbed Pippin by the shoulder and yanked him toward the mast. "Get up there and do your duty, before somebody gets killed."

"We're all going to get killed," Brigid muttered. No one, not even Captain Chase, corrected her.

Wind billowed in the shimmering sails, and the ship surged forward, over the Edge. *Relentless* and her crew passed beyond the borders of the world.

Ilsa looked back once, down at the end of the sea, and her stomach dropped at the otherworldly sight. The ocean stretched out behind her, an endless waterfall in both directions. It was dizzying to see the world as an outsider, a view reserved for God. Ilsa felt like a trespasser in a realm where she did not belong. She gripped the railing in front of her, trying to keep her footing steady and not fall headlong into eternal nothingness. Her vision swam.

Yuri put a heavy, comforting hand on Ilsa's shoulder, just as he had when they'd first sailed beyond the Cliffs of Edgewater and looked back at their towering height. Ilsa placed her hand over his and squeezed.

They'd end this journey right where they started it: side by side.

"Hold steady!" Chase shouted to the crew. "Only a matter of time till he gets tired of us following and decides to do something about it."

A rushing sound filled the ominous silence, followed by a sharp scrape. One of the two remaining chaser boats on *Relentless's* deck lurched forward, then shot skyward with an unsteady, jerking gait as if piloted by inexperienced hands.

"Who launched a chaser?" the captain demanded, whirling on his crew.

"Your first mate, sir," Yuri said, pointing up at the rogue boat.

For half a second Chase's anger flared against Ilsa. But no, she was still standing beside him. That meant...

Chase scowled at the sight of Vandraak clutching the tiller, his tattered black cloak trailing behind him.

"What are you doing?" Chase shouted, rushing to the railing. "I didn't authorize that launch. Get back here with that boat! We've got the fight of our lives on our hands. If we are to have any hope of success, you will await my orders!"

Vandraak pulled the boat to a hovering stop and smiled impassively at Chase, baring his sharp teeth, but he did not move to obey. Chase's temper surged.

"You would defy me? Here?"

"No, Captain," Vandraak said. "I would betray you, here."

His words hit Chase like ice water. He opened his mouth, but no words came.

The dragonblood laughed, a hollow, scraping sound.

"Did you know it is possible to become a dragon?" Vandraak's smile looked especially sharp. "No one's ever succeeded in pulling it off, though. That much concentrated power only comes from one place—an Edge dragon. More specifically, an Edge dragon who has just made a kill. So how do you arrange that and live to reap your reward?"

"Stop it," Chase growled, but Vandraak, of course, went on.

"How do you convince a crew of Hunters to sail out to the Edge to die?" The dragonblood sneered. "I found it easy. All I needed was a madman. Someone foolish, desperate enough to attempt the impossible. Give him a taste of power, just enough to keep him crawling back for more."

Chase paled as the realization sank in. Everything he'd bet his future on, everything he'd sacrificed for...a lie. It had all been a lie. He staggered backward as the dreadful realization slashed his last hope to shreds.

It was then that his first mate—the one he should have trusted all along—stepped forward.

"You're the madman, Vandraak, not Captain Chase." Ilsa shouted. "Turn into a dragon? Rubbish! What makes you believe you'll survive this any more than the rest of us? Get back here and fight with us, and maybe we'll all stand a chance."

"Ha! You!" Vandraak swung his gaze to Ilsa. "You almost thwarted me. I foresaw that you could, so I tried to get you out of the way. You nearly succeeded, too. I saw you that night, in the storms. You almost killed him. If you had, you'd all be safe now, wouldn't you?"

Chase gaped at Ilsa, stunned. She'd tried to kill him? More importantly, what had stayed her hand?

"Captain," Ilsa said, extending imploring hands toward him. "I can explain. I didn't—"

"What does it matter?" Chase pushed her away. "None of it matters." He fought a wave of nausea. Vandraak was right, it would be better if she'd done it. He'd been warned. Over and over, he'd been warned. That was all the mercy he deserved.

Adam Chase hung his head in defeat.

"Your deaths will create a surge of power like none that has ever been." Vandraak's exultant voice continued. "And who will be left to reap it? It is I who will become legend, you fool. I will be a glorious terror; I will stain the seas red with blood. You and your pathetic crew of misfits and stragglers will be but the first drop."

Chase's head jerked up. A flash of resolve shot through him at Vandraak's words:

His crew.

They didn't deserve this end. Chase was the one that had brought them here. He'd gambled with their lives as much as his own. He was a Map's End Hunter. He would not die a coward's death. He would fight for them.

Chase's hand flashed toward the dragonflame pistol at his belt. He whipped the gun out of its holster and fired off a bright blast. The shot erred too wide, streaking off to the starboard of Vandraak's boat. Chase had lost the element of surprise, but no matter. He had another oil cell.

Vandraak laughed as Chase reloaded.

"Hurry up, Captain." the dragonblood's mocking voice seemed to be coming from inside Chase's head. "You're out of time."

Chase looked where Vandraak pointed. The dragon, its attention drawn by the pistol shot, beat its wings with the fury of a hurricane. The monster charged forward with an ear-splitting roar.

Vandraak ducked his chaser out of the beast's path. The dragon didn't even glance the little boat's way as it surged through the sky. But the monster's tail, swinging like a storm-bent cedar, whipped against the chaser's hull.

Vandraak's boat capsized midair. He scrambled to steady it, but the crosswind caused by the dragon's wing was too strong to fight. It tore away his threadbare cloak and tossed it to the wind.

The lines yanked out of Vandraak's clawed grasp, and, with a terrible scream, the dragonblood fell. His arms and legs flailed to no avail, and the swirling ether swallowed him.

His cloak followed much more slowly, drifting side to side like a lost ghost before it, too, vanished from sight.

Chase stared at the place where the dragonblood had disappeared, stunned to silence, not sure if the sudden rush of emotion that flooded through him was horror or relief.

Vandraak was gone. The dragon cultist, killed by the very thing he so desperately craved.

"It's over, Captain." Ilsa murmured from beside him. "You're free."

Chase took a shuddering breath.

"Captain!" Bones shouted, jarring him out of the solemn moment.

Chase looked up just in time to see the dragon closing in, a terrible flash of white and teeth.

"Brace your—!" He never finished the warning.

Avatheon rammed the ship. With a great cry of splintering wood, *Relentless's* ribs broke. Chase hit the deck hard. Bright flashes exploded in his vision as he crashed to a painful halt against the ship's railing.

With an otherworldly screech of rage, the dragon doubled back. It grazed the rigging as it passed. Razor-edged wings knifed through canvas. Spars buckled and lines snapped. The mast cracked at the middle and fell like a sapling, dragging the skyborne ship's fragile balance with it.

Relentless spiraled in the air, plummeting toward the empty abyss below like a shot bird. Burning debris rained down on the ship, falling like fiery hailstones. Some winked out on impact, but others flared into blazes that spread across the deck.

Chase rolled onto his side, his body wracked with shooting pain. His vision swam. He clutched his head, fighting for consciousness, and blinked hard. A shape came into focus, lying a few feet away from him on the deck. The fragmented end of Tasha's harpoon, lying forgotten where he'd thrown it, what seemed like a lifetime ago.

He stretched out his shaking hand and grasped the broken shaft like a lifeline. The weathered wood was marred with dozens of small hashmarks.

Victories.

Chase clenched his teeth and steeled his courage. The old harpoon was broken beyond repair, but it had led the life of a champion. Perhaps it had one last fight in it.

Chase planted the point of the barb on the deck and leaned heavily on the broken end. He yanked himself up and swept a final gaze over the broken remains of his ship. A strange detachment settled over his heart—as if the battle had already happened, and he was watching the end of his own life though a memory.

"Get those fires out! If they reach the oil, the whole ship will blow!"

The shout cut through the haze in his mind. Chase whipped his gaze toward the sound.

Ilsa.

She stood on the burning, broken quarterdeck, yanking at the helm in a monumental effort to right the ship.

"Starling!" Chase took the steps to the quarterdeck two at a time, desperation filling him with a surge of strength he hadn't felt in over a year. He hardly felt the painful protest in his leg.

Ilsa whipped her head up. Her face was streaked with sweat and ash, pale as the beast itself, but fighting. Fighting for them all.

Chase grasped the spokes beside her, lending his strength to hers. He strained against the ship's natural bent to spiral endlessly downward. Together, they pulled the ship back upright. Ilsa staggered backward, breathing hard.

"Thank you," she said. She pushed her windswept hair off of her forehead and started off toward the closest patch of flame.

"Wait." Chase put a hand on her shoulder to stop her.

"We have to put out—"

"Get the crew out of here," he ordered, cutting her off. "Take the ship to the surface."

"But without the mast we haven't got enough sail power—"

"Just do what you can." Chase interrupted. He looked out at the dragon. The beast had turned, readying itself for another charge. "And I'll do what I must."

Chase drew the pistol from his belt and pushed it toward Ilsa. "It's been an honor sailing with you, Captain Starling."

"Captain!"

Chase didn't turn at Ilsa's shout. The captain stumbled towards the last chaser boat. He heaved himself over the gunwale and engaged the oil valve. The chaser's sail billowed with shimmering power. It blasted from the deck of the ship, trailing a bright streak through the predawn sky.

"What's he doing?" Nell wailed. "Has the captain abandoned us here to die?"

Chase's boat darted toward the dragon, then pulled up sharply in a jagged, unpredictable maneuver. The White Dragon snarled, its attention captured by the chaser's swift movement. Chase dove, and, amazingly, the dragon followed.

"No." Yuri pointed. "He draws it off."

"He's luring it," Ilsa breathed, hardly believing it herself. "He's giving us a chance to escape."

"Escape?" Bones snapped. "Escape to where? Even if we could land, we'd sink like a rock. We're no longer seaworthy."

The question hung in the air, echoed on every face. They looked to her, Ilsa realized with a start.

Captain Starling.

There was no time to protest, no excuse she could offer. Her own weakness didn't matter anymore. All she knew was that she would spend every drop of what strength she had left protecting her crew.

All of her crew.

"We've got to—" Ilsa began, but an almighty roar snatched away the rest of her words. Yuri clamped his stony hands over Ilsa's ears in an attempt to shield her from the deafening shriek, but even with his protection the sound left her reeling.

Avatheon writhed in the air, thrashing wildly as if in agony. It didn't take Ilsa long to discover why.

A harpoon, or at least a shattered fragment of one, protruded from the beast's right eye. Chase's boat wheeled away from the dragon's head, attempting to make a quick escape, but the monster struck blindly at the boat that had stung him.

In a horrible flash, the chaser snapped between the dragon's jaws, reduced to a hundred thousand splinters in less time than it took to blink. Chase vanished.

"Adam!" Ilsa cried.

"He's gone!" Radney gasped. "He's been killed!"

No. Please, no.

"No, look!" Yuri pointed toward the dragon. "There!"

Ilsa strained her eyes to see what he'd seen. To her, it was just a dark streak against the dragon's whiteness. Then, with a start, she realized what it was: Captain Chase, clinging for his life to the rough scales of the dragon's face. She only caught a brief glimpse before the dragon turned and dove out of sight beneath the boat, but just seeing him alive was more than enough.

"I'm going after him! Have we got any boats?" Ilsa demanded.

"Captain took the last one." Bones confirmed her fear.

"We'll take the whole ship, then. Yuri, take the helm and—"

"Incoming!" Brigid's shouted warning came too late.

The dragon's second blow struck from below. The ship split apart from the bottom, cracking into two pieces.

The impact flung Ilsa backward, sending her sprawling to the careening deck. The others fared no better. Pip Steelkilt was thrown from the rigging; he caught onto a loose line and barely saved himself from hurtling overboard. His brother hauled him back aboard, but it was nowhere near to safety.

The center of the ship was gone. In its place was a jagged, gaping chasm torn straight through the hull to the emptiness below. Ilsa, Brigid, and the brothers stood on one side of the bottomless gulf, with Yuri, Nell, and Bones stranded on the other.

The dragon circled in the sky beneath the ship, like a shark waiting to strike.

We need something to get us down. We need... Ilsa cast about frantically, looking for something—anything—that could help. Her gaze landed on a glowing red gemstone, hung from a cord around Yuri's neck.

Wings. We need wings.

Yuri's whispered instructions came back to Ilsa: *Break the stone. Release the firebird. And let it carry them away.*

"Yuri!" Ilsa shouted. "Don't move!"

Praying for a steady hand, Ilsa aimed the captain's pistol at Yuri's heart. Understanding flashed in his golden eyes and he gave her a tight nod.

She pulled the trigger.

A blast of violet light exploded from the gun, sending a ball of energy hurtling toward Yuri. Her aim was true. The firestone shattered.

An animal cry rose from the ship. Ilsa lost sight of Yuri as a flare of brilliant light engulfed him. Huge, fiery wings, rivaling the dragon's in size, unfolded from the point where the Stoneman stood, giving him the appearance of a burning angel.

The light solidified into the form of a magnificent bird, burning like melted rock, pulsing with intricate patterns of red and gold light that etched across its form like tattoos. The creature—or perhaps, spirit—turned keen eyes on the huddled fugitives on the crumbling deck, its gaze lingering on its master.

"Get on!" Yuri commanded.

The firebird spread its flaming wings across the ship, bridging the chasm between its halves. Yuri picked up Nell and tossed her onto the apparition's back. The others followed, clambering up amid the strange fire that seemed to burn nothing it touched. Ilsa shielded her eyes from the blaze of light that flared from the bird.

"Is that everyone?" Ilsa heard Yuri shout.

"Yes; go!" she called back.

The firebird beat its radiant wings and streaked skyward. Avatheon reeled out of its path with a piercing shriek. The bird swooped down, carrying its passengers back over the Edge to safety.

A hiss of steam erupted from the sea as the burning spirit hit the cold water, instantly hardening to arid, volcanic stone. The buoyant rock bobbed to the surface, creating a huge, bird-shaped raft, with six souls safely aboard. The means Yuri had planned to carry him in death now served as a vehicle to save their lives.

Only Ilsa remained on the dying ship. The others, now safely huddled on the sea far below, would soon realize she wasn't among them.

I'm sorry Yuri, but I would not ask you to follow me now.

She swung herself over the railing and crept along the bowsprit, clinging to the narrow rod with all the strength she had left. Below her, the empty abyss stretched forever; beyond her, the monstrous dragon whirled in the air, preparing to come at the ship again.

Just a bit farther.

Vandraak's capsized chaser, still skyborne, drifted purposelessly in the air below *Relentless*. Ilsa didn't let herself stop to think about what she was about to do. She jumped.

For a horrible half-second, Ilsa was suspended in the endless, featureless sky. Then she landed on the upside-down hull of the abandoned chaser with a jarring smack. The force of her landing tipped the boat enough that she managed to get a grip on the gunwale. She yanked it toward her.

Slowly, painfully, the boat began to turn in the air. Ilsa didn't wait for the chaser to right itself completely. As soon as she could, she scrambled aboard, clinging to the lines to keep from sliding straight off the other side. She hauled in on the jib sheet and shoved at the tiller, then cranked the oil valve to give it a burst of speed. The chaser surged forward, back under control.

Now to face the dragon.

Ilsa whipped her boat around and darted at the beast, circling its massive head.

Where are you?

There. Chase gripped the dragon's face, hanging from one hand beneath its blinded eye. In the other hand, he cradled a bright capsule against his chest. One of the oil cells from his chaser boat.

The captain caught sight of her.

"Ilsa!" he cried. His hair whipped about his face, matching his wild eyes. "Shoot it! Do it now!"

Shoot the capsule? Ilsa didn't know if she'd heard right. The explosion might deter the dragon, that was true enough... but it would undoubtedly kill the captain.

"You can still win this." Chase urged. "Get the oil. Heal yourself. Live."

Ilsa's breath caught. Did he really believe such a thing was still possible, even now? She looked at the oil cell in his hand. Could it really be enough to kill the dragon?

Total, complete restoration. Chase's words echoed in her mind.

A miracle was within her grasp.

"Do it. For both of us," Chase begged. Ilsa was astonished to see tears in his eyes. "Please."

Ilsa knew exactly what he was asking: his life for hers. Let him die, so she might have the chance to live.

She raised the pistol and took aim. Chase shuddered and turned his face away, accepting the end.

But when the pistol snapped off its final shot, no explosion followed. Instead, the dragon roared, tossing its mighty head as the blast caught it in its already-wounded eye.

Chase lost his grip. With a cry, he fell, his outstretched hand straining for something to catch onto, but finding nothing.

Ilsa yanked at the lines, sending her boat in a nose-dive after the captain. She gritted her teeth and braced herself as the chaser plummeted faster and faster. She'd nearly caught up with him. She reached out, straining to close the distance between them. At last, their hands touched. Chase gripped Ilsa, and she yanked him aboard.

Far above, the enraged dragon slammed one last time into *Relentless's* broken hull. The sky split open as the oil-drenched ship exploded with a roar like a thousand thunderclaps. Ilsa didn't look back at the fireworks, but she could see the colors reflecting off of Chase's death-white face.

The dragon, having defeated its irksome foe, shrieked in triumph, beat its wings, and plummeted downward. In a matter of seconds, the great beast had vanished from sight, returned to the mist it had haunted for a thousand years.

The shockwave from the explosion caught Ilsa's sails, propelling the little boat forward—and downward—at an alarming speed. Ilsa had barely realized her chaser was once again over water before it crashed into ocean waves. The impact snapped the chaser's hull in two, plunging its passengers into the frigid sea.

The last thing Ilsa felt before the world went dark was the grip of a strong, stony hand on the back of her collar, pulling her up toward the surface.

Ilsa turned her face toward the lingering sunlight and breathed deeply of the still air. How was it possible for the sea to be so peaceful now, even as the smoke left from *Relentless's* death still stained the sky?

"So, you see, when it rains, we will be able to catch water to drink." Yuri's deep, rumbling voice drew Ilsa's attention. She watched as he stretched out Radney's oilskin cloak between the firebird raft's wing and tail, so that it made a small cavity. "Next, I will show you how to fish with spear and eat it raw."

"Ick!" Nell wrinkled her nose.

"You talk like you've been shipwrecked before," Brigid remarked, sounding a little impressed.

"Once." Yuri nodded. "But that is long story."

"Not like we're going anywhere." Pippin shrugged.

"Very well," Yuri chuckled. "It began when I awoke one morning on an island with no name, not marked on any map. True places never are, you know."

"That's objectively untrue, Yuri." Ilsa interjected, flicking a few droplets of seawater at him. "I did teach geography, you know."

"Ah, but it makes for good story." Yuri sighed. "Fine. I start again. It was not marked on any map, which does not by nature make it more special than other places, which *are* on maps, but perhaps, had the mapmakers known such an island, it would have taken away some of its mystery and—"

"Fine, fine, tell it your way." Ilsa laughed, waving him off. "Pest."

So far, in the hours they'd been adrift, the castaways had all been so relieved to be alive that no one had given much thought to their future survival.

The mood on the raft was surprisingly cheerful, in spite of their dire circumstances: No boats. No food. No water. No way to call for help.

But no dragon; that, at least, was cause for celebration.

As the sun's last rays stretched toward dusk, Yuri spun an outrageous tale that only grew less believable the more he tried to convince his audience it was genuine.

"...I looked down, and I see fishes, not unlike..." Yuri peered into the water, searching for a fish for comparison. "Hm," he mused after a moment. "There are no fishes in this sea."

"What about a bird?" Nell pointed toward a dark shape soaring through the clouds high above. "Could you pretend it was a bird you saw, just for the story?"

"That is no bird."

He'd been quiet all afternoon, but now Captain Chase commanded everyone's attention as he stared skyward. Instantly, the cheery atmosphere evaporated, replaced by cold dread. Everyone looked up, Yuri's story forgotten as their eyes followed the strange shadow.

"What in the blazes?" Bones muttered. "Haven't we had enough bad luck for one day?"

The skyborne shape turned a somersault in the air.

Ilsa scrambled to her feet, her heart flooding with hope. She'd know that silhouette anywhere.

"Mobius!" she cried, stretching her arms toward him. The tammer dove into her arms, nearly knocking her backwards off the raft in his excitement. Ilsa clutched him tightly and buried her face in his fragrant fur, laughing through tears.

"You found us! How did you find us?"

Mobius sprang out of her grasp, as if suddenly remembering something important. He sat in the middle of the bird-shaped raft and looked at each of the castaways in turn. Then, satisfied that everyone was appropriately invested, he gingerly lifted his front foot and extended it to Ilsa.

Tied around his ankle was a bit of twine, threaded with brightly painted beads.

"What's this you've got now?" Ilsa slipped the twine off of Mobius and held it up to the sunlight.

"Tash?" Chase choked out. He took the beads and turned them over in his fingers. "These are hers. Did Tasha send you?"

Mobius ducked his head, looking for all the world like he was nodding.

"If Tasha sent you to find us, then..." Ilsa trailed off. She whisked her gaze up to the horizon. Empty. But she knew if Mobius had made the distance, the *Shepherdess* couldn't be too far beyond sight. "She must be close enough that she saw *Relentless* go down."

Mobius nudged Ilsa with his nose, then extended his foot again. Return message requested.

"Rest a minute," Ilsa said, stroking his soft ears. "And when you're refreshed, go find Tasha and give her..."

Ilsa fished around in her skirt pocket for something to send back, something that Tasha would recognize as a sign that they were alive. Her fingers met a familiar texture, and she pulled it out. Her tattered hair ribbon lay in her hand. Ilsa smiled, pleasantly surprised. She thought it had been lost.

Ilsa tied the ribbon around the tammer's foot.

"Lead her back to us, Moby." Ilsa hugged Mobius again. "We're going to make it."

A cheer rose from the raft-bird. Mobius fairly glowed in the shower of praise as the castaways passed him around, hugging him, ruffling his ears, telling him what a good boy he was.

The only one not celebrating was the captain. Chase sat apart from the rest on the bird's starboard wing, his ivory leg skimming the surface of the sea. Ilsa stepped away from the others and sat beside him wordlessly.

"It was all for nothing, Ilsa," Chase said. He stared out to the empty horizon. "We were so close. But we failed. I've ruined us all, and for what? I will never be healed."

Chase fell silent, staring blankly at the waves. Ilsa sat beside him; for once, the silence between them wasn't heavy with looming dread or unspoken secrets.

"Why wouldn't you kill it?" Chase asked at last, his voice barely above a whisper. He shoved a hand through his tangled hair. "You missed that shot on purpose; don't try to deny it. You shot it in the eye so it would drop me, when you could've easily killed it. You could've had a future, a real future, and you threw it away."

"I know, Captain," Ilsa said softly. She laid her hand over his, and this time, he didn't flinch away. "But a perfect future bought with the blood of my friend is a future I want no part of."

Chase jerked his head up, recognizing her words. He looked at her for a long moment, a thoughtful expression on his face. Finally, he spoke.

"Don't call me that."

"Call you what? My friend?"

"No." Chase shook his head. "Don't call me captain."

Ilsa rolled her eyes and smiled. "Please. She was never my ship. I only lasted as captain for a few minutes before I managed to blow everything up."

Her attempt to coax a smile from him was unsuccessful.

"You were more worthy to lead her than I ever was. You'd make a fine Hunter, if..." Chase swallowed hard.

"What's bothering you, Adam?" Ilsa asked gently.

"You *saved* me, Ilsa Starling." Chase looked her in the eye. "You snatched me from the dragon's jaws. But in order to do it, you traded away your one chance at healing. After everything you've survived on this voyage, you're still going to die."

Ilsa looked out over the waves, toward the Edge and the endless heavens beyond.

"Yes," she agreed. "But first, I intend to live."

Chase sighed. "I'm far too tired for riddles."

"It's no riddle; it's a resolution." Ilsa turned away from the Edge and looked back across the sea to the south. Towards home. "I'm going to treat each day given to me as if it's a gift. No matter how much time I've got left. Two months, ten years, it doesn't matter. I won't recover from my illness, but that doesn't mean I can't be healed."

"Perhaps you are already." Chase looked at Tasha's beads, still cupped in his palm. "Do you think...maybe I could be, too?"

"Not likely," Ilsa said. Chase blinked, taken aback, but Ilsa smiled and went on. "But we've been praying for the impossible since the moment we left port. Your miracle doesn't look like you'd imagined, but you did get one, after all."

"Miss Starling?" Nell interrupted from across the raft. "I think your rabbit might be hurt."

Ilsa turned just as Mobius wriggled out from Nell's grasp. He sat up and puffed out his chest, displaying a bright red sunburst, stark against his white breast. The tammer fairly glowed with pride as he gave his wings a triumphant flap.

"That's not blood," Ilsa said, hardly daring to believe her own eyes. She stroked the mark on Mobius's chest. The blaze was fur, red fur, its color as full and rich as it ever had been. Determined to persist, despite the whiteness that surrounded it.

I intend to live.

Ilsa gathered the tammer into her arms and held him close, planting a kiss on the soft slope between his ears.

"Message received, Mobius."

Message received.

CHAPTER SIXTEEN

Desired Haven

Map's End, Seven Months Later

"YOU ARE CERTAIN I cannot tempt you to join me?"

Yuri leaned heavily on the doorway of the cluttered study. The Stoneman's sad smile betrayed the fact that he already knew the answer to his question.

Ilsa shuffled the papers on the desk before her in an attempt to look busy while she cleared the tightness out of her throat. It was hard to look at him, with his bag packed and slung over his shoulder, knowing that this was where they would finally part ways.

"I think I've had enough death-defying adventure to satisfy me for quite a while yet, Yuri."

His low chuckle rumbled in his chest in the same familiar, comforting way it had the first day she met him.

"Besides," Ilsa glanced around at the mess. The disorganized, ravaged remains of Adam Chase's livelihood lay scattered in every nook of his hastily evacuated study. "I have plenty of work to do here. Sorting through an inheritance is a full-time job, particularly if my benefactor was not very future-minded in the way he left his accounts."

"You believe there is anything worth salvaging?"

"Probably not. Adam and Tash certainly didn't think so. There may not even be enough to pay off the creditors he borrowed from to finance the voyage. But..." Ilsa trailed off. It was hard to explain why she was doing this. No one expected it of her. The crew wasn't waiting around for their wages; they'd been happy enough to have returned home with their lives. Adam and Tasha had been more than willing to wash their hands of the whole mess before setting off to start afresh on the Plains of Adisa. If Ilsa remembered correctly, Adam's exact words had been, "torch the ledgers, for all I care." Even Abel Hawthorne had refused any offer of financial settlement, claiming that the survivors from *Relentless* had more than earned their keep on the return voyage.

"I've left too many things unresolved in my life," Ilsa said. "I want to close this out the right way."

"It is noble task," Yuri said. "Though I cannot say I envy you."

"Well, be grateful it didn't fall to you. Just as I'm thankful not to be journeying deep underground to become king of your terrifying lava realm."

"It will be good to be back in the land of the deep," Yuri said. "Though I do wish I could show it to you." He shook a finger at her. "Mark me, I will, someday. You cannot escape it."

"Sounds like a threat!" Ilsa laughed.

"You are not still afraid my people will eat you, are you?" Yuri raised an eyebrow at her.

"Why shouldn't they?" Ilsa countered, setting aside the stack of dusty records and stepping around to his side of the desk. She leaned against the solid oak, clasping her hands behind her. "Once word gets out I fired a dragonflame pistol at their crown prince—"

Yuri let out a full-chested laugh, so deep and echoing that Ilsa wondered if the downstairs tenants of the two-story flat might interpret the sound as thunder.

Yuri passed his broad hand over the scar that marred his chest, the one mark upon his skin he did not choose to bear. The flame-shaped burn sat exactly where his jeweled pendant used to rest. No longer did it swirl with barely contained power, but rather stood as a silent, permanent memory.

"I will not need dragon tattoo to remind me of our voyage, after all," Yuri said as he patted the scar. His tone was only half-joking. He shifted his pack to his other shoulder. "You see that I carry you with me always."

Ilsa's eyes stung, and she dropped her gaze to the scuffed floorboards. He was really leaving, and she didn't know if she could bear another goodbye.

The floor creaked as Yuri stepped toward her. His thick, stony finger tucked beneath her chin and lifted her gaze back up. Ilsa met Yuri's golden eyes and found that she was not the only one fighting tears.

"You are courageous one, Little Sister," he said. "Do not forget that, even when I am no longer here to remind you."

Yuri folded Ilsa into a thick, rocky embrace. His strength enveloped her, and he stooped to press his forehead against hers in a farewell that said more than words ever could.

The silence left by Yuri's absence wrapped around Ilsa for a long while. She sat motionless at Chase's cluttered desk until the afternoon sun slanted its last rays through the window. The warm glow hit her face, rousing her from her reverie. She shook herself back to awareness and looked around at the daunting piles of records still on the desk before her. Plenty of work left to be done before sundown.

Ilsa rubbed the beginnings of a headache out from between her eyes. Grandfather's watch told her it was just after four. She stood, stretched her aching back, and paced to the window.

Chase's office was situated on one of the island's higher streets. Ilsa looked down at the town of Map's End spread out before her, sweeping her gaze from one end of the island to the other. On the south end, the Edgewater ferry was launching, carrying Yuri back to the mainland to start the first leg of his journey home. On the opposite side, closer to the harbor, bells were ringing in the Hunter's Chapel, celebrating the safe return of yet another Map's End ship.

Ilsa searched the bustling streets until she spotted a familiar freckled face in the crowd.

Nell looked up at the window and waved, as she did every day. Ilsa returned the gesture with a smile.

While Bones and Brigid had signed on for *Shepherdess's* next venture, along with the Steelkilt brothers, Nell had decided that one Hunting voyage was more than enough for her. Now she wove her way through the busy streets then bounced up the front steps of Abel and Mary Hawthorne's townhouse, where she earned her keep helping Mary with housework, cooking, and the care of baby Rachel—now a thriving, beautiful child of seven months.

Ilsa smiled and turned away from the window. It all felt so right. Adam and Tasha had gone home to Tasha's people, where under her loving, dedicated care Adam would start the long process of severing his dependence on medicinal dragon oil and pain-numbing drugs. It would be a hard road, but it was the one he'd chosen, and with Tasha by his side, he'd been willing to face it.

Yuri had been the last to leave, and his departure felt like the closing of a chapter. Each of the *Relentless* survivors was home.

All but two.

"Well, Mobius," Ilsa said. "It's time."

The tammer roused himself from his perch on top of a bookshelf and fluffed up his tousled fur. He sprang down onto the desk and gave himself a good shake before settling. He sat straight, puffing his chest with overstated importance, as he'd done every day since the red-furred sunburst had appeared. Ilsa stroked the mark, bright as a promise.

I intend to live.

With a wide sweep of her arm, Ilsa pushed a mound of paper away, clearing a space on the desk. She set a clean sheet of paper in front of her and took a deep breath.

Paper. Ink. A pen. A prayer.

Ilsa touched the quivering nib of the pen to the paper.

Dear Phillip...

Don't miss the next installment of

ᴄA ᴄLASSIC ᴿETOLD

KILL THE DAWN

by Emily Hayse

After a devastating wound and the loss of his beloved father, Hakkr is trying to pick up the pieces of his life. But when his father's last conquest, a mysterious thrall, shares a terrible secret, Hakkr's life only further unravels as incident after incident leads him to the chilling realization that his people's enemies are not the only ones who want him dead.

Set in a wild northern world of wolf-hunts and Viking warfare, *Kill the Dawn* is a breathtaking new retelling of Shakespeare's Hamlet, full of heart, beauty, and bittersweet sacrifice.

Whether or not the average reader has read *Moby Dick* all the way through, chances are that many of the characters, themes, and plot points from the original novel will still be recognizable in *Chase the Legend*, as will the notable changes and creative liberties I took with Herman Melville's classic story.

Most obviously, Adam Chase represents Melville's iconic Captain Ahab, with a few alterations, such as his age and personal history.

For my protagonist, I borrowed Ishmael, Melville's everyman narrator and occasional author self-insert, and merged him with Mr. Starbuck, the steadfast and soft-spoken mate whose gentle manner is one of the only tempers to Captain Ahab's madness. (The true carbon copy of Mr. Starbuck in my story, George Edwards, was allowed to stay home with his loving wife in my version.) While Ishmael's witty observations make him a great narrator, I have always found Starbuck to be a much more compelling character. His inner conflict between his duty as Ahab's first mate and his rock-solid moral conscience became the basis of Ilsa's character arc.

Two of *Moby Dick's* three beloved harpooners were present in my story: Yuri, of course, represented Queequeg, Ishmael's closest friend, the tattooed Polynesian whose coffin eventually serves as Ishmael's life buoy. Tashtego, the silent American Indian, transformed to Tashtanna, whose personality and position in the story expanded far beyond what Melville allowed her predecessor.

Some of the greatest changes I made to the story were thematic. The themes of healing and threads of chronic illness and disability in *Chase the Legend* are my own. While Ahab's amputation is of course an integral part of his character and a major contributing factor to his madness, Melville does not linger much on it as a theme.

In my story, it was healing itself that became Chase's white whale—the thing he would pursue to his own destruction if left unchecked. I knew from the start that I did not want to give my characters quick and seamless magical healing. Realistic depiction of chronic/terminal illness and disability in fantasy fiction is sorely lacking. If depicted at all, illness and disability tend to resolve magically by the end of the story. This is neither helpful nor respectful to real chronic illness and disability warriors, who find that their experiences living daily with a condition are erased and invalidated. Through Ilsa, I hoped to present a character who could humbly and bravely accept her physical limitations and learn to embrace the truth that her life has meaning and value, without the promise that she will get better in the end. I owe many thanks to Mary Herceg and the organizers of the Diamonds Conference for their help with handling this topic with truth and sensitivity.

Moby Dick is a whale of a book (haha) with too many themes and philosophical points to count. So when I set out to write a retelling, I had to narrow my focus. Eventually, I decided to address two thematic questions I had for the original work:

1. Did Starbuck truly fail, as most literary analysts imply, when he refused to kill Captain Ahab in Chapter 123: "The Musket"?
2. What would it take to save Captain Ahab from himself?

These two questions shaped the direction of the story, and eventually ended up flipping the message of *Moby Dick* on its head entirely. Where *Moby Dick* is a story of defiance—of fate, of the past, of the odds—*Chase the Legend* is a story of dependence—on God, on others, on truth. Where Ishmael is *Moby Dick's* lone survivor, Ilsa, through the willful sacrifice of her chance at physical healing in order to save Adam, becomes *Chase the Legend's* lone casualty.

And thus, I leave you with my answers:

1. No, Starbuck's refusal to kill Ahab showed the strength of his character, not the weakness of his resolve. Surrender of one's will to a higher Authority is not defeat; it is victory.
2. The only thing that could save someone like Ahab is the Gospel. Romans 5:7-8: *"For scarcely for a righteous man will one die: yet peradventure for a good man some would even dare to die. But God commendeth his love toward us, in that, while we were yet sinners, Christ died for us."*

Acknowledgments

To my great Creator: *Soli Deo Gloria.* He gave me this story, and now I give it back to Him. It is my prayer that He will use this book to lift up the downtrodden, encourage the wavering, and point the hurting to the only true source of healing.

To John: how can I even begin to thank you? You're my rock, my support, my biggest fan. You are always by my side, through the late nights, the early mornings, the long disappearances to Panera, and the endless conversations about the moral conundrum of Ahab and Starbuck. You are the only reason this book ever got finished. I love you so much.

To my boys: Sam, who keeps me laughing (and humble) with his words of wisdom, such as: "You never make any sense. But that doesn't mean you're not a good mommy." Hopefully someday this story will make sense to you, buddy. And Wesley, my little snuggle bug, you are living proof that boys grow much faster than books do. Mommy loves you both, plus a hundred and twenty-one whales.

To my parents, sisters, brothers-in-law, grandparents, and whole posse of extended family who have absolute confidence in me. You always believe in me, even when I'm struggling to believe in myself. Thanks for being my built-in fan club, and for being willing to watch my tiny friends on occasion so I can get some drafting done. And special thanks belong to Sarah, Mom, and Kaitlyn, for helping me catch those stubborn typos (and three alternate spellings of the dragon's name.)

To Allison Tebo, the Gandalf to my Bilbo. I can't thank you enough for pulling me out of my comfort zone and leading me on this grand adventure. You believed in my writing enough to invite me along; you forged the path, you defeated the giants of cover design and planning, and you brought me into your fearless Fellowship of authors.

To all the ladies of A Classic Retold: Allison Tebo, Emily Golus, Jenelle Schmidt, Alissa Zavalianos, Nina Clare, Tor Thibeaux, Emily Hayse, and Rosie Grymm. Thank you for your teamwork, inspiration, motivation, ideas, promo graphics, memes, and so much more. And a special thank you belongs to Penny Kearny, who traveled along with us for a good part of the journey and has championed these stories and cheered us on ever since. This group has been life-giving for me over the last two years. Our group chat is one of my favorite hangouts, and I cannot wait to hug you all in person someday. (Though for the time being, I'll have to content myself with hugging your beautiful books.)

To Becca Wierwille and Michaela Bush, my earliest readers: Thank you for your feedback, enthusiasm, and encouragement. Your advice and recommendations took this story from a slapped-together draft to a proper manuscript—and your comments always make me smile.

To Mary Herceg, for believing in these characters and encouraging me to write the story I'd been entrusted with. Our conversations took my nebulous ideas and forged them into something that mattered. You uncovered this story's heart. I don't think it's too much of a stretch to credit you with saving Adam's life. You pulled him from the jaws of the dragon and convinced me that his story wasn't over. Thank you for sharing your heart with me, my friend.

Chase the Legend was born out of a difficult period in my life, one filled with doubt, spiritual fatigue, prolonged discouragement, and physical weakness. But just as Ilsa's story would have been a much darker tale had she not had Yuri and Tasha to come alongside her and speak truth into her life, so was my faith constantly bolstered by godly friends who reminded me of Truth when my path felt dark—Laura Burkhart, Katy Parker, Faith Carranza, and Leslie Stubbs. Thank you for only ever being a phone call away.

Finally, to my readers: thank you for going on this voyage with me. May it push you toward greater dependence on the One who heals all hurts.

HK

About the Author

HANNAH KAYE is a professional daydreamer, homeschool mama, drama teacher, and lover of stories in all forms. She is the author of *The Sadie and Clyde Adventures,* a series of humorous and heartfelt Westerns for middle grade readers. Her stories are largely inspired by her sisters, her Christian faith, and her passion for weaving Truth into fiction. When not spinning tales, Hannah enjoys being outside, especially near water, where she's dabbled in kayaking, sailing, and SCUBA diving. She lives in northeast Oklahoma with her nerdy husband, two young hobbits, a long-legged dog, and several aquariums of tropical fish. She can often be found lurking near a coffee pot, baking elaborate desserts, or playing jigs on the Irish tinwhistle in improbable locations.

You can connect with Hannah online at www.hannahkaye.blog
send her an email at authorhannahkaye@gmail.com
or follow her on Instagram @hkayewrites.

www.ingramcontent.com/pod-product-compliance
Lightning Source LLC
Chambersburg PA
CBHW060528160726
47991CB00001B/228